LIGHTNING BOLT

CHARLIE DEMOTT WILDEY

NFB
Buffalo, New York

Printed in the United States of America

Lightning Bolt/DeMott Wildey 1st Edition

ISBN: 978-1-953610-45-4

> Fiction> Science Fiction
> Fiction> Speculative
> Literary Fiction
> Fiction> Fantasy> Thriller
> Fiction> New Weird

NFB Publishing
119 Dorchester Road
Buffalo, New York 14213
For more information visit Nfbpublishing.com

Chapter 1

THE ORCHESTRAL NOISE OF popping grease on a hot flat top grill filled the tiny shop with the sound of applause. Clattering percussion of a metal spatula tossing meat around the grill. Wyatt held a grilled hero roll in his left hand, layering in cheese and diced fresh onion and sliced green olives before scooping the shaved ham from the grill and squeezing it into the bread. He wrapped it tightly and thumped it definitively onto the counter to be retrieved by a waiting customer who accepted it with a nod before walking off down the street. After scraping the flat top clean, Wyatt opened the refrigerator, grabbed a tall can of beer, opened it, and drank half of it while sitting down on the stool in the back corner.

Wyatt was a slender, casually handsome man, with tawny brown complexion. He was on the young side of thirty, but he carried the weight of the age around his neck every day. His cheekbones were high, his course hair tightly cropped and his eyes tired. As a child Wyatt had been short – now he was probably average height, but he still had that short child baked into his demeanor.

The shop was called "Lil ol' Betsy's" but as far as anyone can tell there never was a Betsy. It was tiny, felt cramped if there were two people inside which usually there weren't. It was open all the time. There was a window for customers on one end and a door for workers to come in and out of on the other. There was no bathroom but there was a porta john in the back alley, brought for some unfinished construction project from who knows when. Wyatt had always wondered what would happen when that thing fills right up, but so far it hadn't been a problem. Must be someone was taking care of it. A mystery too disturbing to consider.

Lil ol' Betsy's made all kinds of sandwiches. They sold coffee and beer and cigarettes and weed and cocaine and potato chips and condoms and paper towels and umbrellas and batteries and sometimes whatever other things would show up from their distributors. The whole shop was about 18 inches higher than the street. Paulie, Wyatt's boss, said it was good for business to be higher up than the customers. Said they trust you more if they need to look up at you and reach up to get their items. "That's why you sit at restaurants and the waiter is standing up," he said, and that didn't seem like a good point, but Paulie seemed to think it was.

The shop found itself on a street in an old neighborhood with lots of small shops and apartments above. Buildings stood shoulder to shoulder, low and wide. Everything in this part of town was a pretty consistent four or five stories tall, and though the facade of each building had some attempt at character it all truly blended together until it just looked like buildings. Some corners had taller apartments that shot up above everything else and otherwise it was just mostly a flat, dim, buzz of architecture. The city had been called New York, but nobody cared enough to do that anymore. The biggest buildings and fanciest designs were mostly on the other side of the river from here. Over on the main island. Things had grown tall in some outer borough neighborhoods, too. Not around this neighborhood. Everywhere you looked a layer of trash had settled like a blanket. Lil ol' Betsy's was just a little shop that was on the way for its customers. If they were going to work or coming home they could stop by. Convenient, adequate, and mostly forgettable.

Wyatt would show up for his shifts, relieving whoever was working the previous shift, and he'd stay there until the next person showed up. He was about halfway through his shift for the day. They were paid in bank receipts since nobody printed new physical money and there was no one to say how much it would even be worth so banks ran everything and it all took place inside their computers. The leftover paper money and coins were collector's items. Over the course of each week Paulie would drop in once during everyone's shifts. He'd give them an envelope with the paycheck in it and next week's schedule written on the outside in pen. This was the only time Wyatt ever saw Paulie, and as far as he had heard from other employees it was the same for them. That's basically the way things went.

It was what now passed as "early morning" and the sun began its dreary climb above the horizon, the sky turning a bit orange as the light hit the dense pollution. It was called "shog" and it made the days shorter. Morning started around 10 a.m. most of the year now. As the day slunk to a start Wyatt could see stray dogs zigzagging across the streets, sniffing around and chasing lizards that skittered around in the trash. There was trash all over the ground and most of it had been packed down under tire and foot after years and years of city traffic.

The street warmed in the gradual strengthening of the morning while Wyatt looked out the window. He watched the dogs, sometimes growling at anyone who got too close and sometimes graciously accepting pats on the head from passersby. Wyatt watched people as the streets, which were never empty, came a bit more alive when the day begrudgingly began. People came out of apartments, went in and out of shops, waited for buses, drove by in cars. The old world had collapsed years ago but everyone still had things they had to do. People were milling around – most of them still worked even – so Wyatt watched people mill. There has always been something indispensable to the human experience about milling around, and more so watching people do it. He finished his beer and tossed it in a bucket under the counter.

A homeless guy came up to the window. Wyatt knew many of the vagrants who hung out in this neighborhood, but this guy didn't look familiar. He clearly hadn't slept in a little while, and he was making these clothes last as long as he could. Still, his hair looked willfully disheveled and he had a beard that some social groups would call "stylish." This man was younger than Wyatt. He couldn't be older than 30 but he was definitely getting close. He had an enamel pin of an octopus on his tattered sweater, near the neck. A lot of homeless folks were federated these days. They wore pins and things to make things easier amongst themselves, sort of uniforms for distinction. Wyatt had a handful of acquaintances who'd been associated with some of the vagrant federations. He couldn't remember if Octopus was one of the ones he'd dealt with in the past or not. Anyway, the homeless guy said "hey camper," meaning Wyatt, "do you all in here sell shoes?"

Generally that was not the type of thing that a place like this sold, but like we said the shop sold whatever came in so it was always worth checking. "That's not usually the type of thing that we sell, but we'll sell whatever comes in so let me check," Wyatt said. He looked down at the homeless man's shoes, and they were clearly so wet that they would never dry out. It looked like the guy could use some new shoes.

After putting another beer for himself onto the counter, Wyatt pulled out a few boxes from under the shelves and sifted around in them, looking for shoes or boots. He found a poncho that he thought might be helpful to the guy so he kept that out. No shoes.

"Hey, what's your name?" Wyatt asked the guy, returning to the window.

"Li," he answered.

"Alright Li, here's what it is today. I do not have shoes here. But I do have this poncho, brand new, still wrapped up, that I can give you for five, or four and a cigarette. I could even knock another one off if you have a lighter."

"I don't have a lighter."

"That's fine. I have lighters. I can give you one if you want one."

"I'd take a lighter."

Wyatt put a lighter on the counter next to the poncho. "Ok, do you need the poncho?"

Li pulled his shoulder bag in front of him to look through it. It looked heavy, but it didn't seem to have much of anything valuable inside. "I'll give you 3.75 and a cigarette."

"Listen, that's a deal. But lemme tell you something. Down on Foster Street there's a bookstore – buncha radicals in there. You know the place?"

"I don't go down Foster."

"Sure, well if you make an exception this one time, stop into the place, it's called the Triangle Silhouette. I gotta buddy that works there, Marcy, and they like to hold on to sundries like this. If you say 'Wyatt down from Lil ol' Betsy's said you might could help' maybe they could help. Alright?"

"Sure, sounds ok," said Li, and he put a very worn out debit card and the cigarette on the counter and put the new poncho and the lighter in his side bag.

"Nice day for a walk," Wyatt said.

Li nodded. "Thanks. You're Wyatt?"

"Yeah, now go on you rascal," Wyatt cracked the new beer and sipped.

Wyatt scanned the card and put the cigarette in his pocket. Li shuffled off over the landscape of trash.

It started to rain, making a gentle patter patter on the ground outside. The sun was still shining that hazy orange, which meant it was shog rain. Moisture got caught in the layer of shog that hung over the city and sometimes it would get cooked up there and evaporate the way it used to say in elementary school books about the water cycle. Sometimes it didn't, so it came back down as rain. Shog rain stank a little, and because the sun was still shining the ground was warm and steam would rise up around ankles. Still, if you looked carefully you could find a rainbow, even during shog rain. Wyatt leaned over the counter and out the window to see as much sky as possible to see if he could spot it, the shop's little awning keeping him dry. The shog rainbow wasn't the same as a real rain rainbow. It was missing some colors. They said if you saw the rainbow, long on green and orange but short on blue and violet, it was bad luck. Wyatt didn't believe in that. He looked as far down the south end of the street and as far down the north end of the street as he could. From his vantage point out the shop window he couldn't see it. The sun must've been behind him or behind the buildings. So he retreated back into the tiny shop and took a long sip from the beer.

Wyatt sat back down on the stool and pulled a book out of his jacket pocket as it hung on the back door. He was reading a collection of prose poems by some writer in the rocky mountain west Wyatt hadn't heard of; it was the recommendation of a friend of his that ran a little independent literature press out there. The collection was called *Finding the 8 of Diamonds.* Some of it was pretty good. A few of the pieces tried too hard, and some of them were a little more earnest than Wyatt usually liked to read. Here and there he found really good lines, though. It was a good little collection. The writer talked often about the encroachment of man into the mountains; the way roads divided ecosystems, how shog seeped into the rocks, and how nature was claiming the parklands back now that they were left unmanaged. It sounded like trash was all over the ground out there, too, and though that wasn't a surprise it did disappoint Wyatt a little bit. He was reading a piece called "Meditations on the Intruder." It was lamenting the pollution and the irreparable damage done to the wilderness surrounding a cabin the writer likes to frequent during extended camping excursions. The piece then turned to acknowledge the cabin itself and the occupants — writer included — as intruders and polluters. She writes that though her goal is to observe and record nature, her presence is a form of encroachment, too. Wyatt found the writing to be a bit clumsy but the insight was clearly rendered.

As he read, two cops came up to his window. Wyatt looked at them, pulled Li's cigarette out of his jacket pocket hanging behind him, and lit it with both indifference and defiance. One of the cops was a guy, his uniform was impeccable and it looked dumb. So clean. All the latest technology. Lights and scanners everywhere on him. His cop hat was on backwards; Wyatt couldn't even guess what he was trying to say with that. The other cop was one of those bot cops. Shaped mostly like a guy, but it had three legs because they never figured out two legs for robots well enough to make it worth it. It had a cop hat. The hat stuck with a magnet on the top like a doofus, but otherwise no uniform. It's uniform was just that it was a bot cop. Nothing else like it. Three legs, a torso, two arms, a head with 360 scanner all the way around instead of a face but they put lights on there when it was talking to people so they had something to look at. It had hands that could grab and do hand things, but also the left hand had a sorta taser and the right hand was a gun. They were bullshit.

"Hey, you fuck," said the cop. The guy cop.

Wyatt got up off the stool. "Yessir?" the cigarette bounced in his lips as he answered.

"Has Paulie been here today?"

"Paulie who?"

The bot cop laughed. It sounded like sandpaper getting electrocuted and Wyatt hated it.

"Paulie who," the guy cop said. "You hear this guy? You know who Paulie."

"You wanna sandwich, boss?" Wyatt asked the bot cop.

"Repeat: has Paulie Burton been seen here today?" was the bot cop's answer. They really didn't talk like robots, the way you picture that. They had very normal sounding voices. They just didn't talk like people.

"No Paulie, no," Wyatt said.

"Well listen, a package came in for him. We've got it at the station. I think it's from the old country. Tell him to come pick it up," said the guy.

"I'll tell him. Is that it? You're scaring away customers."

"I could burn this place to the ground," and he was right. Wyatt knew he wasn't bluffing.

"That'd be a thing to see."

"I can tell you it is," said the bot. Did that count as a joke, Wyatt wondered?

The human cop plucked the cigarette from Wyatt's mouth and holding it slapped him across the face with a brief pop of sparks. "Just tell your old man to come in as soon as he can," said the cop.

Wyatt looked at the crumpled cigarette on the counter, still burning, only a third of it smoked. He nodded without looking up. "Sure thing, boss."

He didn't look back up while the cops walked away. When they were about 20 feet from his window he flicked the cigarette out into the street where it was sniffed and then ignored by a street dog. With a rigid jaw and flushed cheeks he looked up to watch them turn the corner, letting out a frustrated sigh after they were gone.

No one else even looked at the window for the rest of the shift. Twice Wyatt opened the book again and stared at the page before realizing he wasn't reading and then put the book back down in the corner. Time stood completely still and the interior of the tiny convenience shop felt frozen as if preserved for future anthropologists to puzzle over. Wyatt's mind was so focused on distraction that it was completely absent and lingered nowhere. Now and then he'd take an absent-minded sip from the open beer. Outside these walls things continued to swirl and bustle but only as much as they ever did, which was to say not at all in any meaningful sense depending on who you asked. Overhead, above the rooftops surveillance drones surveilled. Wyatt pulled the stool towards the window and leaned on the counter to see as much of the sky as he could. As he sat, the wind meandered around just right to reveal a glimpse of the blue of the sky, something that happened so rarely that it felt like a little treat. Scooting around, visible above the shog, were satellites hanging in the sky where you'd think they'd ought to fall right down. Most were dormant or dead, belonging to now defunct companies or governments, and they just kept drifting around and around until they bumped into something. This must've happened all the time, but Wyatt had never seen it or heard about anyone seeing it. The debris must just burn up before it falls, Wyatt thought as he watched a few satellites disappear behind the orange haze as the sky shifted back, pulling the blanket to hide itself. He made a mental note about how it felt to see the sky for that moment. He wanted to remember it. Maybe he would.

As his shift came to an end he heard a card key being swiped to unlock the employee door behind him. In came Marina, taking off headphones as she closed the door behind her. She was latina, in her mid-30s, very close to Wyatt's age. He enjoyed seeing Marina. She was very pleasant. She was an artist. There was a vibrancy about her personality that he found compelling. It was such a rare thing in people.

"So?" she said.

"It's been fine, mostly normal," he responded. "I saw the sky for a minute," he added because it was still on his mind.

"Oh, still blue?" she asked playfully but with some honesty. She probably hadn't seen it in a long time either.

"Yeah, it was."

He stood up and put on his jacket, stowing the book back in a pocket. He took a deep and dramatic last pull from the beer he had been nursing and was disappointed to find there was only about half a sip left, so he tossed the empty can under the counter. Marina looked around the interior of the shop for a moment before sitting down on the stool by the window.

"Oh," said Wyatt, "the cops came."

"Copz?"

"Yah. They were looking for Paulie. When did you see him last?"

"I dunno, three or four days ago I guess?"

"They said they've got something for him, a package down at the station. I guess if you see him let him know to go grab it."

Marina pulled a cigarette out of her pocket. "K."

There was a jar of adequately rolled joints and spliffs for sale. Wyatt pulled one out and punched it into the register, swiping his card before he left the shop. It was Tuesday, but he didn't work again until Friday this week so it was sort of his weekend. In the alley behind the shop he paused to light the spliff and smoked it on the way to the bus. There was a bus stop at the end of the street, but that line didn't go to his neighborhood. If he walked about six blocks east there was a bus that would take him home without needing to transfer. From past experience that was just about enough time to smoke half the spliff so he could just extinguish it and keep it in his pocket until he got home.

It was now midday, and it was a pleasant day for a walk. The rain had stopped so everything looked laminated if not clean. There were people wandering back and forth all around him. Most neighborhoods in this city had little visual differentiation from any others around it. They all functioned basically the same, with different versions of the same types of apartment buildings and streets and shops and occasionally what had once been parks but now were microscopic feral wildernesses sprung up in the midst of urban decay. Because all neighborhoods were essentially the same there wasn't much reason to venture too far into other areas for most people. This had the interesting effect of creating a much stronger sense of community than had previously existed. To an outsider each neighborhood looked the same, but to that neighborhood's residents ten blocks away might as well be a foreign country with their own customs and habits. Wyatt greatly enjoyed hopping on a bus and heading to a different corner of the city just to walk around and observe the subtle differences in behavior that had developed over the last few decades.

Wyatt walked with one hand in his coat pocket and one hand casually holding the joint between his fingers. From time to time he'd absentmindedly take a pull and exhale. Mostly his eyes were watching the ground in front of him, to avoid stepping on anything dangerous. Thinking back on the homeless man's visit to the shop window and knowing they didn't have any shoes if it came down to it, he was particularly aware of trying to keep his shoes in as good shape as he could. Suddenly, someone called out to him, pulling his eyes up from his shoes. Sitting on a second story fire escape in an alley was a man a bit younger than Wyatt. He was white, wore black jeans, a faded grey shirt, a black wide brimmed gardening hat and no socks. He had a mixed drink in his hand so vibrantly magenta it looked like it glowed amidst its drab surroundings.

"Wyatt! How's it?" he shouted.

It was Roland, a boy with whom Wyatt had briefly fostered a summer fling.

"Wow, Roland! How...uh...How're you?" Wyatt was visibly caught off guard but trying very hard not to look it.

"Pretty good, man."

"I didn't know you were in this neighborhood."

"Yeah just crashing for a little bit here, I've been here a couple weeks. We're hitting the road again at the end of the month."

"Who're you playing with now?"

"We're called the Last Steppers."

"Woah, no way, I've listened to you guys. I think I heard your 7″. Kinda sludgy?"

"Yeah that single was for sure. Most of our stuff is closer to garage punk. Kinda psyched out hardcore."

"Damn, I dig that. Any shows here in the area?"

"No, not lined up right now. We're heading down south for a bunch of stuff all the way down the coast to Florida."

"I hear Florida's getting to be a real mess. Swamps spreading and shit."

"Yeah some of that's true, some of it's a little exaggerated. What're you up to? You live in this neighborhood?"

"No, not really. I live in Sunset Morning. I work not too far from here in a little bodega. I walk up this way to catch the bus at Church Ave."

"Which one are you working in?"

"Lil ol' Betsy's."

"I don't think I've heard of that one."

"It's pretty tiny. Mostly people only stop if they're already walking down that street. Good sandwiches though, if you're ever, you know...hungry."

There was a bit of a pause. Roland took a sip of his bright pink drink and then nodded. Wyatt looked at his phone and took a drag from the still smoldering spliff.

"I actually really gotta head out to catch my bus," Wyatt said.

"Shit, well it was good to see you man. You wanna hang out again while I'm in town?"

Wyatt wasn't sure what exactly he meant by that. "Yeah that'd be cool. Is your number the same?"

"I'm not sure, which one do you have?"

"Umm..." Wyatt scrolled through his contacts, not even sure if he would've had Roland's name even if he did have his number.

"Gimme your number and I'll text you."

"K, you ready?"

Roland put his drink down on a tiny table that shared the fire escape with him, pulled out his phone and nodded. Wyatt said his number. "That's an upstate area code, right? You still have that?"

"Yeah, why not?" Wyatt said, fidgeting a little and glancing in the direction of the bus stop.

"No, it's kinda cool," Roland shrugged, putting his phone in his pocket and taking a cigarette from somewhere inside the apartment in reach of his stool. Wyatt wasn't sure if he had actually put the number into his phone.

"Well I hope to see you before you guys really start stepping."

Roland chuckled as he exhaled cigarette smoke and nodded. He didn't say anything, picked up his drink and took another sip. So Wyatt started walking again.

He replayed the conversation in his head as he approached the bus stop. Should he have said something more? Should he have made sure to get Roland's number? He puffed on his spliff as he stepped up to the corner with the barely intelligible sign marking the place where the bus would stop. Or should stop. There was only about a quarter left of the spliff. As he very slowly let smoke fall up from his mouth he studied the length of the thing. Pondering how his encounter with Roland had cost him a quarter of a spliff more than he usually had smoked by this time. And there was no point to having had the conversation only to fumble through it like that. Part of his brain cursed at another part. But he also thought back to the sharp angle of Roland's jaw and the lethargic look in his brown eyes that had first drawn Wyatt to him at that first show before he even knew Roland was with one of the bands.

With a rumbling burp the bus announced itself around the corner and squealed to a stop six or seven feet past the sign. Wyatt pressed the lit end of the spliff into the wall of the building next to him and stuffed it into his jacket pocket. Trying to forget about what he had already convinced himself was a total failure of an interaction, he waved his phone in front of the payment machine, and a green light turned on indicating it was satisfied with Wyatt's offering.

The bus was almost mostly full. One guy in the back looked like he'd been on for a day or two already; he casually read a newspaper while the whole row of seats had his belongings spread out confidently. There was an aging hipster standing with his bike, a woman about twenty holding a baby and sitting next to a stroller full of groceries, some people sleeping, some people looking out the window, a guy dressed like a businessman looking for a fix, tie loose and all that. Wyatt sought a place to sit in the sweet spot, right before the step up in the middle.

All together the passengers of the bus lurched back and then forward and then settled back into a slightly bouncing stasis as they left the stop. Wyatt watched buildings and windows and people's lives pass him by outside the bus, and he tried to make himself really see it. But his head spun with the wheels and dissipated behind the bus in exhaust. His thoughts went back to nowhere. The bus trekked on, winding through the blocks, gaining and losing passengers.

Then without warning, and obviously without warning, Wyatt's phone buzzed. He pulled it out of his pocket and saw a text from Roland that he did not expect.

we're doing the Lantern tomorrow night for drinks, if you wanna come out

Wyatt smiled and put the phone back in his pocket. He had never heard of that bar. He pulled a small notebook out of his pocket, the cover a little singed and ashed from sharing pocket space with dozens of joints in its lifetime. Despite the bouncing of the bus, Wyatt put pen to paper and wrote a little poem for the remainder of the trip, only looking up to check when he needed to get off.

Chapter 2

WOKE UP EARLY, GETTING *coffee on the way in—* words on Wyatt's phone when he woke up. He groggily pieced the letters together as he deciphered the meaning. It was from Talbot. He could get coffee with Talbot.

I could do that. Brook's? Wyatt responded, laying on his back and holding his phone above his face.

Next to his bed were a few empty beer cans from the previous night. He armed them against his chest to carry them and dropped them into a garbage can on his way to the closet. Without looking he picked out a t-shirt from his bundle of t-shirts and switched into it. It was a grey-green shirt that said "EYE DEW", a mopey band he saw a couple times. They were nice guys.

yeah I'll be there in like 5 minutes, Talbot responded.

Brook's was about a 10 minute walk away, but Talbot always said he was closer than he was. Wyatt knew that Talbot did that because he thought Wyatt was always late. Talbot was saying "5 minutes" meaning "you should leave right now." Wyatt was onto this little tactic, and though he was usually a punctual person it didn't really bother him not to be thought of that way.

Reaching the street, Wyatt was relieved to find the remainder of a joint still in his jacket. He lit it and started walking toward the coffee shop. It was a pleasant morning.

Wyatt got there first, but only by a few moments. Talbot was wearing a dull white oxford button up shirt and a decent pair of slacks. They still made decent slacks at some places. This is what Talbot wore to work. Talbot, like Wyatt, was half black and half white. He was taller than Wyatt and had darker skin, which was noticeable especially when he wore white shirts.

Wyatt was born in a little town upstate. There had been two presidential elections in his lifetime and he remembered one, from when he was in kindergarten, a year or two later school stopped. He was too young to really remember what was different about it. Wyatt was still pretty young when he lost his parents. Someone with no experience or decent temperament tried their hand at burglary and ended up killing Wyatt's parents mostly by accident. Just some idiot. So as a child he went to the city, looking for an aunt he'd heard about but never before met. He settled in as a teenager lurking at punk shows when he met Talbot. They'd been hanging out since.

"Wyatt, my young man," Talbot said.

"Morning Talbot."

"Did I wake you up?"

"No, I was waking up. But reading your text was the first thing I did today. So you can count that if you want."

"Haha, I will count that, yeah."

"How long have you been up?"

"I dunno, a few hours."

"You haven't been sleeping."

"I slept a bit, but I've been waking up pretty early for some reason," Talbot said.

"Sure."

"What've you been listening to?"

"Jeez I don't remember right now. It's been a little while since I listened to anything new, other than a couple shows I've been to," Wyatt answered. It was their turn at the counter. "Hold on, let's do this part," he said to Talbot. "Could I just get a coffee?" he said to the barista.

The barista was an old white man, maybe 60. The man nodded and looked to Talbot.

"Americano?" Talbot said. "I'll pick these up." Wyatt gave a grateful shrug. Talbot picked up the coffee about 4/7ths of the time.

The weathered man behind the counter went about the orders. His arms were lined with faded tattoos. Wyatt's coffee came up first in a cup that held the coffee but was too thin to hold the heat so Wyatt couldn't pick it up. He grabbed it using his canvas tote bag as an ersatz glove and he went to a table by the window. Talbot stood near the counter while his espresso was pounded. Wyatt zoned out.

"You been working on anything?" Talbot asked, while sitting down. He blew on his open coffee cup.

"A lot of time at Betsy's, making sandwiches, but it's been fine," Wyatt said. "I finished that play I was working on, and I'm just trying to figure out how to make it exist."

"Like, looking for a theater and stuff?"

"Yeah I don't know anyone who's done it. But, like, they do all these little plays all the time at those theaters. There must be some way to get one in there."

"Do you ever go to see plays?"

"No not really. I went to one a year or so ago because like a friend of a friend was in it. But I thought the play sucked. That's what made me want to write my own thing in the first place."

"Interesting."

"I mean I'm sure there are great plays all the time. I just don't know. I don't know where they are."

"You should go to see more. Right?"

"No, yeah I know. You're right. Do you go to plays?"

"Me? No not really. I mean I've been to a few here and there. On dates and stuff. I think my mom was way into theater, like back when she was in school. But she never really wanted to talk about it."

"Hm. Yeah I should look around for something that looks interesting and see what the scene's like," Wyatt sipped his coffee, just now cooled down enough to manage. "So, how's work been for you, man?"

"Oh yeah. You know, fine."

"Hitting your, uhh, quarterly goals and stuff?"

Talbot chuckled. "Do you think I work in a cartoon of an office? It's an actual office. Nobody talks about that stuff in real life."

"I haven't seen enough compelling evidence to the contrary."

"Well you've never been in an office of any kind, have you?"

Wyatt conceded and they both laughed.

"What have you been listening to?" Wyatt asked.

"Um, a few things. A lot of metal."

"What kind?"

"Prog, death, blackened death, deathcore. Progg-y death. You know. Bit of column-A, etc."

"I just listened to a really good black prog album a week or two ago. I think it was kinda new. I don't remember who it was."

"Were they local?"

"No, other coast. Portland I think? Don't think of metal from there really."

"There's actually a really good scene there, I went out a couple times a few years back, but it sounds like it's really thriving."

"That's cool. I've never been there."

"I mean, there are a lot of nazis there. Neither of us look white enough to really be safe."

"Terrorist Paraglider. That was the band!" Wyatt said, relieved he had thought of it.

"Oh, oh yeah. They're good. I listened to that record."

"They're not nazis are they?"

"I dunno. It's tough to tell out there. I mean, I figure anyone in that scene must at least tolerate it, so that doesn't bode well. But who knows. There's antifa organized in that city, too."

"Yeah I've read a coupla those zines."

There was a natural lull and both took the opportunity to drink their now lukewarm coffee drinks. Talbot looked at his watch. Talbot was the only person Wyatt knew that wore a watch, and it confused him every single time he saw Talbot lift his wrist to look at it. Talbot's eyes flinched.

"Shit, time to roll out," he said. There was not much urgency in his voice.

"You late?"

"Just kinda on time if I leave right now."

"K, well then. Lemme know what you're getting into this weekend."

"Oh will do," and he left.

Wyatt stayed in the coffee shop. There was some Americano left in Talbots mug so he poured it into his own and took another sip. He suddenly realized he hadn't brought anything with him, so he sort of perked up and straightened his back to look around the coffee shop to see if there was anything to read while he finished. There was a pile of zines on the counter by the artificial creamer. Most looked like corporate advertising designed to look like zines. One was genuine; it was called "Sidewalk Gum" and there were three copies. Wyatt picked it up and shuffled back to his table by the window to read it. It was an earnest collection of poems with a few very hastily rendered drawings scattered throughout. The front cover said "vol. 1", which Wyatt always thought seemed like a bit of wishful thinking, if not hubris. He had published a couple zines, all with different names and ideas, and none marked as the first of a kind. None had taken off or been particularly well received, but by making each a one-off project none seemed to be a failure.

Sitting in the coffee shop without a notebook or a pen Wyatt felt like he had a fierce creative drive that he couldn't harness at this moment. It had been four months since he had an idea he felt interested in working on. Now he felt like he had it in him to put something onto paper, but he didn't have any paper. He got up to flip through the corporate wannabe zines because a lot of the time they only printed on one side of the paper. There was one that was printed to look photocopied and handmade, but it was clearly just a flyer trying to sell discount furniture (or was it a brilliant statement?) that had a bunch of blank pages. So Wyatt nabbed it, picked up a pen from near the counter, and sat back down to his mug of now-cold coffee.

He flipped the flyer open to an empty side of a page and folded the booklet back on itself to get to work. He jotted down a few words, letting them out, and stopped mid sentence. It said-- "a big weird thing"-- before trailing off. His face got hot. What if someone in the coffee shop could see him struggling, or even worse saw what he had written? A big weird thing? What bullshit. He scribbled it out and tried to remember what he had been thinking about before he had paper. At a loss he just started writing about his encounter with the police officer the previous day. He tried to write it in a way that would come off as sardonic and subversive. He really wanted to write something he would be impressed by reading. Before long he had filled all of the empty spaces throughout the book. Rereading it, he hated it. But maybe being written in this weird corporate rag made it interesting? He decided to leave it here to be found. He put his name at the end and scratched out any references to the author of the original zine. It probably wasn't a real person anyway. Or it was just some graphic designer breaking his back for this furniture company and barely affording rent in a marginally nicer part of the city. He got up, returned his mug to the counter, and dropped the new zine there.

As a habitual reflex, Wyatt pulled out his phone and looked at it blankly. There was an email waiting there from a digital lit mag he didn't read called *Reckless Shuffle* that he had submitted a story to. He excitedly slid his thumb across to open the email, and his shoulders sank as he read a fairly standard rejection notice. One of those "thank you for letting us read your piece" and "not the right fit for us at this time" and "the number of submissions we receive" kind of things. He got the idea of it and only skimmed through to the end, and leaving the email in his inbox the phone returned to his pocket.

Next to the coffee shop was a tiny little corner store, a little bigger than Lil ol' Betsy's. They had a bigger selection, but their sandwiches weren't as good. Wyatt went in and bought a pre-rolled joint, a little luxury, and smoked half of it while he walked home. He realized he had accidentally stolen the pen from the Brook's. He'd bring it back tomorrow. Outside his building some guy asked him for a drag, and Wyatt gave it to him.

"Read anything good lately?" Wyatt asked the guy.

"What do you mean?" he answered, holding smoke in his lungs.

"Like any books or anything?"

The guy breathed the smoke out. "No I haven't."

He handed the joint back but Wyatt waved it back to him and went inside.

CHAPTER 3

HE LIVED IN WHAT HAD once been a largely industrial area of the city, but the factories had been closed for a long long time. There were not many grocery stores in the city, and none were close by. At some point young people with fancy sneakers and ideas to make money decided these old factories would be a good place for people to pay to live and they started reviving blocks that had once been industrial by transforming them into residential centers. The neighborhood had been dubbed "Sunset Morning" by a mega-developer at some point, and though their experiment failed, the name stuck.

Wyatt's building was big and square. It took up almost the whole block. Inside was almost a neighborhood of itself: different hallways had different things to say and different people living there.

He walked past the group of six people standing on the sidewalk in front of the building who were always there but were always faces Wyatt had never seen since they were different every time he passed. He walked down the hall and up a flight of stairs and back towards the front of the building. When he got to his floor, a neighbor from down the hall was leaving his apartment with an acoustic guitar in a case and a large bag full of gear.

"Hey Wyatt!" he said.

"Hey there, Brent. Got a gig?"

"Yessir, over at the Shipyard, in the Bush."

"Cool, man. Kick some ass."

"Haha, just for you." Brent was a dork, but he was a good guy. "I've got another show there in a few weeks. You should come check it out, man! I've been working on a bunch of new songs, getting ready to lay down an EP."

Wyatt didn't really like Brent's music, but it had been a long time since he'd been out to one of his shows and he was starting to feel obligated. So he nodded and said he'd try and check it out.

He paused at his door so it could scan the phone in his pocket and unlock, and then he entered his apartment. It was a small room with a kitchen to the right and a bathroom to the left. In the main room was a bed, a small desk and some chairs that had come out of the dumpster behind what used to be a school. He had a bookshelf with books stacked in it, on top of it and in front of it. He had read close to half, maybe. The room was not tidy but was certainly not a mess. It was just barely big enough for the furniture he had. If he really stretched he could probably reach any wall from any spot in the apartment.

Wyatt opened up the laptop that slept on the desk and poured some wine from an open wine bottle into a glass that wasn't a wine glass. When the computer was awake he scrolled through and selected some noisy free jazz, an experimental group from Scandinavia somewhere. It was distorted and chaotic but in a way Wyatt found a little soothing. It drowned out the sort of constant clatter and hum of other apartments along the hall or above and below him. He sat down and pulled up a short story he had started in a notebook and transferred into the computer before it was finished. He reread the last few paragraphs and like plumbing a clogged pipe forced out a few more sentences to push it a little further along. The sentences turned into a couple paragraphs, but then he sputtered out. The bookshelf on the other side of the room reminded him how fragile his claim to being a writer was. It was full of things with other people's names. The majority of his work was still handwritten in notebooks somewhere or locked away in the memory of this laptop. If the laptop took too much of a tumble his writing would pretty much all be gone; there would be no trace of him as a creative for anyone to discover. This was a thought that lingered somewhere in his crowded mind most of the time, sometimes jumping right up to the front whenever a bus drove by too fast, and he imagines getting flattened by it and becoming a part of the litter-covered streets. From writer to road. After leaning back in his chair doing nothing for a few minutes he stood back up.

The doodly music continued and Wyatt tossed his clothes back into the drawers he had pulled them out of and stepped into the tiny bathroom with a tiny shower. The water was fine. He thought about a sci-fi novel he had seen ads for. Rinsing mid-priced soap from his body he wondered if he would like the book. It was getting some good buzz, but he had never heard of the author and didn't like some of the comparisons. Then he heard a knock on his apartment door.

"Yeah?" he called out from the warm water.

"It's me," said a woman's voice. Wyatt recognized it as his friend Lena.

Wyatt leaned from the shower out of the bathroom and pushed a button on the communication panel to briefly unlock the door to let her in while he finished cleaning up. Drying off and stepping out of the shower, Wyatt found Lena sitting at his desk flipping through a sloppy little lit zine Wyatt had picked up at a gallery opening recently. He had only read half of the first story, but he thought it was pretty good.

"Hey," she said, not looking up from the zine.

"So," he said, getting dressed, "how's it going?" A distorted electric guitar played a sliding solo over indecipherable jazz drum rhythms.

Lena was tall and willowy, had reddish brown hair and light skin. Her posture was strong and her movement was fluid. She was wearing denim overalls and a floral patterned shirt. "This is good," she said, referring to the zine. "Who wrote it?"

"Some punk. I picked it up at a gallery, but I don't know who it is. I haven't really read it yet."

"Which gallery?"

"It was Marina's new display at that place up past the canal."

"Oh in Sludgetown."

"Yeah that's the one," Wyatt nodded.

She put the zine down and picked up the book that was next to it on the desk. It was a novel called *Old Rage* written by Edna LeBlanc. "Are you reading this?"

"I am, yeah, about halfway through. It's super good. Have you read it?"

"I've read some of her short stories but none of her novels. I've heard a lot about this one. People like it."

"Yeah, me too. I'm people. It's really great, almost discouraging. I read stuff like this and I'm like, fuck, what's the point? I can't do this."

She chuckled. "Mhmm. I know what you mean sometimes."

"Anyway, what're you doing tonight?"

She put the book back and stood up. "I'm not really sure, I've just been inside most of the day so I was getting antsy."

"What were you working on?"

"Not as much as I wish. I was doing some drawing, but I don't know if I liked any of it. What'd you do today?"

"Just making sandwiches. I only got home a few minutes before you came over."

"Did you ever meet Dan Fuller?"

"I'm not sure, who is he?"

"He's a writer. Poet. He's doing a reading along with some other weirdos at The Last Coffee Shop."

"Oh, tonight?"

"Yeah."

"I'd check that out. When?"

"I dunno. Soon-ish. It'll take a little while to get over there," Lena said.

"Cool! I'm all set, let's head over there," and they left Wyatt's apartment to crunch back out onto the trash covered sidewalk.

They'd have to take a bus to a subway terminal and a train the rest of the way to the Old University District where The Last Coffee Shop was.

It was nearly five in the evening and the sky was receding into a green, hazy night. Street lamps lit up and crackled, in patches, inconsistent and lethargic. Some entire streets remained dim. Each street lamp that was lit glowed with a slightly different hue than its neighbor. Air traffic remained constant all through the night. Small drones and other flying things kept buzzing around: watching, listening or just buzzing and not paying attention to them at all. As they turned a corner, Wyatt saw that there was a bus waiting at the stop. He took a few stutter steps to run for it before the bus left and turned to see if Lena would run too. She looked at him with a face that clearly did not intend on running, so Wyatt lurched back to a walking pace. He didn't really want to run for it, but he felt like he had to show that he would have been willing to. Accordingly the bus chugged away, spitting up debris behind it like dust behind a hurrying cartoon. As he watched the dim red tail lights disappear into the gloam, Wyatt suddenly remembered the half-smoked joint still in his jacket pocket, casually putting it to his lips and lighting it. He pulled smoke into his lungs and while holding it in his chest offered it to Lena, who took a small drag and handed it back as they arrived at the bus stop to wait.

"Have you been painting lately?" Wyatt asked.

"No, I actually started doing some photography."

"Where'd you find a camera?"

"We were picking through an abandoned estate up on the Sound. Some rich guy had been dead for like 10 years and nobody came to get his stuff."

"Ooooo spoooooky!" Wyatt said, holding his hands up like a tormented ghoul. "Was he still in there?"

"No, but his stink was," Lena smiled, shoving ghost-Wyatt away. "I was in the second or third trip in there, so I think they pushed the body out onto the water before I got there. There was a ton of crazy shit. I picked up a lot of books you should take a look through."

"Wow, yeah I'd love to. That sounds rad."

"What about you – have you been writing?" she asked.

"Well not as much, I've got a script I'm trying to get produced, that's kinda what I'm working on."

"What is it?"

"It's experimental theater. Just like some people living in this apocalyptic wasteland with an anthropomorphized dog-man."

"Did I read a draft of that? The dog-person sounds familiar."

"Maybe a long time ago, I kept quitting, it took me forever to finish. I think it's pretty good. I really like it. Are there any new theaters you know about that might take it? I've pretty much done the rounds at all of the places I know about and I haven't been able to get anyone to take it on."

"Do you wanna direct?"

"No, I don't think I'd be any good at that. I wouldn't mind co-producing maybe, but most tend to have directors they call on for stuff. I just wanna hand over the script and be like 'bye, have fun, see you in 12 weeks' or whatever."

"I can ask around a little bit. I don't know that I have connections to any theaters you wouldn't have already talked to."

One of the passing cars jerked off the road and pulled over right in front of Wyatt and Lena. It had no front passenger window. The driver leaned to the window and shouted over to them, "Taxi, if you need a ride. Don't wait for the bus."

Wyatt was nervous about this type of thing. He looked over at Lena. She looked back at the driver with the confidence of someone who had a switchblade in her pocket.

"How much? We're going to the Old University District."

"Alright," the driver said. "How's about $15 sound, huh?"

Lena looked at Wyatt. "I'll pick this up if you pay to get me into the show."

Wyatt took one last drag from his roachy little joint and nodded, doing his best to hide that he didn't want to do it. He hated riding in these weirdos' cars. These drivers didn't usually have the intention of hurting anyone, but they were almost always strung out or drunk. Wyatt knew at least a couple people who had to swim their way out of private taxi rides.

This guy had most of his teeth and that was a pretty good sign. He had a beard that was trimmed unevenly, and hair tied up into a knot. He was dressed just like anybody. Shirt, pants, whatever. Wyatt noticed a very old tattoo on the guy's wrist of a very specific design he didn't recognize. It was faded and indecipherable now but clearly was a symbol denoting some kind of allegiance, current or long prior. It was a neat bit of ingenuity that the car had no front passenger side window, or just a convenient coincidence. It made it easier and faster for the driver to shout at potential clients on the street, but it also discouraged people from sitting in that front seat which was probably best for everyone. The car was a dull grey and had taken on so much grime of the atmosphere it practically wore the city like a coat. Inside was fairly tidy. There was no litter to speak of. Everything was worn down to its limit with many of the seams having been re-sewn by hand and every removable panel gone. It smelled, but it didn't stink. A mix between that smell of a wormy sidewalk after rain and a record store.

He knew where he was going and he drove pretty well, whipping between lanes with abandon. They'd have to cross the bridge over the East River to get to the University district, which was a little more dangerous in a car than it was in a bus, but for some reason Wyatt felt like this driver knew what he was doing.

As the car started to come to the bridge Wyatt could see that there was a makeshift barricade set up at the end. There were seven kids, looked to be around ten years old, all wearing Prussian-style helmets, holding weapons, and managing a gate they had clearly built. They were stopping at each car, halfheartedly threatening the drivers with violence and collecting a bridge toll in exchange for safe passage. Payment was collected electronically with a magnetic swiper a few gang members held. It seemed like they let buses go without trouble; most bus drivers were armed and truly did not give a shit about hurting anyone who threatened them. Ten year olds included. Certain important hubs and annexes in the city existed at the mercy of dozens of gangs. Usually 12-14 year-olds, sometimes younger, and often dressed in some kind of matching themed costumes. Cowboys, clowns, safari hunters, things like that. They roamed around on bridges, at important subway stops and especially in office neighborhoods where there was still a little bit of money to steal. They were sometimes violent, but they were never tough. Just kids who had found what felt like a pretty fun job. They didn't want to get hurt, so they wouldn't usually risk that.

There were not many cars ahead of them, so they were only waiting about 15 minutes before they reached the gate. Lena put her hand in her pocket, reaching for her switchblade Wyatt guessed. Noticing that, Wyatt took in a sharp, nervous breath. The driver's temperament was unchanged as far as Wyatt could see, but he wasn't sure if he should rest assured by his confidence or feel fear at his recklessness. Creeping, the car approached the gate. All intact windows remained closed. The front passenger's side window remained missing. One of the Prussian costumed kids bent over slightly to peer into the broken window, making eye contact with each passenger. He looked to be about 13-years-old probably. Others circled the car. Some carried pistols. There were wrenches in holsters, hatchets, knives, hammers and baseball bats wrapped in wire. All of the weapons were designed to be visible even when not wielded. Their purpose was to intimidate. Most had been customized in some way and to Wyatt most of the customizations didn't seem to make the weapons any more functional. The driver looked straight ahead out the windshield with lazy assuredness. The car came to a stop. One of the young gang members stood directly in front of them, and two more joined his side. They were looking at where license plates used to go: middle of the front bumper. Wyatt saw them confer with each other before the first, standing in the middle, looked up to make eye contact with their driver. A prussian helmet nodded. The driver responded in kind. And the gate was opened for them to drive through. Lena took her hand out of her pocket.

"That was smooth," Wyatt said to the driver.

"I drive for the gangs sometimes, when they need it. So they gave me a universal pass. Mutually beneficial."

And so at that, they set across the bridge. Out the window Wyatt could see the ruins of older bridges, one to their north and one to the south, no longer drivable. They were now homeless camps. Ropes ran across them so that supplies could be shuttled over the gaps. The bridge they drove on was lined with debris and the remnants of stripped down dead cars on all sides. The road was bumpy but easy to drive. Bus companies paid to clear off the lanes and would occasionally slather new pavement or structural reinforcement to keep it passable. Below them, the water was a slurry of grime, litter and bodies. It looked like you could hop right across the water on the islands of trash wandering around on the surface. It was a deep black-green that reflected an oily rainbow when the sun caught it. Ducks had adapted thicker bed of feathers in order to endure swimming in it, and a constant swarm of gulls twisted above the water, picking at food-ish bits that floated by. There weren't many fish left anywhere though. As they drove, they passed other gang members from other troupes who paid little attention to them. They just bounced and jostled across the uneven road surface until they got to the other side. There was no gate on this side, so when they got to the shore of the big island they just drove on.

Old University District wasn't far from the bridge. It was close to what used to be a park in the southern half of the island. The park hadn't been tended by anyone in decades, so nature was clawing its dominance back in the area. Trees were overgrown and unforgiving. Their roots slowly chewed on nearby pavement, so surrounding blocks were surrendering to the new jungle. This university had shut down a long time ago, as long as Wyatt could remember. But the professors and students who had been there at the time just never left, so the culture of the neighborhood still bore the influence from the institution that had once been there.

The Last Coffee Shop on the Left had been part of the university campus at one point. The university didn't close all at once. It died one piece at a time: a few programs ended, some of the colleges closed, the bookstore dried up. Eventually it was gone, but a few remnants held on. What had once been a cafeteria was still a community kitchen where you could get a cheap meal if you didn't mind the risk of getting raided by the police once in a while – other eateries in the area hated people getting free food so they'd hire the cops to go in and wreck the place occasionally. Dorms were now apartments or squats. And long after the rest of the infrastructure of the university had crumbled and blown away in the wind, the Last Coffee Shop remained a fixture in the area. The driver zigzagged his way there, scraping through alleys that barely had enough room for a car. He seemed to have an encyclopedic awareness of where roadblocks were and made his way to their destination with deceptive deliberation.

"Well friends, we did it," the driver said as he skidded to a stop down the block from the place.

"Glad you found us," said Lena, tapping her phone on the payment square on the back of the seat. "Thanks much."

"Thank you," Wyatt said, as he climbed out.

The architecture in this part of the city was much older and more elegant than Wyatt's neighborhood. But it was worn down by years of apathy and acidic air pollution. The streets were paved with a layer of trash just like back in his neighborhood. People still walked around and drove to jobs and drove home, streets and sidewalks were crowded with hustle and bustle. There were a lot of young people who lived and played here. Lots of them were from families of old wealth and they held onto the theater of the old upper class, even though no one really had much money anywhere anymore. They performed upper class intellectual. Once there had been the "haves" and "have nots." Now there were pretty much "have nots" and "have even less." Somewhere there were the "haves," but Wyatt had never even heard of anyone who had any idea who or where.

Someone was waiting, working the door – a spindly guy in his mid-twenties. He had a worn-out baseball cap on his head, a cigarette in his mouth and a few tattoos on his arms placed strategically to appear slapdash. The front of the place was nice and it stuck out. The windows were cleaned every day, and the name "The Last Coffee Shop on the Left" was painted across in large letters approximating elegance. There was a painter they brought in every few weeks to re-do the lettering because the air peeled away at it so quickly.

"Here for the show?"

"Yeah," said Wyatt, pulling out his phone to pay. "I'm paying for both of us."

The guy nodded and exhaled cigarette smoke, doing his best to blow it away from them, but an imperceptible breeze still pulled it into Wyatt's eyes and stung. He palmed in his left hand a black device, about the size of a golf ball, that he used to accept payment from Wyatt's phone. "Right on," he said when the light turned from green to red, acknowledging the transaction. "Take these. Put 'em on your wrists," he handed them two twine bracelets. "The show's in the back room so you'll need this to get in there. You can hang out in the coffee shop before or after."

Wyatt and Lena took the twine and cinched them to their wrists and stepped inside. It was a very cozy and pleasant space. There was red cloth draped across the ceiling, almost completely covering the drab, mass produced tiles. Walls alternated between exposed brick and exposed beams. The wooden sections of the walls were covered in amateur art and posters for everything ever. There were huge, soft chairs and sofas around the perimeter, but regulars knew that the comfier the chair the more likely it was to have bugs, so Wyatt only sat in the wooden chairs at tables in the middle of the room. The barista behind the counter was a woman, probably in her early fifties with hair grey and wispy, tied back to reveal a friendly and relaxed face. Wyatt had been here a number of times but he had never seen the same barista more than once. Instinctively, he and Lena stepped to the counter, staring past the barista at the menu with that squint that communicates, "I'm reading the menu. I'm not ready to order yet." Wyatt knew he just wanted a coffee. He looked to Lena before saying anything. She was still looking at the menu.

"You want anything?" he asked her.

"Yeah I'll have a flat white," Lena answered.

Wyatt looked at the barista, and she smiled, kindly. "I'll have just a coffee, in a mug. And we'll also get a flat white."

"Alright, I'll get your coffee first," the barista said, pulling a mug from a shelf and filling it up from a carafe. This was the type of place with a bunch of mismatched mugs. She handed him a green mug with the focus grouped logo from some company nobody had ever heard of. "Yours will be right up."

Wyatt picked up the coffee and held it close to his face. He wasn't really blowing on it or even taking in the aroma, just feeling the heat at his upper lip out of habit. They stepped to the other end of the counter as the espresso machine grinded and steamed.

"So who is it you know on this show?" Wyatt asked.

"Dan Fuller."

"How do you know him?"

"I don't remember. I think I met him through the Litter Bachs, do you remember them?"

"Oh hell yeah, they were great. I've got that 7-inch they pressed, think it was the only release they put out. I still listen to it sometimes."

"Yeah. I don't know any of the other people tonight."

Wyatt looked at the poster for the show hanging by the cash register. "Oh! I know Rebecca Pabst."

"Oh cool, how?"

"I mean, I've read some of her stuff. I don't know her. She had a short story in a zine my buddy Branson put out not too long ago. I think I liked it."

"Flat white for you," the barista delivered the steaming, muddy drink to the end of the counter for Lena.

"Thanks," she said, taking it. They walked to a table. There was only one available. The rest were occupied. Some were clearly killing time until the show, and others were lurkers who'd be there all night.

"Hey do you remember that band the Torqués?" Wyatt asked as they sat down.

"No, I don't know."

"Oh, well there was this guy, Roland…"

"Oh ok, I see, that's ringing bells! Real dark brown eyes?"

"Yeah that's him."

"You guys were hooking up for a summer or something?"

"Uhhh… yeah," he blushed a tiny bit, but took a sip of coffee to hide it. "What about him?"

"I dunno. Nothing. He's with a new band I guess. They're in town for a little bit and then heading out on a little tour."

"Ooooh… you wanna relight the fire?" Lena smiled.

"No, I don't know," Wyatt fidgetted. "He invited me out tomorrow. I guess some of them are going to a place called the Lantern. Have you ever heard of that place?"

"The Lantern? I don't know it, no. Who's going?"

"Just some other punks I think. I don't know who he's hanging out with these days. It's been a few years since I've seen him at all. Every damn six blocks has its own punk scene."

Lena sipped the espresso, and there was a pause in the conversation. Wyatt looked at her mug. It said "World's Worldiest World" on it, and it kind of pissed him off. He pulled out his phone to look up where The Lantern was. It was right in Sludgetown.

"Yeah I know what you mean. Do you want me to come along?" Lena put her mug down on the table.

"Oh, I hadn't thought about it. Would it be weird to go by myself? Or is it weird to bring someone?"

"It depends on what your goal is I guess."

"I don't have a goal. I dunno. Are you doing anything tomorrow?"

"Nothing especially, no. I'd come if you want, I like hanging out in that area."

Wyatt thought about it, staring back and forth between the two coffee mugs on the table and the map on his phone. "Yeah come along. I hate being in a group where I only know one person."

"Sure, I'm there."

"You wanna eat in Sludgetown first?"

"I can do that, yeah. You know any good spots?"

"There's a really good falafel place."

Lena nodded while sipping some more of her drink. The shop was starting to get bustlier and people were moseying to the back room gradually.

"Well, what do you think?" Wyatt said. "Should we head back and post up somewhere?"

"Yeah, let's do it."

Lena nudged her chair back towards the table a few inches with her hip as they stood up and they walked to the back room. A barely attentive hipster glanced at their twine wrist bands before losing herself back into a vintage copy of Time Magazine from 30 years ago. This room was decorated with richly colored blankets draped in a circle to evoke some kind of large yurt. On the far side of the room was a small platform about a foot high, barely big enough for a three person band. There were a couple rows of wooden folding chairs ringing around the outside and the rest of the seating was pillows and thick rugs. There were cliques of people murmuring and a few soloists with nobody to murmur to. One guy was reading. A couple people scribbled in notebooks. As Wyatt sipped his coffee, Lena recognized someone sitting with a group of two others. She smiled and waved to the group, Wyatt following in her wake as if pulled by gravity as she walked to greet them.

"Hey Qat, what's up?" Lena crouched to hug them.

"Lena! Hey," Qat said, returning the hug graciously. "I was hoping you'd be here."

"Oh yeah? Am I in trouble?"

"No, I was just thinking about your photography. I want to see it. I was talking about it to someone."

Qat had flawless bronze skin and vibrant, perceptive eyes. They were wearing an elegantly flowing jumper and loose, rattling jewelry. Their head was buzzed and intricate tattoos were visible on their scalp under the short trim of hair.

"Wow, cool! Yeah I'm still figuring some of it out. It's basically impossible to find the right cables to hook anything up to anything, so I'm not sure what I'm gonna do."

"Oh no," Qat sighed.

"This is my friend Wyatt. He's a writer."

"Hi, Cat," Wyatt said, spelling the name wrong in his head. He'd be embarrassed to know.

"Hi, Wyatt. Good to meet you! Lena, do you know Tom or Curtiss?" Qat gestured to the men they were with. Two beautiful young weirdos, probably 22 or 23. One had porcelain complexion and a perfectly quaffed shock of red hair. The other had deep black skin and a tight haircut. Looked like actor types.

"No, I don't think so. Hi!" Lena said. "Tom, Curtiss, I'm Lena. And this is still Wyatt."

"Hey, Wyatt," said either Tom or Curtiss, whomever was black. Wyatt didn't catch which name belonged to which of the two.

"Hello, everyone," Wyatt said. "Lots of names for the reader to keep straight. Hope it's not too confusing." They sort of chuckled.

"So," Qat addressed Lena again. "What's this problem with cables?"

"Well, as it is I can only collect pictures in the camera, and view them on this tiny little screen," she answered, pulling the camera out of her bag. "It's been so long since anybody used any of these things, so it's really hard to get the pictures off the camera. I'll have to track down a computer and a cable that can download the pictures. And then I'll still need to figure out printing."

"Printing photographs," Qat said with quiet amusement that drifted out of their mouth.

"I mean I really only started taking pictures in these last few weeks, so I haven't even started trying to figure that out."

"Lena," Wyatt said, "I know this tinkerer who collects old computer stuff. He squats in my neighborhood in an abandoned mechanic's garage. We should look there."

"Oh holy shit, yeah that sounds great."

"Aren't you glad I asked about it," Qat said with a sly grin.

"You said you're a writer?" said Tom or Curtiss. The white one this time. Wyatt was a little startled being addressed. "Yeah, I mean sorta. I write."

"Anywhere I may have read something of yours?" the same Tom or Curtiss asked.

A question Wyatt never loved answering. "Not really anywhere, lately. Unless you picked up one of my zines from the record shop in my neighborhood."

"What do you write?"

"Just...write I guess. Some zines, poetry, short stories. I've been in a few little journals here and there. I have this play I'm working on."

"Oh, theater? Curtiss and I are actors," said Tom, now identified as the red headed one.

'Of course,' Wyatt briefly thought with an internal snort before saying "Are you? That makes sense. Where do you perform?"

"Why does that make sense?" asked Curtiss.

"Well, you're both beautiful. Ya know," Wyatt shrugged, "like actor types." Wyatt wasn't sure if that sounded like a compliment or whether or not he meant it as one. They didn't seem to register it as compliment or insult. "Where do you work mostly?"

"We're not committed to any particular theater," Curtiss said, his voice smooth and long.

"A variety of black boxes and DIY spaces mostly," said Tom. "Generally on this side of the river."

"Any shows coming up?" Wyatt asked.

"We just recently started rehearsing for a new project directed by Wolf Wolf."

"Oh my god, she's working on a new project?" Lena seemed genuinely interested.

"Yes, it's been quite some time," Qat said with a wistfulness in their voice.

"Would it be possible for me to come to a rehearsal? To see the space?" Wyatt asked.

"No, no I don't think so," Curtiss said so quickly there was no daylight between the question and the answer.

"Wolf Wolf is very particular," Lena said.

"She doesn't usually want people to see anything during the process," Tom added. "Sometimes I feel like if she could do rehearsals without even the actors she'd prefer that."

"Sure, ok yeah I understand that."

Wyatt was frustrated and the conversation slowed. He felt like it was his fault, and he felt an anxiety bubble in the back of his neck. It was with huge relief to Wyatt that Qat spoke up again.

"The last Wolf Wolf production was truly an experience," they said.

"Did we go see that together?" Lena asked. "Has she done something since *Infinitely Swinging Shutters*?"

"No that was it, I think you were there, yes. Miraculous wasn't it?"

"Oh my god, I'd never seen anything like it," Lena turned to the actors. "You're both in her new project?"

Tom nodded and Curtiss said "yes- a humbling opportunity."

Wyatt had never heard of Wolf Wolf and he was terrified by the reverence that she commanded from this audience. Suddenly he hated every word of his play.

"We'll go see it when it premiers," Lena said to Wyatt. "It'll be important to see."

"Have we seen you about?" Curtiss asked Wyatt. "Are you often at shows?"

"No. I mean I would guess not. I'm not a part of that scene specifically, no."

"What brought you to write a piece for theater then, if that isn't a place you find yourself spending time?"

"I think I got tired of seeing my words on a page. Like, how do I know if anyone is dealing with it at all if it's just trapped there in a page? I wanted to be able to see something I wrote and watch other people see it."

"That's a risk— could be the thing gets performed and no one is there," said Qat. Everything they said sounded like someone added chapters to the Tao Te Ching. "Then the mystery of whether or not people engage with your work has been solved and you know for certain the answer is that they are not."

"A calculated risk I guess. Then I'll know. I can always go back to zines."

"I've read zines that completely changed my perspective," they said.

"Any of mine?" he asked, with just enough sarcasm.

Qat laughed. "I don't remember."

Then the lights dimmed and the show began. One by one writers and performers took the stage and poured their work out into the room. Wyatt did not connect with most of it. Here and there he would find moments and nuggets that he could hold and examine and sort of nod his head about. Mostly he found it uncompelling. Dan Fuller, ostensibly who he was there to see, was just one of those love poem guys. There was an audience for that stuff, but it was not for Wyatt. There were a few that had searing honesty, tackling brutal subject matter with naked courage. But they lacked artistry to his ears. One performer had a digital sampler that she'd play non-sequitur noise loops throughout her pieces. That was something. They all felt hard worked. Sometimes to a fault. The sweat of the process shone through in the work. There must be value to that, Wyatt considered, but he wasn't sure it was enough to qualify any of it as good art. Maybe he was being too harsh, and as he critiqued what he saw on stage he doubted the value of his own work.

And the lights came up to end the show. The name he had recognized from the poster didn't end up being there. Absentmindedly, Wyatt took a sip from his completely empty coffee mug and then looked inside with disappointment, seeing the bottom of the mug and nothing else. The room was settling into that milling around phase that happens after something. No one in Wyatt's group had started talking about the show yet. Qat saw Wyatt's unsuccessful attempt at the coffee and asked if he wanted to join them to the cafe for more. Wyatt agreed.

"So were you here to see someone specific?" Qat asked him as the two walked to the barista's counter.

"No, just sort of here for the whole thing," he answered. "Lena is friends with Dan Fuller, and I'm kind of just tagging along with her. Interested as a writer, but these were mostly new faces to me. What about you? Did you know someone in the show?"

"Yes, I'm friends with Maria Lopez."

"Which one was that?" he asked and then turned to the barista, "Can I just get a refill of the house blend in here?" sliding his mug across.

"With the loop machine."

"Oh! I think that was actually my favorite of the night," he said. "I do mean that. I'm not just trying to be agreeable. I'm kind of relieved that one was the one you were here for because I didn't get much out of any of the others." He lowered his voice as he spoke, not wanting to upset friends or relatives of the other writers in earshot.

Wyatt's mug was returned to him and Qat stepped up to the counter for their turn. With coffees in hand they found a comfortable spot to linger. They stood leaning together on a support beam somewhere in the middle of the room.

"So, Wyatt," Qat said, "tell me about this theater project."

He summarized it for them.

"That sounds interesting. I'm sure I know some people who'd be interested in taking a look."

It sounded promising to Wyatt but he didn't have the presence of mind to do anything about it that night.

CHAPTER 4

MORNING ARRIVED WITH THE gentle melodic squawk of Wyatt's cell phone alarm. His hand turned it off before his brain had caught up with his eyes. It was a cloudy day, but not unpleasant. Wyatt slid his feet to the floor and reached over to his desk to put on some old music on his aging, un-branded, bootleg laptop. He shuffled to the bathroom to take a shower that went from steamy to tepid ⅔ of the way through. He stayed in until the water started to sputter and turn cloudy. Each apartment in the building was allotted a certain amount of water per day. It wasn't much, but it was supposedly clean.

After drying off, Wyatt spent an indeterminate amount of time looking at his closet deciding what to wear. The music played on in the background -- a playlist, not an album, so he had no frame of reference for how much time or how many songs had passed by the time he had picked a black pair of jeans and an unpatterned flannel shirt. The laptop speakers rattled out a drum fill and jumped back into the chorus for a brief second before going silent with a thump as Wyatt closed the lid. All morning Wyatt was mentally trying to keep Roland at arms length distance in his mind and not fixate on their planned meeting that evening. He grabbed his notebook and a couple pens to head out the door.

By his building's standards it was still pretty early. Most people who lived here slept pretty late, aside from those who were already at work somewhere. The sun was scratching through, and the shog was wearing thin. There was a food cart run by a Kurdish man that made breakfast sandwiches in Sunset Morning, never at the same corner. It was part of the morning ritual on days Wyatt didn't work to walk around until he found it. The guy made a great little sandwich for just a couple bucks.

"Where do you get your eggs?" Wyatt asked him one time while he prepared the sandwich, a year or so ago.

"Ahh the eggs, that is a secret. I can't have you going and taking my eggs now, can I? Bad for business."

"Do you just find them or something?"

The man laughed, he seemed like he was really having fun, and that made Wyatt smile. He answered over the sound of the metal spatula smacking the small cooktop. "There is a building, used to be apartments, and my wife's cousin runs a business there. He raises chickens. They run all around."

"Wow, nearby?"

"What did I say? I can't tell you."

"No, that's fine. It's just nice to know they come from somewhere."

"Everything comes from somewhere, but these eggs come from real live birds."

"If I look around hard enough, I bet I could find it," Wyatt joked, mischievously.

"Sure, I'm sure. Just follow the smell of the chicken shit," he said as he handed Wyatt the hot sandwich wrapped in foil, gleaming with butter.

This time, when Wyatt spotted the cart on the end of the block he just walked up and the guy said "egg and cheese?"

"Yeah, yes please. Thanks," Wyatt answered. And they stood without talking while butter was scraped across the sizzling cooktop, eggs were pulled from the cooler at the front of the cart and cracked open, butter was pushed onto the stale roll before they were pressed onto the corner of the grill, cheese was unevenly sliced off a sizable brick that must last weeks, the eggs were flipped with no theatrics, cheese wedged into roll before the eggs were slid in, and then with a flurry of foil the sandwich was wrapped. It was messy, deliberate, efficient and always resulted in a delicious sandwich. Wyatt loved these sandwiches. He paid and took it, unwrapping it immediately and walking toward a now-shuttered cafe around the corner.

This cafe was closed by the time Wyatt moved into the neighborhood, so at least 3 years now, and had remained dormant. It was a good place to sit. Wyatt brushed some litter off a seat, sat down with his sandwich and placed his notebook deliberately onto the table. There were four tables outside. Two on either side of the door chained shut. They were corralled by impermanent, fence-like railings that had once housed decorative fabric but remained now as nothing but a frame, wearing a soft looking coat of rust as if it was skin. He always sat at the two outside tables, alternating with no method and always deliberately choosing a chair he had not sat in the time before to the best of his memory. Every time he came there was a new layer of trash to be brushed off, no matter what chair he picked. It drifted down out of the sky or something, covered every undisturbed surface in the world.

The air was full of what now passed as silence. With your ear tuned you'd hear an eternal span of traffic stretching on forever, on the roads and in the air. And if you really listened you could hear a constant sizzle of the trash. It was cooking in the heat and in the acid in the air, always breaking down and decaying. It was constant, so it was hard to hear. But sometimes Wyatt held his breath and listened for the buzz, just to hear it. Today he did not. Today he just ate his egg sandwich, and it was quiet.

After finishing his sandwich and tossing the crumpled up foil out into the street to assimilate down, he slid his notebook in front of him and opened to the first empty page. He looked at it for a long time before even taking a pen into his hand. Even while holding the pen, the page remained blank, the whiteness shining in the morning sun for what could've been a decade. Needing to make some kind of movement, Wyatt flipped back a few pages to read what he had written last time he had written. He was in the middle of a short story about an office worker who at night walked around his neighborhood and burned down abandoned buildings. He hadn't even gotten to the part about burning down the buildings yet. He was still setting up the office stuff. With stories like that Wyatt always told himself the writing would go much faster once the action really got going, that it was this groundwork laying that was the most laborious and took the most effort to write. It was true that he spent much more time writing first acts than third acts. But that might not have been related.

He didn't feel like he had it in his head what to do with the next pages, how to make progress on this story. So usually what he did at these times was write a few poems. It was not easier to write poems, but it was easier to finish a poem. For every 10 poems Wyatt wrote into a notebook maybe he would transcribe one of them into a laptop to be shown to anyone else. So he flipped some random pages forward, which he always did with poetry -- leaving the blank pages for prose or something otherwise long form. Forcing himself, he put the pen down onto the stupid fucking blank page.

He started to write forced, surreal imagery. Trying so hard to break his mind away from things he could see, or things he had seen or had been thinking about. He completed a few poems and suddenly was driven to flip back in the notebook to the end of the short story. With only some confidence the pen scratched across the notebook, line by line, building the story. Wyatt checked his phone for time more often than he wanted to, but even with frequent checks he never made any note of how long he had been sitting or how long he had been productive.

As the morning pushed on there was no change in traffic. This was not a busy street, but there were passersby with irregularity. The air grew warmer but not uncomfortable. Wyatt wrote for as long as he could think, and then he wrote for about another page more. He liked the story and just wanted to get it moving. He wrote that his character stopped by a hardware store on the way home to buy some supplies for his nocturnal activities but realized that he honestly didn't know what things someone would need to burn down a building. The guy wasn't a terrorist, he didn't want to hurt anyone, just clear out some of the empty shells that cluttered up the landscape. Like a surgeon removing sick tissue. Chopping off the gangrenous part of a leg. Wyatt sat back and looked away from his notebook, keeping one hand on it. He'd have to do some research. He'd have to learn about burning down buildings. Who could he ask about that? There must be some political idealist or performance artist he knew who had burned downed empty buildings to say something or say nothing. Down the hall were a couple guys who had lived in art collectives; it was worth asking them.

With a gentle pulsing, Wyatt's phone slid abruptly into his attention. He pulled it out of his pocket to see a text from Paulie, his boss from Lil ol' Betsy's.

I heard the cops stopped by the shop for me?? he said, with the manic panic Wyatt knew he spoke with.

yah, that's right. They had something for you?

did they say anything else?

no just that they could burn the place to the ground.

There was a pause before the response came.

u dumb fuck Paulie replied.

Wyatt assumed that meant everything was ok. He didn't really understand the relationship Paulie had with the cops. The line of questioning would've gone further if Paulie was concerned about something. For a few minutes he sat there in the aftermath of the text conversation and let the relative quiet of the morning rise back up around him.

A car passed driven by someone that Wyatt once knew. As he watched the driver pass by at car speed there was a sudden, brutal, percussive crash on the sidewalk a few feet from where he sat. Wyatt bounced from shock. In a splash of debris a medium sized delivery drone, about the size of a bicycle, clattered to the ground. Pieces of trash and drone rained down onto Wyatt, crouching for cover. After the chorus of rubble pitter-pattered to the ground the area was quieter than the world had ever been. Wyatt let out an uneven breath that had begun to tighten in his chest.

He looked around, studying the sky for clues, or for other potential dangers or just for something because he didn't know what to do with the frantic energy and the burst of adrenaline. Convinced that there would be no encore performance, Wyatt hurriedly collected his things and started to walk away. After getting a few steps from the crash site, Wyatt turned back to quickly inspect the wreckage for anything of value. If it was a delivery drone it might've been carrying something he could take. Buried in the rubble of the demolished drone there was a package. Using a piece of debris, he sliced open the side of the cardboard box to see what the contents were or had been. There was a lot of packing material which Wyatt pulled out like animal guts until eventually finding inside a stack of ceramic tiles. Some were cracked and others were not. They were clearly very old, maybe hundreds of years old. Some were painted with a quaint, farmhouse style decoration like you might imagine seeing in an old magazine from before. Wyatt could not imagine a single situation in which someone would pay to have these shipped somewhere. The initial panic from the explosion returned as a general fear that tightened into a clot in Wyatt's chest and stomach. Maybe fear of getting caught stealing the package, combined with fear of more collapsing drones. He quickly grabbed as many as he could and slid them into his bag before heading away again towards Lena's apartment, a couple neighborhoods north of his own.

Now in the back of his mind were two competing anxieties: death by collapsing, aerial garbage and the pending evening with Roland et al., though he did not know who was included in "al." He tried to keep both thoughts as far away from his head as possible, building moats of other topics as a defensive measure. He tried to think about his writing, and about the performances from last night, and about the ceramic tiles that weighed down his tote bag, and how much he likes those egg sandwiches. Each of the distractions co-existed and bounced back and forth between the two lurking stresses. This is the game his mind played until he reached the subway line that would bring him to Lena's neighborhood.

The subways were owned by a company called "the Subway Company." They basically controlled the tunnels. It was a little corpo-fascist kingdom down there. Any of the tunnels they controlled. Some leftover tunnels, from when the city operated transit, were empty and lawless. Subway lines operated by the Sub Co. were rigid and orderly. There were very few employees. Trains were operated by pre-programmed algorithms. Maintenance was carried out by drones piloted from a central office by a handful of operators. The only humans who worked in the tunnels were police officers hired for security. Trains arrived according to a strict schedule. People waited quietly, allowed passengers to exit the trains first and then boarded in an orderly fashion. Police would routinely and brutally punish anyone who stepped out of line. Drones would pop out of their little storage pockets in the walls and ceilings to clean up spots of blood after the cops had enforced order.

The subway was expensive now, not necessarily as a result of the cost of operation, but deliberately as a measure of keeping out undesirables. Sometimes the copz would drag out customers who looked too homeless or even vaguely lower class. Wyatt couldn't afford to ride as often as he did, but he knew someone who could hack cards. It was dangerous, but he'd never been questioned. After swiping his card the turnstile produced a proud, utilitarian thunk as it unlocked–like the sound of a bone breaking–and he entered the tunnel. He was relieved that while underground no sky trash could crush and maim him, but he was always unnerved by being in the subway. It was often the best way to get somewhere, but Wyatt could feel that this environment was designed to be hostile to some in order to cater to others. Wyatt could pass. Could perform like he belonged here. Still every minute spent underground was spent in fear of a copz billy klub.

With a smooth, neon-sounding hum the subway slid down the tunnel and up to the platform. Silently, the doors opened and respectable looking people wearing clean shoes stepped off with hollow confidence. Once passengers were done exiting, those waiting to board did so, Wyatt melding into the group as invisibly as possible. He looked for a good corner spot but saw they were all occupied by boring occupants. So he just sat down anywhere.

Lena's neighborhood was about a 15-minute ride north but on the same side of the river as Sunset Morning. After sitting down, he pulled out his notebook and stared down at an empty page for the duration of the trip. Then, an alarmingly pleasant synthesized voice announced his stop, and he hurried off the train. It had started raining while he was underground, and he muttered "shit" when he saw the wet trickling onto the stairs as he climbed back to the sky. He paused near the top of the stairwell, just out of the rain, trying to get cell coverage to text Lena. It took his phone several minutes to click back onto the network.

Hey, he tapped. *It's raining. you at your place if I come over?*

Wyatt puttered around on a phone game, connecting dots with his thumb while he waited for a response, occasionally glancing up at the thick grey quilt of the sky. People passing up and down the stairs to and from the subway glanced at him incredulously. After a few moments Wyatt noticed a cop was standing at the bottom of the stairs frowning up at him. Probably he had another 60 seconds or so before the cop shouted something at him and less than a minute after that before the cop started up the stairs toward him. His stomach started to churn until finally Lena chimed back *yah cmon up.*

Hurriedly, he stuffed his phone into his pocket and scooted the rest of the way up the stairs and into the rain. It stung a little, and it stank a lot. The glimmer was beautiful. Her apartment was one block up and three blocks over. With his hands in his pockets, he shuffled as quickly as possible: gliding, scraping over the kipple, leaving a faint trail like in snow. There were a lot of dogs in this neighborhood. The dogs would fill in behind him, sniffing his wake for morsels to eat. In the nooks between buildings or camped on the more undrivable roads fallen into disrepair were homeless people of all ages, simply making do. This is always how things were here.

When he reached Lena's building, Wyatt reached for the old-fashioned doorbell panel—with its quaint columns of buttons for each resident—and pushed the button representing her. There was a longer pause than Wyatt expected before the door buzzed open, considering that he was supposedly expected. But he barely finished thinking the thought before forgetting it again, entering the building and exiting the rain. Her building had no elevator—or at least no working elevator, but there were a number of mysterious old doors that could have been elevators—so he climbed the five flights of stairs to Lena's floor. After knocking there was again a pause before Lena answered. She opened the door, absent-mindedly, and just said "come on in" before receding back into her apartment. So he slid in and closed the door behind him. It was a three bedroom apartment with about 11 people living in it at any time. Someone was cooking food, someone else was sleeping on the floor.

Lena was in her room sitting on her bed looking at an old TV that was hooked up to her laptop. Something was on the TV. "Can I get a lil drink?" Wyatt asked, with a vocal emoji to punctuate the sentence cutely.

"Sure," she answered, still without paying much attention.

He meandered into the corner where the kitchen and refrigerator were to retrieve a beer.

"Have you seen the news?" she asked without blinking.

"No, I haven't really looked at my phone since I got off the train," Wyatt answered, not counting the dot game. "It was raining a little."

"Something's happening."

"Hm?"

Wyatt sidled up next to Lena to look at the TV. It was one of those citizen reporters, sitting in an apartment at a desk and talking in the old fashioned news way that still popped up every once in a while. There was footage of a big, black circle floating just above the water. Wyatt didn't know what he was looking at. The reporter seemed confused, was speaking vaguely, but seemed giddy to be able to be sharing whatever it was she was talking about. The circle had some texture, spiraling into the center like a toilet flushing. Slowly spinning.

"What's it?" he said.

"No one really knows. These things just showed up an hour ago."

"What things?"

"No, I dunno. These huge gates just opened up. Four that we know about so far, kinda scattered around."

"Gates," Wyatt sipped his beer.

"Yeah, that's what they're calling them. They're just these big openings out of nowhere. A few have had these demon things come out of them."

Wyatt liked this. "Demons?" he chuckled.

"Look. I don't know," she would not break eye contact with the TV.

The TV reporter said, "Ok, let's put that footage back up. This was recorded by a hobbyist who had a camera near Corn Beach."

The news feed showed what was meant to be a close up of the "gates," but it was zoomed in to just reveal a swirling mess that the camera couldn't quite translate into an image. The gate was above the water a ways off the shore at Corn Beach, a ways south of them, where an amusement park sort of was. The footage was shaky and frantic.

"Oh," Wyatt muttered seeing the thing. "Shit."

The reporter described what she'd heard about the demon, but no footage was available of the thing that'd come from the gate. Apparently it was a damp looking red color, very close to black. Three legs moved with irregularity— a pattern that truly could not be deciphered— the legs bottomed by what looked like hooves. There was a body and a series of maybe four tyrannosaurus-looking arms all around. Then on the head, no face, no ears, no mouth. Two antenna, or antlers, or some other things. And they seem to be strolling around the area confidently now. There was no frame of reference for size of the gate in the footage, being shot at that distance and just out across water. It looked small in the hugeness of the ocean horizon. The reporter started to list off and thank a number of business sponsors. Then they started to read ad copy.

"It sounds like there are a few different kinds, but these demons are just walking around, coming out of the gates all around the world," Lena said. There was a calm in her voice. No, a fascination. An interest that overwhelmed fear.

Wyatt did not have interest outweighing his fear. "Are we going to die?"

he asked matter of factly.

"I don't think so. They don't think so."

"They?"

"I dunno. These bozos on the news."

"What if, like, they're just trying to keep the peace? Keep us from panicking and rioting and shit. Journalistic integrity or whatever."

Lena sort of chuckled.

Wyatt waited.

"No, so far nobody has been attacked by them. The gates did some damage in other places. But the demons are just walking around."

"They're just walking around? What the fuck?"

There was quiet in the apartment except for the chatter of the news explaining how little they knew, the sound of the ancient furnace circulating air and the clatter of drones just outside the window. "I need to go over there I think," Lena said.

"Fucking damn it," Wyatt said.

"I know it's kinda far south from here, but I gotta see it. I can't just go eat falafel and come out to a bar tonight, with that fucking thing down there."

"Should I...come?"

"Yeah you can. Why not? I mean it'll at least be interesting, right? The most interesting thing that has ever happened."

"But, what if…" Wyatt was scared the demons would kill them, but it felt so strange to try to form those words with his mouth that he had just used to order and eat a breakfast sandwich earlier in the day.

"Come with me, there's some bikes nearby. We can ride from here to the beach and back up to...where was your date again?"

"It's not a date. Sludgetown, the Lantern."

"Right Sludgetown. K, well that's kind of the opposite direction, but we can scoot right back up that way pretty easily."

"Ride the backs of the demons."

She laughed. "If they're headed north, why not?"

Wyatt hated it, but he knew she had to see it down there. And Wyatt wanted to see, too. Of course he needed to. Traffic was going to be a damned nightmare, Wyatt thought.

"Earlier they said the camera guy's name, who shot that footage, and I looked him up. He goes by the name Ricky Switch. I think I found him. Maybe we can try to meet him," Lena said.

"Sure, alright, we'll look for him down there I guess."

"He's probably still there," Lena said while starting to get ready to go.

Wyatt hadn't really settled into the apartment or put anything down, so he just stood up and shuffled to the door. When he stood up the weight of his tote made him remember those tiles. "Oh," he said, "I've... er ... I have these ceramic tiles. Can I leave these here for now?" and he pulled them out of his bag with both hands.

"Where'd you get those?" she asked, loading up a little bag with her camera and some other things.

"I was writing this morning, at that dead cafe I go to, and a drone crashed a couple feet away from me. Like really close"

"Oh shit, you're alright?"

"Yeah nothing hit me. It was a delivery drone, so I checked what was inside, and it was these tiles. So, I dunno, I took 'em."

"Sure yeah. Of course. Leave them here for now."

And unceremoniously, Lena opened the door of her apartment and left, with Wyatt following her instinctively. Didn't she think it was weird about those tiles?

"What's going to be the best way there on a day like today?" Lena asked, already walking south as soon as she got outside.

"A day like today?" Wyatt repeated, joking and thinking. "Do you figure busses are still running?"

"Of course they are. I think I know the fastest route we can take a bike. Just follow me."

Lena was in a bike stealing clique called Gorilla Bishop Punchers. So when she said, "take a bike," it was literal. She had a little clipper in her bag almost all the time that could cut most bike locks. But she rarely needed it.

There were almost always bikes around.

"Yeah sure, that's fine."

"I left two behind my building the other day. Let's see if they're there."

"Rode two bikes home?"

"It was me and someone else."

"Oh word, right on. Nice work," Wyatt assumed it was coital.

Just where they ought to be were two recently stolen bicycles that hadn't yet been re-stolen by anyone else. They weren't attractive specimens, almost every part on it had at some point belonged to a different bicycle. Both were frankenstein monster bikes. Lena knew what to look for though, so they would ride well. Chances are if they were hobbled together like this it was by someone who knew how to work on a bike. So despite the motley appearance, they were probably in better shape than most bikes that were all one color.

Checking her phone for directions, Lena mounted the bicycle with the prowess of a veteran cowboy climbing on a horse. Wyatt got on the other bike with the confidence of someone who sometimes rode a bike as a method of transportation. Pocketing the phone, Lena said, "ok I think we can just take the old Ocean Parkway straight down. Shouldn't be too much trouble today."

The two shoved off and started the trip rolling south to the beach. From Lena's apartment building they had to ride a few blocks to get to the edge of Prospect Park, and then the old parkway was just on the south end of that. It had been a fairly busy road, but as the number of running cars had started to dwindle, especially in this area, the parkway started filling up with meanderers. It was now to the point that there was so much on the parkway that wasn't a car that if a car chanced through they would avoid the parkway and take side streets because it was quicker. Bikes were king, so they were able to make fairly good time. Lena was an incredibly proficient rider, but Wyatt had been along with her enough to know how to stay just a length or two behind.

As they rode south, Wyatt watched Lena but kept his attention focused as far into the distance as he could see. Looking for any shape that felt out of place, looking to see the intruders. He strained his ears to hear them. He saw nothing but the tired neighborhood as it stood yesterday. Heard the din of mundane city. Still he remained transfixed when he saw a flicker in the sky, a pulse of yellow that appeared for less than a second and disappeared in an instant. The world seemed to take a breath. Cars and pedestrians continued shuffling around. The air felt more humid. Birds all sat still and quiet. Above the skyline rose an immense shape. Dark, dark red, almost black. Its figure was incomprehensible. Beautiful in a way, but very terrifying. Lena, after a brief hesitation, quickened her pace and pushed on directly toward the thing. Wyatt followed.

CHAPTER 5

THEY HAD ARRIVED AT the beach. Along the way they had caught glimpses of the large demon ahead of them but never enough to decipher its shape. Huge apartment complexes lined the edge of the beach. Finally Lena and Wyatt cleared the buildings and reached the boardwalk. The ocean opened up before them, a vast expanse.

And there they were: the demons. Casually strolling across the scene. Wyatt did a quick look and counted nine— eight smaller ones and the one Great Demon. The smaller ones had been described on the television. They were about 10 or 15 feet tall, Wyatt guessed. Their bodies had a kind of glow that he couldn't quite understand. From their inky bodies emitted some kind of luminescence. Wyatt dismounted from the bicycle and Lena stopped to do the same.

"Fuck," Lena said. A tiny smirk decorated her lips. They tucked their bikes between some buildings and chained them to a pipe.

Walking side by side, Lena and Wyatt moved closer to the beach. Their pace was drifting and dreamlike, as if they were floating towards this new mystery by a power not their own. The sounds of the beach were the same as they might always be, only muffled. Muted. Demons skittered around in and out of view. Some were holding things, what looked like large orbs and crates. One Minor Demon was digging. Their three legs moved like a spider's. Though there was no recognizable face, Wyatt noticed that the orientation of their antler-like headgear seemed to indicate what direction they were looking. The demons would look around like a cat exploring a new room, observing every object around them. They seemed to all be completely disregarding human beings but carefully observing the landscape. Walking along the boardwalk toward the old amusement park, Wyatt saw that there were now demons in almost every direction he could look, but there was no fear in the air.

"Look at the sand," Lena said. "They aren't leaving footprints."

Wyatt saw that she was right. He looked around and up at the nearby apartment buildings. "I don't feel like there are more people here, do you?"

"Oh I didn't even think of that. No you're right. Maybe some."

"There's definitely people watching, but it's hard to tell if they aren't just people from the neighborhood. Most of the balconies are empty. I mean there aren't really people watching from balconies."

Lena retrieved the camera from her backpack and looked at the viewfinder. "We're too far. Do you think we can get closer? Maybe to that one that's building a sandcastle or whatever?"

"Sure, let's."

"Also keep your eyes open for the guy who got that footage we saw on TV."

"What's he look like?"

"I dunno, a guy holding a camera."

"Oh, OK yeah."

The two stepped down from the boardwalk and onto the cluttered and crunchy beach. Like the sidewalks, the beach was coated in trash. There were piles of garbage lining the coast like a fence where the waves had deposited whatever they've carried in their watery bellies. In the middle of the beach, at a place that seemed randomly chosen, a demon scooped sand with one of its three legs and both arms. It had dug a hole big enough to crawl down into. It was deeper than it was wide and the edges of the hole were stark and crisp. It was an exceptionally well dug hole. As Lena got closer, she woke up the camera with a pleasant little beep. Still walking, she took a picture and looked down at the screen to review it.

"...holy shit," she said.

"What?"

"I dunno. Just fucks me up. Taking a picture of this thing. It's fucking weird."

"Weirder than just like seeing them at all?"

"Yeah. I mean, now there's a picture of it. We're not imagining it."

"Unless you're just imagining that picture."

"I dunno. There's just something about putting that thing in this camera."

"Yeah, I hear you," Wyatt agreed.

They drew closer to the thing and its hole. Wyatt started to walk more slowly when they got within 20 or 30 yards. This near, Wyatt noticed the sound: a gentle, odd musicality that was in the air around the demon. Maybe the sound of its breathing? Maybe it was humming under its breath. There was no melody, just a vaguely pleasant tone vacillating, subtle, filling the air around it. Lena took a few more pictures, trying different compositions and adjusting settings in the camera's esoteric menu. Wyatt stopped walking. Lena kept going. It did not seem to notice that they were there. The demon did not alter its behavior in any way. There was no indication of a change in attention, no modulating in the pace of its dig. Lena stood immediately next to it. Wyatt stayed back. She reached her hand out and touched it. It was pale against the swallowingly black surface of the demon. For a moment nothing happened. Then it twitched and shook her off, like a horse shooing away a fly.

"It's cold," she said. "Cool, like a little bit cool. Like an apple."

Wyatt couldn't remember the last time he touched an apple, but he understood what she meant. After the demon shook Lena off, it continued digging as if they weren't there at all. Lena took some more pictures, walking all around the perimeter of the hole. Looking up, Wyatt noticed the enormous demon was striding gracefully toward the ocean, stepping directly over where they stood. Its footsteps made no noise, but its immense movement did seem to push a sound through the air. As it walked above them, Wyatt watched its massive form. Lena pointed the camera up but didn't take any pictures. It walked onto the water as if it simply were more beach. Reaching the gate, the demon unfolded two huge limbs, grabbed the edges of the gate and pulled it wide like a curtain.

A beep from Lena's camera and the artificial sound of a shutter.

The demon disappeared inside the widened opening which then shrank to its original size. It was gone, but still the dozens of smaller demons continued their abstract work. Wyatt looked at his phone to check the time, but even after looking at it he didn't really take in the information or make any decisions based on it.

Drifting from the hole digging demon, Lena started on down the beach and so Wyatt did too. Her camera was in her hand, and occasionally she would look through the viewfinder but decide it wouldn't be worth the picture and drop it back down. Her elbows remained at a 90 degree angle, at the ready. In this way the two traced along the beach at the steady pace of the curious.

They pushed a pile of tied up plastic bags off a bench and just sat. They observed the coming and going of the demons until eventually their movements became just another part of the environment, though uncanny. City squirrels would dance around them. Wyatt noticed birds watching them warily.

"Well here they are," Lena said after a while.

"Yah."

"What do you think?"

"Still working on that, honestly."

"Yeah."

"You got answers?" Wyatt asked.

"No, no answers. None of those."

"Think this changes anything?"

"About what?"

"Just, anything?"

"Oh, like, do I believe in god now kind of thing?"

"Yah, I guess like that."

"It definitely makes things confusing," Lena said. "Like, what, now there's gotta be a hell? I dunno. It's fucked up."

"They can't be from hell. Not like, actual hell."

"Why not? Demons? Where did they come from?"

"I dunno. The depths. Or like something cosmic. Shit, maybe they're really angels. If they're from hell why aren't they hurting anything? They're just walking around. Carrying stuff, digging holes."

"They're building hell here."

"Rent got too high down there or something?"

"Could be getting crowded," Lena joked, her voice stayed serious.

"Sure so they came here. The most expensive and crowded place in human history."

They shared a microscopic moment of laughter.

"Well. Whatever it is. It feels big. Like in terms of scope," Wyatt said. "Makes this big dumb planet we're on, makes it feel like it matters less."

"Mhmm."

"I think I'd always figured, like, look I understand how big...how big the universe is. Or whatever. You know, like in satellite pictures, or when you hear stuff about how many lightyears away anything is. So I always had this intellectual understanding that we were here but there must be all this other stuff going on somewhere else.."

"Right."

"But that was always in the back of my mind. Or not in my mind at all. And now it's in my mind. It's like walking around on this beach that used to be so boring I never even bothered to make the trip down here."

"It's like the most confusing thing to ever happen in human history," Lena said.

"I kinda hate it."

"I think I'm thrilled."

"Yeah," Wyatt said. "That makes sense."

A demon stepped directly over them. Lena watched it. Wyatt watched the ocean. He felt like it was his responsibility to write something about this if he were to keep calling himself a writer. So he dragged the notebook from his bag and opened to a blank page. His hand held a pen that did not move. After a long time Wyatt just started pulling the pen across the paper, but he did not make any letters or words. He just wanted ink on the paper. Eventually he finished. He felt like this page was done. About half of the page was now black. It looked like something with paws was locked in a room and scratched on the door to try and get out. Just an etched, desperate non-pattern. While Wyatt was looking at the page, Lena glanced over and saw it.

"I like that."

Wyatt didn't hear her. "What?"

"That's pretty good. That page. It feels like sitting here. I agree with it."

Studying the ink more, Wyatt said, "Yeah, I guess you're right. That's what it is."

"Hey, go stand out on the beach and hold it in front of you. I'll take a picture of you and the demons behind you."

"Ok, sure."

He obliged, lurching up from the bench to go a few yards out onto the beach. Lena pivoted around him to find the angle that had the most demons the most clearly in the background. She took four pictures and was satisfied.

"Should we go?"

"Yeah," Wyatt answered, putting his notebook into his bag and shouldering it. Together they walked back to their stowed bikes.

CHAPTER 6

WYATT REMEMBERED THE IDEA of time for the first time in hours as they rode their bikes away from the demon beach. He remembered that he was heading somewhere specific, to meet up with Roland. He wasn't just heading away from the beach and what they had experienced there. But the gate and its demons took up so much real estate in his mind that it felt silly to try and force those mundane ideas back in. What about Roland and his friends? Would today's revelations change their plans? His throat felt dry.

"Hey Lena," he called ahead. "I gotta stop at a bodega. I need a drink."

"K," she said, and they rode up to the next corner store.

"I think I oughtta text Roland and see if they're still even going out."

"Why wouldn't they? Because of the demons or something?"

"Yeah I dunno, maybe," he walked into the bodega and back to the coolers of beer.

"Do you still want to go out?"

Wyatt opened the cooler and inspected the options carefully. "Um-mmm," he grabbed a beer with a stylishly minimal design. "Yeah, I think I do. I do. It just seems like... like that's all I can think about or whatever. Those fucking things. Makes hanging out seem dumb."

"Just text the guy and see what he thinks. If they're still hanging out we'll go from there."

Wyatt paid for the beer and went back outside. The weather was almost perfect— not too hot so the garbage didn't smell, and it was very pleasant feeling. After cracking open the can and taking a drink from the beer, Wyatt went back in for a cigarette. The counter guy looked like he could be someone Wyatt and Lena knew. He wasn't, but he looked like he could be.

With the beer in one hand he pulled his phone out with the other. His thumb hovered over the screen while he thought about what to say, his mind wandering and needing constant policing to keep it on the task at hand. Finally he tapped to Roland's text thread and typed simply *y'all still going out tonight for drinks?* before putting his phone back and drinking more beer.

"Can I get a loosey, too?"

A cigarette was politely handed over, paid for, and Wyatt turned to leave before pivoting back one more time.

"Hey, man," he said to the counter guy.

"What's up?"

"Did you hear about the demons?"

"Down on the beach? Yeah."

"And, like, what do you think?"

"Shit, I can't stop thinking about it kind of."

"Right?"

"It's got me a little fucked up."

"Does it scare you?"

"No," said the guy at the counter. "It's not scary. Just kind of frustrating."

"Frustrating? Yeah. I guess you're right. That is what it is," and Wyatt left.

"Here's my suggestion: we go out," Lena said. "Either it'll be a good way to get your mind off it for a while, or it will be a good chance to keep talking about it with people if that's what you want. I think both are good options."

He nodded, sipping again from the can. "Yeah. Want some?" offering her the can.

"How much is left?"

"I dunno. Some."

"No thanks." She pulled out a cigarette.

Music was playing from inside the convenience store. Lena was still outside on her bike, looking at the pictures she had taken on the tiny digital viewfinder on the ancient camera. As Wyatt left the store he finished the beer and placed the empty can gingerly on the ground next to the open door of the bodega. "So?" she said. There was a buzzing sound in the air. It was new, or at least Wyatt thought it seemed new.

"You're right, let's go up there. It beats writhing in panic I guess."

"What's the best way from here?"

Wyatt's phone buzzed. It had a text back from Roland that said *yeah dude!*

"Let's just take the Old Belt," Wyatt climbed on his bike, lit the cigarette, and they both pushed off.

The Old Belt had been a highway that ran like a spine along the west and south edges of this part of the city near the water. At some point it stopped being maintained and it had been impassable by car for decades. Looked like a dried up river bed hovering above the rest of the city. For pedestrians and especially able cyclists it made an easy way of getting around the neighborhoods it was designed to traverse originally. What had been pavement was now basically dirt. Shrubbery and stumpy trees grew along the Belt's length, choking in the smog but growing despite and maybe in spite of it. A car hadn't driven on this road in at least 15 or 20 years, but it was still commonly used by other travelers so there was a bit of trail. Wyatt loved the Old Belt. It reminded him that humans were part of nature and that eventually when they were gone it would all just keep being nature without them. It was comforting to see trees growing here, the lizards that lived in the little wilderness. One day it would collapse. As they scaled the mountain of the onramp up to the elevated highway Wyatt looked over his shoulder back towards the beach. They were now a couple miles away from the beach. Still at this distance he could see the huge lumbering shape of the great demon as it marched in and out from shore. It's movements seemed aimless and still— in a way deliberate. He thought he could even still hear that buzzing sound. One of the smaller demons had crawled on top of the apartment buildings and was casually leaping across rooflines, pausing occasionally, appearing to survey the landscape. Lena retrieved her camera and took some pictures of the city skyline featuring the ocean, the setting sun, and now an immense and bizarre beast.

The bike ride took just under an hour. It was a straightforward trip that involved simply following the trail that had been cut through the overgrowth on the Old Belt by the hundreds of bicycles that had come before them. As they rode north, the sun gracefully slid west until the sky to their left was a pale orange haze and the sky to their right was dark and blue. Drones would crisscross above them and some would zip beneath the Belt following the roads below. Cars still ruled the roads. The noise of the city was a constant din. A gang of costumed tweens scampered across rooftops nearby and police sirens shrieked "woop woop" here and there. Shog kept the sun's warmth hanging in the air late into the evening. It was a beautiful day for a bike ride. The Old Belt passed directly over the Sunset Morning neighborhood but Wyatt's apartment building wasn't visible from the trail. He knew that it was waiting for him, just to the east, and it was always comforting to be near his home neighborhood. Sunset Morning was bordered to the north by Sludgetown and passing through meant they had nearly reached their destination. They rode over a large park spanning dozens of blocks that had once been a cemetery but was now essentially a forest that still bore the name of the cemetery it had been: Green Wood. Not far past Green Wood, the Old Belt curved west and passed over the canal. Right before that turn, Wyatt and Lena would bike down the off ramps and into Sludgetown. This required more skill and attention than the rest of the trip, since the ramps were no more smooth than the rest of the Belt but taking the ramps was like climbing or descending a mountain slope. Going down you could gain quite a bit of speed, and without careful riding it was easy to wipe out.

Sludgetown was a neighborhood just in from the shore that straddled an industrial canal. What had once been an area dense with factories and transportation companies eventually became a hip place for young rich people, as the factories all closed down. Over time as things started crashing, the rich people left or died, and it settled back into being an industrial graveyard. The canal and its filth remained. Sometimes the water would just sit there and other times it would torrent inexplicably like a raging canyon river.

Once the neighborhood yuppies emptied out, people started squatting and using empty buildings for galleries and theaters. There was always the fear that if enough rich people saw what was happening they'd swoop back in, but Wyatt had started to doubt the idea that the wealthy still existed enough to have any interest in a place like this.

Lena deftly slid off the Old Belt's off ramp and was deposited into Sludgetown with Wyatt close behind. He pulled up to ride alongside her. The neighborhood was cluttered with trash but distinct trash from other areas in the city. The garbage in this neighborhood seemed to have a different texture, and the odor was unique, but there was as much of both as existed in every other part of town. The smell was distinctly aquatic, rank with algae and whatever else had been flowing through the canal for many long generations. No families lived in this neighborhood, only young people. Wyatt was older than most of the people on the streets who were all in their late teens or early twenties. Cars could be heard driving nearby, but the street they were on was made impassable by vehicles that had died and become landscape themselves. Rusted frames of cars, trucks, and vans, stripped of parts were now being swallowed by urban plantlife. Each vehicle was like a tiny, unplanned park. Squirrels hopped in and out of them.

Gently Wyatt edged ahead of Lena to guide the way without aggressively taking the lead. They were only a couple blocks from the main cultural stretch at the heart of Sludgetown. Being from the bordering neighborhood, Wyatt knew Sludgetown fairly well. There was a relatively vibrant artistic scene in this area, but as Wyatt aged out of his twenties he started to feel out of place. Still there were a lot of good places to eat. He pulled them past the falafel place and around a corner into an alley.

"We should be fine to park here," he said, dismounting. "That's the place back there."

The day was coming to a gentle close though light hung in the clouds with reluctance. As the air became dim, street lamps took up their buzzing, nightly work. A rather unpleasant beep greeted Wyatt and Lena as they entered the Mediterranean restaurant. It was a small space, mostly countertop. There was a cooler with vaguely branded sodas, one hightop table along the murky window to the street. They placed their orders and were handed dripping falafel pouched in pita which was in turn pouched in foil and took up position leaning on the table. The falafel was good.

"This is a good falafel," Lena said.

"Mhmm," Wyatt agreed, chewing.

They both ate.

"I gotta go back down there." Lena was looking off into the distance, maybe to give the impression of someone deep in thought.

"To the beach? Right now?"

"No I don't mean today. But like, tomorrow. Morning."

"Ok, sure."

"I need to get more pictures and see if I can find Ricky Switch."

"Who the hell is Ricky Switch?"

"The guy who got that first footage from the news. They said his name was Ricky Switch. I want to talk to him about cameras. I think I really want to work on this stuff. This insanity is ripe for the capturing."

"Convenient you got that little camera just in time for this shit."

"I know! It's almost like it was meant to be or something."

"That's a bonkers idea."

"What is?"

"*Meant to be.* Like…" Wyatt trailed off. He didn't know what else to say.

"Sure, I know what you mean. Still, this is a project I definitely want to work on."

They finished eating the falafel, both still thinking about it. After a very thorough hand wiping, Wyatt created a small mound of spent napkins and pulled out his phone. They were almost right on time which meant they were way too early, but he looked up the Lantern to see how far it was from the restaurant. It was only a 10 minute walk, and if they went there right now they would for sure be getting there first, and Wyatt didn't want to do that. He remembered his friend Marina— she had something displayed in a gallery in the neighborhood. Lena hadn't seen it. It would be worth checking in on it. So Wyatt explained how they'd be early and pitched the idea of going to the gallery, and Lena agreed. The gallery was not far out of the way, really just a few blocks from both the restaurant and bar that were the pair's destinations. As the night thickened, they weaved through the neighborhood that was bristling with young life.

Along the way they passed a group of uniformed police officers, including one bot cop, kicking and stomping some grounded victim. There was shouting from the cops and yelping from the person on the ground. The bot cop just tazing the shit out of the guy, really showing some restraint. Wyatt had been at the bottom of that pile before and had lost friends to it. But he knew there was nothing he and Lena could do by themselves, not the way they were. What could they do other than piss off the blue and get stomped themselves? Wyatt tried to leave the pit in his stomach back with the copz and they kept walking. Around them everyone else mostly did the same. The police violence faded into the street like garbage underfoot. It didn't take long before the demons invaded his brainspace again.

"Do you think it feels different here today?" Lena asked. "When was the last time you were around here?"

"I can't tell. I was here like a month ago or something. Maybe they don't know about it yet."

"You think they don't?"

Wyatt looked into the faces of the twenty-somethings walking by and around them. He saw a lot of different things and varying degrees of hurrying or wandering.

"Hm," he said, having drawn no conclusion. "Could be different."

They arrived at the gallery which was lit but appeared empty. Marina's art was on the wall that it had been displayed on, the other walls seemed to be between exhibits. Lena went in first and Wyatt after. Inside it was quiet and remarkably empty. Blank feeling. After the door closed, someone came from the back somewhere to check on them. An older Asian man.

"Hi, can I help you?" he said.

"I just wanted to show my friend Marina's exhibit," Wyatt answered.

"Oh, you just made it. It's coming down tomorrow. You know Marina?"

"Yeah, I know her. We work at the same bodega and stuff."

"When's the last time you saw her?"

"The other day," shrugged Wyatt.

"We haven't heard from her," the gallery man said. "Trying to figure out what to do with her work after tomorrow. We've got some other shit in the back ready to go up."

Lena jumped in with "don't you have some room to hold it, like for a few days or something."

"Sure, sort of," the man said. He was apparently concerned he had come off too angry and was now working to sound more accommodating. "Just we haven't been able to get in touch with her. I want to make sure she gets her work back."

"I'll ask around," Wyatt said.

"A couple pieces sold, we have some money for her."

"I'll lead with that, yeah."

And the gallery man disappeared again into the back, leaving the two alone with the art. It was a collection of very gloppy oil paintings, thick and almost dripping with paint. Almost all depicted babies – some human babies and some baby birds – towering over their surroundings. Some were crushing buildings, others blissfully unaware of the miniature worlds in which they sat. Miniscule, finely painted masses were running in terror. The tiny crowds were painted in much greater detail than everything else.

Wyatt went into gallery walk: hands behind his back, moving at a slow and deliberate pace, occasionally leaning in toward a piece to observe up close. He had seen it all before, at the opening, but it was still good work. Lena stepped very close to each painting and spent a long time pouring over them individually.

"Shit, I forgot how good Marina is," she said while walking between two pieces.

"Yeah, I like this a lot."

"I haven't seen her stuff in a while."

After looking at each of the paintings Wyatt fixated on the empty walls opposite Marina's work. He got lost in it. As he stared at the white wall he started to notice the cracks in the concrete. He observed the difference in whiteness where spotlights lit and where they didn't. The casual fade from dim to lighted. The blank wall, for all its blankness, took on so much character. And then as he continued to stare, it again became a blank wall. He saw that even in the shadows, the wall was the same thick and deliberately plain painted blankness. Meant to disappear and be ignored behind whatever was displayed on it. No different in light or not. Reaching into his jacket pocket he found he didn't have anything to smoke.

Lena kept looking at each painting very closely and eventually Wyatt resorted to putzing around on his phone. After studying every piece, Lena walked back across them all one more time before standing back to the middle of the room and observing them all as a collection. Satisfied she said "these are awesome."

Wyatt nodded in genuine agreement. It was now a thick, black night and the windows had become mirrors – warped and smudged. After silently deciding to leave the gallery, Wyatt and Lena went back outside, the man from the gallery briefly peaking his head out once again upon hearing the door before disappearing a final time. Without knowing exactly where to go, Wyatt had the confidence and the lack of concern to start walking in the direction he thought would get them there. If the place was called The Lantern, he hoped there would be a lantern and they'd just look for that.

They zigzagged through Sludgetown as the neighborhood's nightlife continued to simmer, scraping on top of the litter carpet. Occasionally Lena or Wyatt would stop to look at something in a smudged front window of a shop or read a handmade poster on a post.

Peering down the block to their left Wyatt saw, bright white and shining against the murk of night, an elegant and ancient looking lantern. Like something from outside Buckingham Palace or some shit. That must be it, he figured. After gesturing vaguely with his head and shoulders, Lena turned with him down the street toward the lamp.

There was no sign or indication that this was the right place, but it definitely was. Outside the bar were a few groups, no bigger than four punks each, standing around, smoking. Some smoked cigarettes, others joints or bowls, and one circle seemed to be smoking a new synthetic that Wyatt didn't recognize. He didn't keep up with designer drugs, partially because he knew people who'd died from them but mostly because he just didn't have the energy for that as a hobby.

"Look at that light," Wyatt said as they came up on the entrance.

"Yeah, must be the place," Lena responded.

"No I mean, the color of that light, I've never seen a bulb that color. Such a clean light."

"Oh, you're right."

"I wonder where they even get bulbs like that." Wyatt was still looking over his shoulder up at the lantern even as he held the door open for Lena. She entered and he followed her inside.

The ceilings and the lights were low. The corners of the room disappeared into total darkness and a dim red glow of indeterminate source cast sketchy outlines on all the furniture. There was just enough to navigate the crowded space. The space was longer than it was wide. Felt about like being in a bus. Along most of the length of one side was the bar, tended by two tenders and a bar back with face tattoos. Scattered throughout the rest of the space were hightop tables with three stools at each. Every stool in the bar was occupied, and most people were standing. In the very back were a few very worn down couches and a coffee table that probably hundreds of people had bumped their shins on. The table was adorned with a dozen magazines, though it was never bright enough inside to read them and they were so soaked with beer it would be impossible to anyway. This was a non-smoking bar.

After a first scan of the room Wyatt didn't see Roland or anyone he recognized. He glanced to Lena and saw her doing similar reconnaissance and coming to the same conclusion. It was just loud enough inside the bar that you had to almost yell to be heard, not so bad as to strain your voice. Wyatt asked who was getting the first drink. Lena suggested she get the first so when they were hanging out with Roland when it was time for the second round it could be Wyatt who was seen getting the drinks that time. It made sense to Wyatt. Lena got a cloudy, amber beer and Wyatt got a middling whisky in a glass with a little too much ice.

With drinks in hand they began the mostly sideways journey into the foreign land of the new bar, searching for the person Wyatt knew. Eventually, surrounding the last table before the couches, he saw Roland. The crowd was organic, amorphous, and he had no idea how many of the people around Roland were with him -- where his group ended and the bar's general population began. With an anxious heat at the back of his neck, Wyatt approached the group. It was with some relief to Wyatt that Roland looked at them as they approached with recognition in his face.

"Hey, Wyatt," he said, granting permission into the group. "Cool you came out."

"Yeah, man," Wyatt said. "This seems like a neat spot, I've never been here."

"Oh yeah, it's one of the places I kinda gravitate back to whenever I'm in town. Doesn't seem to change."

"Most places haven't for a while," Wyatt said.

"That's probably true. But especially this bar it feels like. So anyway, this is my band: Kirt, Eli and Richard. And my buddy Kalman, he's a writer," Roland pointed, holding a beer, around the table to each member of the group. Kirt was tall and pale. Eli was black and wore all grey. Richard was the guy in the band with long hair. All of them looked like they were in a punk band together. Kalman didn't, but he wore the plain, worker's clothes of someone who probably used to dress like a punk; a durable chino and a well-worn wool shirt with the sleeves rolled halfway up his forearms. He wore wire frame glasses and his hair was cut short. Wyatt was already having a hard time remembering which name went to which body.

"Good to meet everybody," he said. "This is my friend Lena, she's an artist."

"Oh, what kind of art?" asked Kirt.

"Photography right now," Lena answered.

"Woah, photography?" Kalman was visibly excited. "How?"

"I found a digital camera at an old house we were rummaging through."

"So when do you all head out on tour again?" Wyatt asked.

"Couple weeks?" Roland answered, seeming a little unsure himself and looking to Richard for confirmation.

"Yeah, first show is in Old New Haven, on the 28th," Richard nodded after sipping a beer and wiping a bit of foam from his mustache.

"Oh, supposed to be a bunch of punks up there, right? Isn't there a pretty healthy grindcore scene?" Wyatt asked.

"A lot of grind and noise," Richard said. "Stuff like that."

"And how many shows are lined up?" Wyatt was asking questions because as long as he had a question to ask the conversation kept moving.

"I think we've got 8 shows so far, but I know people in a few of the other towns on the way down the coast so I'm hoping to line up some stuff as we go. House shows and stuff."

Kalman turned back to talk about photography. "Lena?" he double checked getting the name right. Wyatt was impressed that he had the name in grasp already. "What have you been doing pictures of? Are you working on anything specific with it?"

"I had been sort of fiddling around for the last couple weeks, but I mean, after today I want to start working on a photo essay about those demons down at the beach."

"Oh shit!" Eli dribbled whisky on his hand. "I fucking heard about that!"

"About what?" Kirt asked.

"Well, um," Lena paused to think about how to explain it. "Earlier today these gates opened up in a few spots around the world, and these demons have been coming in and out. One of the gates is down at the old Corn Beach."

Wyatt watched the group as Lena delivered the news. Eli was clearly fascinated. He had heard about it somewhere. Richard was trying to figure it out. It didn't seem like Kalman or Kirt had known about it, and it didn't seem like Roland was listening to it now.

"Where did you hear this?" Richard asked, skeptically.

"On the news first, then we went down to see it," Lena said.

"You saw them?" Eli was thrilled.

"Yeah, that's where we were right before this," Wyatt said. "Well, I mean, we were down there and then we got some dinner."

"What did you have for dinner?" Roland sort of joked.

"What are they doing?" Kirt asked.

Lena answered "I don't think anyone knows yet. I mean I can't tell, we haven't heard anything."

"They're just kind of walking around," Wyatt said. "I think it looked like some were carrying stuff. One was digging a hole."

"A hole?"

"Yeah, a hole in the sand."

"*Demons*?" Kalman really leaned into the word.

"I don't know," Lena shrugged. "Yeah."

"They're completely colorless, dark," Wyatt was trying his best to explain what they had seen but was having trouble putting it into words. "A weird shape. Definitely nothing like anything on this planet. Strange legs, three legs, they walk in a weird rhythm. No face I could recognize. Antlers, t-rex sorta hands. Coming in and out of these portal things. The smaller ones were as about twice as tall as me..."

"The small ones were two times your height?" Kalman interrupted with a touch of distress.

"Yeah, right?" Wyatt looked to Lena.

"Yes."

"And there were bigger ones?" Eli asked. "How big were they?"

"I guess like... building sized?" Lena had difficulty saying it. She had seen them but it still felt unbelievable to say out loud.

"Holy fuck," something was starting to set in for Kirt.

They all kept drinking.

Obviously this was the only thing Wyatt wanted to talk about, it had only superficially left his mind during their initial small talk. Still he resented that the topic had stopped the conversation. The damage was irreparable.

"So, this happened today?" Roland asked.

"Yeah, I've actually had a hell of a day. This morning a drone fell out of the sky and landed like five feet away from me. Then I went over to Lena's and found out we're getting invaded by demons. I went to see them, and now I'm here."

"Fuck, I forgot about the drone thing," Lena said.

"Like a surveillance drone?" asked Roland.

"No, delivery."

"Oh did you check what was in it?"

"Yeah, antique-looking ceramic tiles. They're at Lena's still."

"You took 'em?" said Eli, and Wyatt nodded while sipping. Eli laughed. "Nice!"

"So these demons," Kalman said with his drink on the table, gesturing now with both hands as he spoke. "They slide out of these portals. And they're just walking around? Doing some kind of project? Has anyone gotten hurt?"

"I don't think so," Wyatt looked again to Lena, who he felt was the expert on it at this point.

"Not as far as I'd heard, I think," she said. "The first thing I heard was that maybe there was some damage in other places caused by the gates when they opened. But the one here is out in the water. When we were there they were walking around, some were on top of buildings, they were all doing stuff, but none of them had damaged anything. I don't even know if they knew we were there to be honest."

"Wait, the gates were in the water?" Eli asked.

"The one here is, yeah."

"How did they get to the beach and around the buildings and stuff?"

"They just walked," Wyatt said.

"Like they can breathe underwater?"

"No. I mean, maybe. Maybe they can. I mean when we saw them, they were just walking on the water just like it was the ground."

"What the fuck?" Eli was smiling.

"Is that what demons do?" Kalman asked. "I thought that it was the guy from the other team that did the walk on water trick."

"Well," Richard said, "Shit."

Roland added, "that's wild."

"I want to see them," said Eli. "Which beach? With the old amusement park?"

"Yeah that's the one," Wyatt said. "We rode our bikes from there up here on the old belt. Pretty easy ride."

"Finally, the demons have come," Kalman picked his drink back up. "I didn't expect it, but now that they're here it feels like it was only a matter of time. You can only live in a world like this for so long before eventually it really comes."

"Maybe they're here to push a big old 'reset' button," Kirt suggested.

"That could be," Wyatt said. "We fucked it all up to the point that the land lord was finally like 'enough, get out, we gotta clean this place up,' and sent in the trans-dimensional repo team."

"I'm gonna write a song about it!" Eli said.

"Fuck no," Roland nearly shouted, just having finished his drink. "Every shitty band I hate opening for is gonna have a dumb ass song about it. Can't wait to ignore some prog metal opera record that talks about the real-life demons for 90 minutes. I'mma get another drink, anyone need anything?" Kirt drained a little of the drink in his glass. Richard's drink was almost empty. Wyatt's whisky was now mostly melted ice, but Lena had only drank half her beer so he'd keep sipping it. The rest weren't really paying attention to their drinks. So Richard ordered a beer in a can. Kirt and Roland began the trip to the bar. After they left there was a discernible and momentary pause. Everyone left in the group was still considering the world that they now understood they shared, considering their place in relation to a world that felt changed.

"So," Kalman said after what may have only been a minute, "you are doing photography. Of these *demons* now," he said with a definite fascination with the word still.

"I think so, yeah," Lena answered. "I was sort of getting bored of the media I'd been working with. I hadn't painted anything I was proud of in like a year, and I tried other things and I just couldn't make anything I liked. So I found this camera and I was really quite taken with the whole mechanism of photography. It was just that, at first. No real direction, just a new medium I was getting some energy from. And then, now, today…you know. This thing happened."

"Wait, do you have pictures of them now?" Eli asked.

"Sort of," Lena started to pull the camera from its bag. "There's this tiny little view finder. I can show you them on this. So far that's all I can do."

She swiveled to the other side of the table to display the camera's small screen for them. Her thumb clicked through the pictures at a deliberate rhythm - giving enough time to see the pictures but not enough time to study them. While she guided her audience through the afternoon's photographs Wyatt watched their faces: Eli with glee and some fear, Richard wide eyed, and Kalman stern, solemn.

"What are you going to do with the pictures?" Richard asked.

"That's still the question. I just started doing this, and right now I don't have a way of getting the pictures off the camera to put them anywhere."

"Do you have plans to display them?" Kalman asked.

"I'd definitely like to when I'm ready. Wyatt knows a guy who collects old computer cables and stuff. He might have something I can use."

"And then what with them?"

"That's a good question. I've only sort of thought about that part. I can print them. That could be interesting. The camera is inherently just a distorted sort of false representation of the moment. It's already corrupted, digital, fuzzy. And printing it would add another filter of haze. At that point the pictures would be so far from the original moment, that really could be an idea worth exploring."

"Yes. Interesting to think of it that way. Photography used to be so close to the original, capturing it. Compared to painting or whatever else," Kalman mused along.

"Or there's the idea of projecting them," she said. "Get a big screen or just a blank gallery wall. One huge projected image, a slide show of all of them. That would really make for a curated experience. I choose the order people see them in and how long."

"People would come and go," Richard said. "Not always see it from the beginning."

"That's true. I'd have to account for that."

"If you got as many screens as you had pictures, you could display them all just the way paintings are exhibited," Wyatt suggested. "All at once, in a gallery. On a bunch of TVs or laptop screens."

It seemed like Lena genuinely had not thought of that as a possibility. The extra apparatus was enough of a hurdle that the idea had never been given real estate in her mind. But now she was putting herself in a gallery, surrounded by the flickering screens of an assortment of old devices repurposed to create a photo essay. Not printed, without that extra step further removing the piece from the original time and space of a finger pushing a button and an image captured by an electronic eye. Without dripping ink. Instead the distortion of a blue screen. Ephemeral. Disappearing as soon as it's unplugged and then only in the mind of the viewer and hidden in the cryptic glyphs only the camera could read. This idea was interesting for Lena.

"A lot of screens," Richard said, pointing out the obvious difficulty.

"I bet we could find cheap screens. If you want to do it that way it can just be a part of the project. Part of the exhibit is the work you put into gathering and repurposing old screens."

"I mean there are old screens everywhere," Kalman agreed. "Lots don't work, but lots do. Tons of old laptops, but the problem isn't the screen. If you can hook that up to something else, you know? Bada bing or something like that."

Roland and Kirt returned with two drinks each. Kirt gave Richard the beer he had ordered and Roland slid a drink across the table to Wyatt. It was the bar's version of the bright pink cocktail Roland had been sipping on the fire escape when Wyatt walked by. He was surprised. Roland looked at him with a wry smile and a wink, so Wyatt sipped the drink to find it was delicious and not as sweet as it looked.

"Thanks," he said. "This is great."

"My secret drink here. Not on the menu," Roland said.

"So, what about you guys?" Wyatt addressed the band as a unit.

"What?" Eli asked.

"I mean about this. What do you think? Any impact on the tour?"

Eli and Roland were confused but not aggressively. "No," Roland shrugged. "I don't think so. We're looking forward to getting back on the road."

"As long as demons don't take the van," Eli said.

"I think there's probably going to be some logistics that'll change," Richard added. "But what's a tour without a flat tire or something."

"A flat tire?" Wyatt said. "For real?"

"You know what I mean," Richard said. "I get it, it's a huge deal. It's not the same. But like, I think we gotta keep doing it, right?"

"Yeah, man," Roland said. "We're gonna play. Do this tour and then I guess we'll have to go from there. See what's going on."

That was the last thing anyone said to the whole group until the end of the night. The seven people would morph in and out of two and three person conversations, occasionally interrupted by the introduction of a passing acquaintance through the bar's crowded belly. Wyatt collected another round of drinks for himself and Lena, and returned the favor by getting one for Roland. The night grew fuzzy, wobbly, but not messy. Lena and Eli found a rapport, and eventually Wyatt found himself standing shoulder to shoulder with Roland but mostly engaged in conversation with Kalman.

"So you're a writer?" Wyatt interrogated.

"I am," he replied with a confidence Wyatt would never have answering the same question.

"What types of stuff? Working on anything now?"

"There's a short story collection I'm having proofread, and I just started a new novel. Aside from that there's always the informal schedule of zines."

"Very cool, I wonder if I have any of your zines."

"They're called *Talmudic*. I put them around as much as I can."

"That does actually sound familiar. I'll look through my collection when I get home."

"Are you a zinester?"

"Sometimes. I've done a few, yeah. Contributed to some. I pick up a bunch. The last one I made was called *The Rasp*. It was three years ago I printed that, shit. Do you want to talk about your book or not?"

"It's still very early on, but I guess I can start talking about it a little," Kalman put his drink down and picked it up between almost every time he talked. "It's a bit of a fantasy novel, in an old tradition, but I really wanted to explore the relationship between religion and gender. So there are two sort of competing religions in this world: one that is rigidly patriarchal and one of them every member is gender fluid — they take a sacrament that alters their body so that their sexual anatomy can fluctuate."

"Wow, that sounds really interesting. Are you interested in having some-one take a look at it when it's further along?"

"Oh, ok, sure. You'd like to help with proofreading or something?"

"I'd be willing to. I enjoy that. I've been editor on a few of my friends' projects. Mostly short story collections."

"Let's stay in touch on that. And you write? That was said?"

"Yeah."

"So, zines you mentioned, what else have you been doing?"

"I have this play I wrote. I'm trying to figure out how to get connected to a director or theater to see if something can be done with it."

"Theater! Very interesting. Are you big into theater?"

"No," Wyatt shrugged, "not really in particular. I was just at this point where I had been putting my work out in the same way for years and getting so little feedback. You know, people liked it sometimes, but then it was like, ok what do I do with this? I think I've always had this fear that if I die, like get hit by a bus on the way home, none of my writing will really even stick around and all the work I've done will just be gone. You hear that shit about like oh Franz Kafka or fucking Van Gogh didn't get famous until after they died. But they had still published a ton of work, their work existed, so it could be found. With me it's like I haven't left anything to discover. So I really just started thinking about how to get a more intense level of feedback, and I decided it was performance. An audience. Roping in performers so they're forced to be a part of it, and it's not just in my own head anymore."

"Yes, very interesting. Instant feedback. Are you making any progress on getting the thing done?"

Wyatt chuckled, "probably not, no. I met a few people in the theater scene the other night and we talked about it. Have you heard of Wolf Wolf?"

"No," Kalman said simply.

"She's a big deal, I guess, in that world. They talk about her like she's this city's Bertolt fucking Brecht. I know some people who are sort of adjacent to her a little bit, and I'm hoping I can meet someone that can help."

Roland swiveled from his conversation to join theirs. "And what now after this?" he asked Wyatt.

"After what?"

"The demon shit. Does that change anything for you and your writing?"

"Almost definitely," Wyatt shook his head, unable to form a thought from the ideas smothering his brain. "I just don't have any idea how. It'll probably take a while to figure what that'll look like. Are you guys touring new material?"

"Some new, some old. A healthy dose of covers in the set lists lately."

"Have you recorded the new stuff? What's the most recent thing you've printed?"

"Did you say you had that 7" from a couple years ago?"

"Yeah I do."

"We did a split 12-inch since then with Dog Doom," Roland said the other band's name with a feigned confidence that wanted to assume people had heard of them but a look that knew most people had not.

"You don't know any theater people, do you Roland?" Wyatt asked.

"Haha, shit no. Sorry man, I'm not smart enough for that shit."

"Oh well."

"If you get it together and have something performed sometime when I'm in town I'd come see it."

And that sentence marked the end of meaningful progress across all the group's conversations. People said things here and there, but no more conversations were really had. Drinks were finished, ideas were agreed with and actions were taken to close tabs and prepare to go. Roland pulled an immaculately rolled blunt out of an ornate, antique looking cigarette box and stationed it in the corner of his mouth as the group migrated to the door. Some members of the band waved to other corners of the bar as they did so.

Outside, Roland lit the blunt and exhaled a waft of sweet, thick smoke. Wordlessly he handed it to Wyatt, who accepted. Wyatt looked to Lena who was still chatting with Eli. When she saw his glance, she returned a look that confirmed she would be fine on her own the remainder of the evening. Since Sunset Morning was only about a 15 minute walk from Sludgetown, Wyatt started walking south, and Roland joined him. Without talking much, the two shared Roland's weed on the way to Wyatt's apartment and arriving home spent the night together.

CHAPTER 7

DEEP INTO MORNING WYATT started to wake up and found that Roland was still sleeping. He got out of bed and made some effort at tidying up the small space of his apartment. Roland began to stir and looked around. There was a poster on the ground in front of the door. It was from Brent, the musician who lived down the hall. He'd slid it under the door, a poster for the show he'd mentioned.

"Good morning," Wyatt said.

"Good morning," Roland rubbed his eyes and stretched. He looked around the apartment. "Nice place."

"Thanks, it gets the job done. There's never enough clean water, but you know. It's safe and pretty quiet."

"Yeah, a good little neighborhood seems like," Roland got out of bed and started getting dressed. He picked up the poster and started to read it. "Any good breakfast around here?"

"Oh, hell yeah. You don't name a neighborhood 'Sunset Morning' if there aren't good spots for breakfast. There's a killer street cart that makes breakfast sandwiches and there's a good little diner down the block. You know, the greasy counter, couple booths, coffee. That kind of thing. It's cheap."

"Cool, yeah. You wanna go there?"

"Absolutely, always down for that," Wyatt grabbed a shirt from the back of his desk chair and buttoned it up.

He took a notebook from a shelf and dropped it into a tote bag to join the Edna LeBlanc novel and felt around to make sure there was a pen already in the bag. There were two, so he shouldered the tote.

"Mind if I brush my teeth first?" Roland asked.

"Oh no problem. Hold on," Wyatt opened a drawer in his kitchen and pulled a new toothbrush out of an already open two pack, handing the toothbrush to Roland and dispensing the now empty packaging. Roland disappeared into the bathroom and Wyatt sorted through his zines trying to remember the name Kalman had said. *Talmudic.* That was it. He did have one. At least one. *Talmudic 13.* He flipped through it. It looked familiar. Roland returned.

"What's that?"

"Oh it's one of your friend Kalman's zines."

"Did he give you one?"

"No I already had it," he slipped that into his bag. "Ready?"

"Let's do it."

And they left the apartment. A new group of people stood on the street in front of his building. They were older than Wyatt, decently dressed. He was confused about what they were doing there. It was raining today, but only barely. They were only just damp by the time they reached the diner. The diner was called simply "DINER." They went in and found it to be full.

A waiter saw them and said "Just the two of you?" Wyatt nodded, and the waiter looked at a booth that had finished their meal and now sat finishing their coffee and said, "Should only be a few minutes."

Wyatt absentmindedly looked at his phone but did nothing on it. They lingered together near the entrance, too groggy for conversation. After some amount of time, the two seated patrons stood, put jackets on their backs, hats on their heads and cigarettes in their mouths. An androgynous teenager cleared away their leftover dishes, eating some leftover french fries before wiping the table with a damp rag. A nod from the original waiter indicated they were free to take their seats.

The diner found itself in a room with very little flourish or style. Almost every interior decision was made to keep things clean and quiet inside. Windows were always closed and ceiling fans were always on. It was open 24 hours. The vinyl booth seats had almost no cushion. They felt like vinyl had been used to upholster park benches. The tabletops had that speckled pattern designed to hide imperfections. It was a dirty and comfortable place. The food was always good. The prices were incoherent, inconsistent, but mostly fair. Wyatt ate here often. The staff here were some of the only people in his neighborhood that he recognized.

"We allowed to smoke in here?" Roland asked the waiter as they received their menus.

"Not usually. Ventilation isn't that good."

"No worries, man," Roland flashed a charming smile.

Wyatt was leafing through Kalman's zine and Roland picked up one of the menus.

"What's good here?"

"The diner food,"

"Well," Roland said, pausing between each word as his eyes darted back and forth across the menu, "I can get down with that."

The waiter returned with cups of what looked like pretty clean water. Not all restaurants served good water necessarily, but the restaurants that stuck around for any amount of time knew that your customers were more likely to come back if they didn't get the shits from bad water. Wyatt had a running list in his head of the places that seemed to filter pretty well.

"Any other drinks?" he asked?

"Black coffee please," Wyatt answered.

"Orange juice?" was Roland's order.

Roland put his menu down on top of Wyatt's at the end of the table and drank his entire cup of water. The door rang and two cops came in, two human cops. Wyatt had been coming to this place for years, four years maybe, and he had never seen cops here. The temperature of the whole restaurant changed. Every patron shifted in every seat. All eyes became alert. It was likely that almost everyone in this diner had been brutalized to some extent or another by the city's police army. Wyatt's back was to the door, but he saw the shift in Roland's face. He watched the warped reflection in an old, smudged mirror so he didn't have to turn around to see.

It was with unexpected authority that the waiter on shift stepped up to them. He had the confidence of someone who had dealt with this before and someone who knew the cooking staff was armed and watching from the shadows. "Yeah?" he said to them.

"We're looking for someone," the shorter of the two cops said. Other than their height the two were basically indistinguishable.

"They're not here."

"Well, well, you don't know who I'm looking for."

"I know they're not here."

"Someone went and got themselves murdered two nights ago."

"Did you do it?" the waiter asked.

The cop was frustrated, but he must have known that inside that diner they didn't have the upper hand like they usually did out on the streets. He must have known how it would play out if he got rough. One of the cops said something, but Wyatt and Roland were too far away to hear it. The cop handed a piece of paper over to the waiter. It had a picture on it. The waiter shook his head and handed it back.

"Alright, well you tell all your little scuz balls we're looking for her. We know she hangs out in this neighborhood sometimes."

"Why don't you check your little cameras?" the waiter said with a smirk in his voice.

It was hard for Wyatt to see their reaction, but he felt a sharp inhale happen around him. This statement from the waiter was an aggressive move and the cops were angry about it. A broad motion from one of the cops knocked over a rack of individually wrapped cookies that slid across the floor. Nobody in the diner moved. The cops exited.

A ring indicated that the door shut and three customers immediately got up and helped the waiter pick up the cookies. The tension flew out of the diner like a balloon being let go. Everyone made an effort to act like it had not happened at all, only trace amounts of residue left in the energy of the space.

The waiter brought over a mug of coffee and a plastic glass of orange juice.

"Sorry about that, usually doesn't happen."

"Hey no worries man," Roland assuring that they were unoffended.

"I've been coming here for a while, never seen fuzz in here," Wyatt said, taking a sip from his coffee. It was surprisingly good coffee. Always was at this diner.

"It's nothing. I don't think they're coming back."

"What was that bit about the cameras?" Wyatt asked with a slightly hushed voice.

The waiter leaned half a step toward them. "Me and a few other radicals recently scrambled all the cameras on this block."

"That fucking rules," Wyatt said. "I love that shit."

"Anyway," he said, stepping back again, "you all getting some food?"

"Yeah," Roland pulled the menu back toward him, "Can I get the Neighborhood Burger, with hashbrowns instead of fries?"

"Mhmm," the waiter said without writing anything down.

"And I'll get the Breakfast Standard."

"Eggs?"

"Scrambled, with cheese."

"Toast?"

"Rye."

"Potatoes?"

"French fries."

"Perfect. I'll be right back."

As the two sat in the silence left by the waiter's departure, Wyatt looked at the pebbled plastic glass of orange juice cradled loosely in Roland's hand.

He'd never thought about the idea that they'd have orange juice here. Wyatt had never seen an orange.

"How's the OJ?" he asked.

"Oh, you know. It's alright. It's that frozen stuff out of the can like your grandma always had."

"I forgot about that shit, wow. I loved it."

"Wanna sip?"

Roland slid it across the table and Wyatt tried some. It tasted bright.

"Damn, that's kinda good. I mean I know it's not actually good, but like it does kinda hit the spot a little bit doesn't it?"

"It does in a way."

"Do you drink coffee?"

"Sometimes."

"They actually have really good coffee here. Since it started getting hot enough there are some good coffee farms in the valley upstate. They get beans from there."

Roland blew on the mug and took a gentle sip. His eyebrows raised and he nodded in approval.

"So, my friend," Roland said. "What do you have planned next?"

"Well," Wyatt paused, drinking the dark coffee. "I guess I'm going to have to figure that all out now. I mean I'm working on getting this play off the ground, and I have a few other projects I could stand to finish up. But now these demons. I mean it is sort of fucking with my head. On one side it just shrinks everything. Especially live performance, because how much can a moment in a theater mean in a universe that doesn't give a shit about holding to the narrative we've had for all of human history. But then there's also like, if something this fucking bonkers can just happen, that's maybe sort of thrilling. And it sort of demands we do our best as a species or something. Gotta make something about it. I'll probably hang out with Lena as she works on her stuff with them. But you know, when she gets working on a project she can get pretty focused on it. I might go weeks without hearing from her. So really I have no idea what things are going to look like now."

"I meant like after breakfast."

"Oh. Um. Well I've got the afternoon free and then I work tonight at the shop till midnight."

"You dig that job?"

"It's fine. Pretty low commitment. Fun weird stuff comes through inventory every once in a while. I like making sandwiches, I think I'm really good at it."

"Yeah? That's pretty cool. Do you have regulars?"

"A bunch, yeah. I mean it's just like this little shop on a block. A lot of people who live or work nearby stop on the way for a bite. I know their faces."

"Do you know their orders?"

"Not many. I'm not good at that. A lot of them get different things every time. The menu changes. There's a few people I know. This one guy always gets a breakfast wrap with seitan and he puts on red sauce."

"Is it more fun to do a sandwich or a wrap?"

"I think I like both. There's like a challenge to it. With the sandwich you need to build it in a way that it's big enough to be filling but still manageable and not too messy. With the wrap you've got this nice little fold technique that keeps everything in, and the real trick is to lay out the ingredients in a way that you'd get each flavor in every bite."

"Wow, there's a lot to it."

"It's just like anything, you can always find ways to do it better. I've just been working on it since I got the job. People know we have good sandwiches, we all really do our best to live up to it I guess."

"How long have you worked there?"

"Yikes, four years now I guess? I mean, I get money if I do like a reading, or my stories get picked up in lit mags every once in a while. But it's been a steady thing that leaves me enough time to work on my own stuff, you know?"

"I hear that man, I dig it."

"What about you guys? After the tour, something in mind? Is there like a day job you come back to between stuff?"

"I got a few things here and there. I've worked in some print shops and that's a good deal I can pop in and out of if we're not on tour. I don't really know, man. We haven't got anything lined up after this and to be honest we haven't really had a lot of electricity around writing new material. Sometimes a tour will wake that back up but sometimes it just really drains you. This might be it for these guys for a while."

"Well what do you *want* to do? You want to keep playing?"

"For sure, it's always the thing I wanna be doing."

The waiter delivered food to the table, placing the meals on the wrong side of the table, opposite the person who'd ordered it. It wasn't from lack of effort or misremembering. There was just always someone else gesturing for something and the waiter rarely had the luxury of looking where he was going. None of the dishes matched. The food looked dull, but it looked authentic. After sliding the plates across the table to each other, Wyatt and Roland squared up to their meals.

"Can you start writing some stuff and just see if that gets the machine cooking for everyone else?" Wyatt asked, taking the fork and knife politely in his hands.

"I don't know that I've got the juice right now either. Maybe we do all gotta take a little break," Roland picked up a piece of hashbrown with his hands and dropped it in his mouth. He raised his eyebrows and nodded in approval as he chewed.

"So are you coming back here after the tour? What do you consider home base?"

"Dude, honestly I'm not sure. I guess Connecticut? That's where most of my stuff is, I got a storage locker and a few apartments that have spare rooms I can always sleep in," Roland took a large bite from his burger.

"I've never been to Connecticut," Wyatt's fork navigated his plate and took a bite of the very fluffy, very cheesy eggs. This cook knew a breakfast. The cheese was well placed. It made a difference. Some diners just put the cheese on, but here they understood where it needed to be.

"You can come check it out after the tour. If you don't mind camping you can make the bike ride in a couple days, I've done it a few times. The trail is solid and safe."

"Oh that would be interesting. Might do me some good," Wyatt sipped some coffee. The waiter was passing by with the pot for a refill for another table so he held up his mug to ask for a warm up.

"Yeah, I mean, my guess is we'll do this tour and all kinda go back to wherever we feel like going back to, and either we'll just keep playing until we've got something worth performing again or I'll slide in with someone else and see what else I can do."

"Just keep moving like that?"

"It's what works best for me most of the time. I take a breather here and there but I get pretty antsy and I get back on it again, you know? Just gotta see where my mind's at when we're done with these shows. Figure out a plan from there."

"Yeah."

"This burger kicks ass. This is a good spot man."

Wyatt was eating some fries and nodded. "For sure, I love having this place around the corner."

"You always bring people here?"

"Sure, if there's people to bring and they want a meal."

Roland smiled.

"Been cops around this area lately it feels like," Wyatt said looking at the door where the confrontation had happened.

"Weird. No cops in Connecticut. Some old army guys play around like that sometimes, but nothing like here."

"Oh shit!"

"What?" Roland was a little startled.

"I left those fucking tiles at Lena's. Damn it."

"Tiles?"

"Yeah, did I tell that story? Delivery drone crashed right next to me yesterday. The package was full of these vintage ceramic tiles. They were beautiful. So I grabbed them, but I didn't want to bring them with me to the beach."

"Demon beach," Roland had finished the burger and was wiping his fingers with a napkin.

"Lena is probably on her way there right now, so I'll have to get those things later."

"Well speaking of on the way- I'd better see what the rest of the boys are up to. Keep 'em out of trouble."

"Yeah sure. It's been good."

"We'll get together again before I'm on the road."

"I'll probably be back at the beach again, maybe tomorrow. You wanna come see it?"

"Hm. I guess it would be worth it. I'll ask the dudes to see if they want to come. Yeah we'll see, maybe," Roland stood up and pulled out his wallet. Wyatt put up a hand in protest, but the gesture was overridden. Roland gave Wyatt a kiss and a smile, paid at the register, and then left. Wyatt watched as Roland exited, looked down at his mostly empty coffee mug, and scribbled a very short poem in his notebook. He read the poem back in his head and underlined a few words he wanted to try workshopping later.

THE ALLEY leading to Lil ol' Betsy's backdoor was unchanged from the way it had been at the end of his previous shift. No indication that this was a door in an alley in a world now cohabitated by demons. No trace of their activity. Their strange music was not found on the air. When Wyatt knocked to let the previous shift know he was there to relieve them of their duty, the door flung open instantly. It was Ted, a younger, wirey little white guy. He looked frazzled, a complete wreck. Ted wasn't always what Wyatt would call "put together," but this was something.

"Hey man. How was the shift?" Wyatt asked with a cautious slant.

"Fuck. It was fine. Normal I guess."

"You heard about the beach?"

"Damn it, I'm... I dunno. I don't know."

"Mhmm. I get you."

"I see it in people's faces. Some of them *know* they're freaking out, some don't. And, actually, you wanna know the worst?"

"Worst?"

"Some people's faces aren't different. That's the one breaking my head."

"Well, try and chill tonight. Take care of yourself Teddy."

"Can't, got my other job."

Another job? Wyatt didn't know he had another job. "Take it easy anyway. Here," Wyatt reached into the shop and grabbed a jar of saké and handed it to him, "on the house."

Ted nodded and took it. "See you 'round Wyatt."

The saké had come in randomly one time. A Japanese restaurant nearby closed and a lot of their inventory and incoming shipments just got picked up by shops on the block.

Climbing into the shop and closing the door, Wyatt slumped onto the stool and took what felt like his first deep breath in 24 hours. He slid his phone across the scanner for payment and pulled a sloppy blunt out of the jar on the counter. After tucking in the wrap a little neater, he lit it and brought a long drag into his lungs. His body felt confused. Out of instinct he drew the writing notebook from his tote, took a pen in his hand, but then he found nothing and wrote nothing. A small bit of ash fell from the blunt in his lips onto the blank page.He brushed it away, leaving a smudge. With frustration he closed this notebook and put it on the counter, staring out the window at the street. The building across the way was empty and had been for a while. It didn't even have squatters. It had always been the building across the street. Always been there. Today there was a strangeness about the building, as Wyatt sat staring. He saw the craft of it. That plans had been made and executed in order to construct it. Workers of skill performed the magic trick of turning bricks and rebar and whatever into a structure that stood there still. Empty now, uncared for, slowly chewed apart by an unfriendly atmosphere.

An office worker approached the window. "Can I get a sandwich?" he asked.

"Of course, what are you in the mood for?" Wyatt answered, leaning forward with a smile. Wyatt studied the man's face to see if he could detect some hint of awareness about the change in the world. He couldn't tell what he saw. The man seemed hungry, and maybe that was it.

"Can I get ham and provolone?"

"Hot or cold?"

"Cold."

"Sure thing," Wyatt stowed the blunt in an ashtray by the back door, washed his hands and grabbed a sandwich roll in one hand and a knife in the other with complementary, graceful swoops. He laid down the slices of ham, folding them into their place before arranging the provolone in an interlocking pattern on top. He laid the cheese slices opposite ways on a cold sub to provide more even coverage.

"Veggies?"

"What do you have in there today?"

"Looks like mostly the usuals."

"How fresh are the greens?"

They were not particularly fresh. Wyatt made a 'so-so' motion with his hand. He appreciated that this man knew how to order a hero in a reliable way to ensure a level of quality.

"Ok, let's do banana peppers, black olive and cucumber."

Banana peppers and black olives came out of cans, pickled, so they were guaranteed to be solid. Cucumbers could be grown in a greenhouse any-where in the city so it was a pretty safe vegetable, too. He knew what he was doing. He even gave the vegetables in the right order: cucumber goes on after the black olive so they don't roll around on the flat surface on top. The guy was a fucking pro.

"Sauces?" Wyatt asked.

"Mayo and some oregano."

Damn. The sandwich was a treat to make. This guy was going to like it; he'd done a nice job putting it together. Wyatt squirted the mayo across like an artistic statement and carefully shook oregano from the shaker to ensure that it was soaked into the mayonnaise. "That it?" he asked.

"Yeah. That's it. And a beer."

"What kind?"

"I dunno, whatever is best with the sandwich."

Wyatt wrapped up the sandwich and looked over his shoulder to examine the beer inventory. He picked a lager of middling quality. Something with a bit of flavor, but crisp enough to just make a canvas for the sandwich. He put both items down by the window. "Eight bucks."

The man held up his phone to be scanned, and sent $10 so that a two dollar tip would automatically get sent to Wyatt's paycheck. He grabbed both items and nodded with a slight smile before leaving.

For the next bunch of minutes Wyatt remained seated on the stool, and that was it. In his periphery he was aware of silhouettes crossing back and forth in front of the shop window. From time to time he'd look at his phone and see nothing new on it.

"Hey Wyatt," came all of the sudden from the street. It was Talbot.

"Woah, Talbot! How are you today?"

"I'm good, thought I'd swing over and see if you were in the window."

"Can I get you anything?"

"Cup of coffee?" he handed Wyatt a thermos.

Wyatt took it, "anything in it?"

"Nah, not today."

"Did you, uh, hear about the thing?"

"I did, yeah."

"It's nuts, right?"

"Fucking insane," Talbot shook his head.

Wyatt handed the coffee back. "I went down there with Lena."

"You saw them?"

"Mhmm. Lena touched one."

"She touched it? Is she ok?"

"Yeah they don't really seem to be doing anything dangerous. It sort of shook her off like a horse annoyed that a fly's on its ass."

"Wow. I've been reading stuff about them. Seen some of the videos."

"What have you been reading, what are they saying?"

"No one knows what they're saying. There's some fear mongery non-sense, religious fervor and stuff like that. And then obviously just a lot of clever people writing up think pieces, trying to find a unique angle or some hook."

"Hm."

"Don't write about it."

"Me?"

"Yeah, I get the impulse. It's the craziest thing that's ever happened. That doesn't make it interesting to write about I think. By the time the pen hits the paper it's already turned into something that's been driven into the ground by hacks," Talbot said as he popped the top off the thermos and blew onto the opening.

"That makes sense. I can't think of anything I'd do with it."

Talbot sipped some coffee. Someone else came to the window. A woman, maybe around forty.

"Candy bar," the other person said.

Wyatt knew this person. They never said the name of a candy bar, but he had gotten pretty good at guessing the kind she wanted. He looked at the rack and picked up the one with just nougat and nothing else. She looked at it, made a decision, and accepted the selection in exchange for a dollar.

"Anyway, what are you up to today?" Wyatt asked Talbot.

"Just finishing work."

"How was it in there?"

"Oh it's alright. Been kind of annoying. They made some changes that make some of the little things harder. I had a form that gets submitted after every order request and it used to go through this online system, but one person did one thing wrong and a shipment went to the wrong Smyrna, so now we need to physically bring a printed copy of order requests down to the office every day. I get it, but it's a drag."

"The wrong Smyrna."

"Delaware instead of Iowa."

"Guess that gets you some good exercise, walking the paperwork over where it's supposed to go."

Talbot laughed and drank more coffee.

"Lena's going to do like a photo project about it."

"That's really cool, does she have a gallery lined up? I haven't looked at photos in... fuck knows."

"No, she hasn't even figured out how to exhibit them. We were talking about it. That might be what she's figuring out today. Not hack when Lena does something with it?"

"Well no. I mean mostly because of the medium. It's novel. Lena always chooses interesting work, I find."

Wyatt nodded.

"Keep me posted about that project as she works on it. I'd come out to an opening."

"Yeah for sure, I will. You don't think they have old video gear or monitors at your office do you? Old stuff that no one keeps track of?"

"Hm. That's interesting. We might. I can look around. There are a few old floors that the company owns but we don't really use anymore. It's storage. Sometimes we have to go get old files from there. Maybe I can sneak around some of the rooms and see what else is there."

"Cool, yeah lemme know."

"Will do," Talbot sipped his coffee. "Alright man. I gotta get moving. See you later."

"Have a good one," Wyatt said, and then he was alone again.

It was a long time before anyone else came to the window. Wyatt sat and he smoked and he watched people walk down and up the street. The general meandering of the space. After some time he remembered the zine from Kalman in his bag and he pulled it out. For some time he looked at the cover. It was like old leather had been photocopied onto the paper and in large, carefully placed letters it said simply "TALMUDIC, VOL. 13". Wyatt was impressed. 13 volumes? He'd never even gone on a date with the same person 13 times. Had Kalman really done 13 editions of this? Or did he just pick the numbers he felt suited the project when it was done? Who knows. Maybe it was even more than 13, maybe this wasn't the latest. Could be 32 volumes. Or more.

Thumbing through the booklet, Wyatt saw that the content of the zine was a diverse collection of prose and poetry in many forms. There were no visual components. It was just words. No comics, cartoon, doodles, designs. It was devoted to the word. He stopped flipping through at random a little more than halfway through and picked a poem to read. It was brief. Less than a page and it described the flowing of water from a roof, down a gutter, into the street and ultimately into a storm drain. There was a clarity in the language that Wyatt found compelling, captivating. It was a beautiful piece.

Before anyone else came to the window Wyatt had read the entire zine and was already revisiting the bits he'd been struck by the most. Kalman's name didn't appear until the final page. For the rest of his shift Wyatt simply read and thought about the words Kalman had committed to this smudged, photocopied page. A few more times customers would come and buy something, and then he'd return to the writing.

It wasn't until he heard the strange music that he really shook back to focusing on where he was. It was like falling off a roof and into his body. A slight crescendo of the musical tonality from the beach grew. Wyatt leaned as far out his window as he could and looked down the street both ways.g Sure enough, there was one of the demons, one of the Minor Demons. Still towering over the people and cars that were there, it lurched and wandered back and forth from side to side. The cars all stopped. Everything stopped. Everyone watched. Everyone watched as it reached out its peculiar hand to grab hold of a tree, watched it bend the tree at a delicate angle and let go, leaving it growing at a diagonal halfway up its trunk. It continued along, stopping to gently nudge parks cars sliding them onto sidewalks, as if re-adjusting furniture.

The street dogs took some notice of the visitor. A few sniffed it. Wyatt could not tell if it knew the dogs were there. Was there anything in the old lore about demons and their feelings toward dogs? Wyatt thought he remembered something about mummies not liking cats. Or maybe they worshipped cats? The demon seemed to pay no attention to the dogs or any other passersby. Then, all of the sudden, it started to climb up the side of the building. It jumped across to a building on the other side of the street. It's jump made Wyatt shudder a bit. The arc of the jump and the motion of the act of jumping did not seem to match. There was no recoil. Just a little twist and it was in the air. No flapping or gliding, just a momentum that carried it across. It climbed to the roof and continued along until it was out of sight.

Some people pretty much just got back to whatever they were doing. Wyatt saw some shaking their heads in confusion as they did so. Other people took longer before moving again. Two people were very distressed by it. One was a child who was crying now. The other was a well-dressed older woman who was hitting herself on the face. She was screaming and bending over. Traffic parted around her like a rock in the middle of a river. Wyatt had to look away.

There was a slight tremble in his hands. What was the demon doing? It seemed that they had begun moving further from the beach. He looked over at the tree the demon had bent. It was being engulfed in new growth, and the branches had sprung buds of blossom. The tree seemed to give off a slight hum, just a small hint of the song in the air around the demons as they traveled. The tree had learned the demon's song.

CHAPTER 8

WEEKS WENT BY. WYATT would go back and forth to work, spending as much time as he could being creatively productive. It seemed the same could be said of the Demons who all continued in and out of their gates and busied themselves making bewildering alterations to the world they visited. Neighborhoods would be completely changed: angles of roads, shapes of buildings, colors of fauna.

Some changes were only perceptible to those who lived there and could see the subtlety of the work. Others were grand changes that the mind struggled to understand. Structures would bend but remain intact. Entire blocks twisted so the doors that once faced east now faced south. Occasionally whole buildings had been flattened. There was no definite answer about what happened to the people who had lived in those buildings. Wyatt had heard some stories that the people simply woke up one day somewhere else, with all their stuff strewn about. Other theories were less optimistic and assumed that wherever the buildings had gone, the residents had gone as well, never to be seen or heard from again. Many of the changes were in less populated areas, but it did not seem that the demons paid any mind to the presence or absence of humankind in their business.

It was impossible to get a clear idea of what the Demons were doing in the other parts of the world where the gates had opened up. Nobody seemed to have any narrative. It was only clear that the Demons had some sort of project, they were working on something, and there didn't seem to be any human on earth who understood what.

In this time Wyatt would fill spare moments with attempts to write. He had outlined several ideas and started a few, but none had gotten far. Most didn't stick around for long. The play remained his focus, but the theater seemed to stay out of reach. It was a realm that seemed closed off to him, impenetrable. And of course a large portion of his time was spent at the bodega. He continued to make the best sandwiches he could.

There were times that the world of theater seemed so distant, so willingly isolated, that he was only a breath away from giving up entirely. A "who do they think they are?" kind of thing. How dare they? What was the point of a performance art if you shut the doors to anyone not already part of this manufactured scene? Wyatt would fabricate this elitist narrative and spiral into it and wrap a blanket around himself down there. The theater scene was broad, with more venues than even a devoted theater goer could keep track of, and truthfully Wyatt didn't make as much an effort to become part of the scene as he felt like he did. Only occasionally going to shows that he was rarely impressed by. He'd show up by himself, sit down, read the self-printed playbills and then leave when the production was over. Always he hoped he'd see someone he recognized and he'd strike up conversation, but he never did.

On a random, hazy weekday, Wyatt was entering a coffee shop that Qat was exiting. He had not seen them since the reading at the Last Coffee Shop with Lena a month or so before.

"Qat!" he said reflexively.

"Oh, hi! Wyatt! Right?" they responded. Qat was holding a coffee thermos. It was very worn. Like an old tractor. They were dressed in a deliberately vintage trenchcoat that looked miraculously cool. Wyatt remembered as a kid looking at comic book detectives and being excited to be the age when a trenchcoat would work, and for him it just never did. Qat had it cinched tightly around their waste cutting an hourglass silhouette. A floral scarf was wrapped around their neck and tucked into the front of the jacket.

"You on the way anywhere?"

"I'm actually headed to work."

"I never thought about you having a daily grind like that."

"Honestly, that's flattering. I'm in retail. Over on the main city island. It's a pain in the ass to get to. What are you doing?" they asked.

"Literally just going to this coffee shop. My plans ended there. You take a bus or something?"

"My employer pays for the train, enough of us live over on this side of the river."

There was one reliable train that bridged over from here to there. It was pretty exclusive. Wyatt had never taken it. He made an impressed face and Qat dismissed it with an eye roll. "You wanna hold up just a minute," Wyatt asked. "I can grab a quick cuppa and we can do a walk-and-talk."

"Sure I can do that. Don't get anything fancy that'll take a long time to make."

"I'm a black coffee kinda guy, if you can believe it. I'll go grab it." And he did. He exited the shop to find Qat there waiting, blowing on the top of their coffee, still hot. "Alright, lead on."

Qat started off in the direction of the train stop and Wyatt walked alongside.

"So," he said, "have you been around to any good shows lately?"

"I've been out and about. Things are definitely different feeling in the community these days."

"Because of the... uhh.."

"Yeah, exactly. Everyone has a different sort of reaction."

"That makes sense. What's it mean for you?"

"I don't know that it means much for me to be honest. I definitely get it, I see the magnitude of it. I would expect it to impact what gets created. But I guess for me the art is still about the artist and the audience. It's sort of already its own demon world before the demons showed up."

Wyatt's coffee was too hot to sip but he tried anyway, feeling the air on his lip and retreating the cup from his mouth.

"Are you still working?"

"I've been trying. Starting a lot of things. I think the thing I'm still really invested in is producing that play."

"Where have you been trying?"

"Well I go out to shows now and then, sort of do the rounds at theaters. But I don't know anyone, and I still feel like those doors are shut. Is Wolf Wolf still working on that production?"

"It's been delayed. She's been reworking the whole project since the event."

"Hm."

"Curtiss and Tom have been having a tough time. They poured a lot into that production and now everything's in limbo. Their art is performing, and they are beholden to having something to work on. That show being put on hold really took a chunk out of them. I hope it comes together."

"Damn, yeah that sounds like a drag. I get it– it's a bummer for the scene. I think I'm really fascinated by the times creativity is beholden to other people. Even with solitary art forms at a certain point it isn't solitary. Like with writing, once I'm done with something it's just sort of up to publishers what happens next. Out of my hands, you know? Like it's not an actor's fault if a play falls through, and now their art is gone."

"Mhmm," they said. "I think the collaboration is a huge part of the satisfaction, but you're right, there's always a step in creativity that takes it away from the creative. There's other works going on. I'm actually going to something tomorrow night at the Buttress Theater. You should come. Very subversive, somewhat surreal, from what I've been hearing. I can introduce you to some people. If they are just finishing a project there will be people looking for something new to chew on. Could be a good opportunity."

"Wow, thank you. Yeah I'll definitely come."

They continued to snake through a neighborhood that Wyatt was not very familiar with. They walked below the elevated train line and occasionally it would rumble so envelopingly that the conversation would stop for the duration and pick up again once the train had passed. Teenage gangsters dressed in black jumped from nearby buildings to the railway and skittered back and forth. A realization came like a prick to the back of Wyatt's neck as he saw a second gang, these dressed as cowboys, pouring out from alleys on both sides of the street. A battle was breaking out.

Gunfire erupted, thunderous, echoing in the canyon of the city street as the two groups clashed. With small, stolen handguns and the occasional rifle the gangs fired at each other, running between positions of cover. Glass of car windows burst out onto the street, and people on the sidewalks screamed and ran. At the moment the battle began, Wyatt and Qat quickened their pace to move away from the bullets, ducking for cover behind a stoop. Qat plugged their ears. There were shouts indiscernible to Wyatt between the gangs and amongst themselves. Orders and threats barked. Stray bullets punctured walls, kicked up bits of trash from the ground and ricocheted off of metal. The closest cars were getting perforated by gunshots. Bullets crackled precipitously, from all directions. Different sounds from each weapon, joining together but not harmonizing. Just bang, pow, boom, echo, grunts, screams, footsteps running. Overwhelming, deadly noise.

Wyatt heard a heavy thud and saw, peeking out between the railing posts, that one of the kids from the subway overpass had tumbled, either from gunfire or just losing his balance, and fell from his position and splattered onto the street. Tires screeched as cars stopped, not wanting to get any closer. The sound of garbage sliding as traffic skidded to a halt. More screams, from gang members and from randoms who were in the wrong place like Qat and Wyatt had happened to be. He checked on Qat— they weren't hurt— and then he looked across and saw people tucked into every safe corner. A group had started to accumulate at the end of the opposite block: either pedestrians waiting until it was safe to pass or a curious audience. The percussive gunfire continued, echoed through the streets. A young, curious face of a child looked down from an apartment window four stories up. Shots slowed down, and there was more breath between each blast of gunfire. When it stopped, people started to move again. Wyatt stood up and looked around. Qat was pensive but eventually stood also, and they started walking again.

The battle probably only lasted a few minutes, and it appeared the cowboys had lost. Some had seemed to escape and none were left to tend to the one wounded but it looked like most had not survived. Attacking from the ground like that was stupid. A much weaker position. Probably the ones dressed in black would double back around in a few minutes and finish off any others they found.

Wyatt shook some coffee off his hand that had spilled as they avoided the fight and sipped from his cup, still kind of warm. Qat was still tense from the whole thing. Though they continued walking, their eyes remained behind, looking at every corner and nook. Qat explained that they had spent a good portion of their childhood in such a gang.

"Oh really?" Wyatt was surprised.

"Yeah. I had a good family, and things were sort of still just starting to go the way it went. My family was maybe one of the last few middle class families before it fully imploded. But as other kids were losing everything and the gangs were starting, I guess I romanticized it a bit."

"Sure. People were fascinated. I feel like I remember it like it was a TV show."

"It's pretty gross to think about now. But I got into it just because it seemed pretty cool to be involved with. All the other kids were squatting and had nowhere to go. If they didn't gang up they had no food or anywhere to safely sleep. I went home to my family's apartment. I dunno. I definitely still feel it in my bones somewhere whenever I see the kids out there."

"Do you know anyone who's still in it?"

"I don't think so. People fall out of it. Or get killed I guess. I definitely didn't really stay in touch with most of the girls for long."

"Are the gangs not close like that?"

"While you're in it, you are. Obviously you need to trust them to protect you in a fight. And they will. And you'll protect them, you know? Maybe some of them do stay close. Stay friends for years for real."

"Maybe there's a support group."

"I doubt it. I think people just find their way into something else. The performance arts were my support group. When I was done, when I knew I couldn't stay doing it, that's where I ended up and I've been there ever since."

Wyatt was curious what it was that pushed them out. If there was a specific event or encounter that made them hang up the novelty costume their gang wore. He guessed that if they wanted to talk about it they'd bring it up, and he left it at that. Maybe someday he'd ask, he thought.

They reached the train stop. Qat had finished their coffee and tucked the travel mug into their tote bag. It was a zigzag of stairs to reach the platform above them. Qat pulled a metro card out of their purse to prepare for the climb. The two said their farewells and expressed that they had mutually enjoyed the walk-and-talk, all things considered. Glad everyone was safe. Qat confirmed the information for the show they had mentioned. It was called "Origin of Dawn," and then they started toward the climb to the train. A faint rumble to the east indicated that the timing was good, and a train would soon arrive. So Wyatt waved, sipped more coffee and started walking, unsure of where he was going, and spent the next portion of the day meandering home.

The next evening he looked up the Flying Buttress theater and took a car there. It was pretty far north in an area now just called "the Tip," but the neighborhood was dense with art culture so he trekked up there from time to time. There were always reasons to be around the tip. It bore that regrettable name because it was the furthest north in this section of the city, and it was shaped by a river that curved along its northern border, making it a sort of peninsula that fit like a puzzle piece into the next burrough. The river ran inland, curving up before plunging south again, making a stubborn frown on the map.

As the name implied, the Flying Buttress was a theater that had once been an ancient church. Church buildings, where they still stood, were mostly empty but many had been converted into other uses. Some were even still churches. Wyatt chuckled to himself thinking about how they were dealing with these last few months. Was it good for churches? They had a new thing to yell about. When Wyatt approached he saw a lot of what were obviously weirdos who were part of the theater scene. There were many young people, but he was pleasantly surprised to see middle aged and older theater goers. There were slender women with curly white hair wearing flowing floral dresses or corduroy. Old mustachioed men with ancient sport coats, worn nearly through at every corner. Maybe a dozen curated looking people standing around, talking and smoking cigarettes and wooden pipes. He felt a sort of excitement just at seeing the place and the people. This felt like a real thing.

The venue was clinging with desperation to hold on to its stability. Every individual piece had been rebuilt or replaced. Nothing was quite even. The whole building slanted slightly to the left. But great care had been taken to maintain as much of the original shapes and impressions as possible.

Wyatt did not recognize anybody outside. He reached into his pocket to get a blunt and his phone. This was a reflex. There were no messages on his phone but he lit the blunt. Inside he found Qat, surrounded, as they usually seemed to be, by an adoring group of hangers on. Qat definitely drew people to them. He nervously approached the group but was quickly assimilated into the circle. Qat greeted him with a smile and introduced him to everybody. How did they remember all of these names? Their memory was incredible.

"So, Wyatt, this is Dev Agarwal. He wrote this play."

"Hey Dev!" Wyatt said.

Dev was maybe a bit older than Wyatt. He was very handsome, had thick black hair in a stylish coiff and a rigid jaw. "Cool to meet you Wyatt. Thanks for coming."

"I'm excited to be here. I'd love to chat with you sometime about all this. I'm sure the night of can be anxious, but I'll buy you a drink."

"Absolutely, I'll take a drink that you buy me. We usually go to the Tap and Mallet after shows. It's just across the park. Please come."

The rest of the time before the show was spent talking shapes around many topics. With a group that large a subject would be brought to the center. People would sort of dip their feet into it, occasionally taking a few steps in, before retreating for the waters of a new channel of discussion. The energy was comfortable, and Wyatt found himself in a sort of flow state in the conversation.

Time came for seats to be taken, and the crowd made the belabored shuffle through the foyer and into the theater. The seats were almost all occupied. The group that followed Qat sat in an amorphous mass that blended into the rest of the audience. So as the lights dimmed the auditorium was filled with the quiet echo of anticipation. The emptiness of the space overflowing with the energy of a full, silent audience. Wyatt had come to love this moment, the deep breath before a show burst into the air in front of him. There was a difference with this show. His expectations were more focused. Instead of wandering into a show, he had been called to attend this. There was some idea that it was going to be something of value.

And it began. The light rose on lavish sets, depicting a vibrant setting of the European renaissance. It told the story of a nobleman who had grown tired of being alive but felt suicide to be too boring or low class. So the nobleman spent the duration of the play trying to convince other members of the upper class to murder him. In the end he found himself ill from tainted meat, stumbling drunk in the cold, dying in the middle of a field and plowed into the soil the next morning.

It left Wyatt feeling exhilarated in a way no piece of art had in months. Maybe longer. This was a complete work of art. A collaborative triumph. It's not that it was a transcendental masterpiece, or the greatest piece of theater of the generation, or anything hyperbolic. It was just the right piece for that moment. It was riveting to experience.

As the stage went dark and light slid back into the theater, Wyatt at first didn't move. Chatter began to seep from the ground and into the mouths of the audience in pockets. He turned his attention to the playbill, trying to stay with the play for a few more moments before talking to anyone else. The group he sat amongst started to talk and eventually someone addressed him.

"What did you think?"

Wyatt sat for a moment before answering, "I enjoyed it very much."

The people around him crepitated in discussion about the work, interpreting and reinterpreting what they had seen from their vantage points and from each other's. Occasionally Wyatt would add a thought or pose a question. The group made the unspoken decision to rise from their seats and migrate to the foyer and eventually out into the night before their regular haunt.

It was a bar called Tap and Mallet. Immaculately lit – giving the impression of dimness while feeling bright and secure. There were combinations of booths and tables, all wide and tall for groups of varying sizes. The leather on the seats was soft and worn down, the wood weathered and rounded from years of wear. There was a large outdoor area behind the bar with picnic tables and sloppy, amateur murals on every brick wall rising to the sky. Wyatt ordered a dark beer for himself and found a place two thirds of the way from the edge of the group. Many began to smoke so Wyatt did, too.

As the discussion continued it veered on and off the topic of the play they had seen. Eventually, conversation skirted on the topic of the demons. Wyatt listened to see what they thought, but nobody really got into it. He felt confused. No… unsatisfied, maybe. The demons had, since the arrival, been in his brain like a rock stuck in his shoe or a shirt tag that won't stay in place. Maybe he had hoped they had some theory that could finally put it to rest for him. It seemed that to them it was just another thing that happens. It was what was happening now. It impacted the world, but only impacted them as far as them as individuals as far as it affected someone's art.

With a bit of a pop the performers and crew of the play suddenly appeared in the yard and were greeted with enthusiasm. Wyatt felt at this moment separate from the group, a visitor here. He felt drawn gravitationally to Qat, the only person he sort of knew, hoping for a bit of permission to be here because they had invited him. The new arrivals eventually settled into the population and conversation resumed as it had, though Wyatt could feel that the energy had a new buzz about it. It was more boisterous. He clocked where Dev sat and began to strategize what social navigation he'd need to do to talk to him. The idea was to time finishing his own drink just as Dev was about halfway through his. That way he'd get a refill and be back just in time to bring Dev a second round.

Wyatt sidled to the bar and ordered two sort of fancy beers. Something crafty a few guys made in an old warehouse nearby. It took a long time to get the bartender's attention but eventually the drinks arrived, so Wyatt returned to the table and was relieved to see an open space near Dev and that there was an empty beer bottle in front of him.

Putting the drink down on the table next to the empty, Wyatt said, "As promised."

Wyatt saw some very fast math in Dev's face, racing to remember who Wyatt was. "Ah, perfect!" he said quickly. "A good looking beer, thank you."

"The show was great— really interesting work."

"Thank you! It's been a long time coming with this one."

"Have you written something that's been performed at this theater before?"

"I have," he said. "A number of times. It's one of my home bases."

"I apologize in advance. I'm going to bombard you with questions."

Dev chuckled into his glass as he took a drink and then said, "By all means, my friend."

"When you have something you want to have performed, do you go to the theater first? Or do you look for someone to produce or direct or something?"

"Ok, yeah. Well it's different every time I guess. Well not every time, but there's a few ways it might go. I'm usually working on writing a couple things, so most of the time I have one or two finished pieces that I think are just about ready to be exhibited. Since I've performed at some of these spaces, every once in a while they'll have an opening in the schedule six months down the line or something. That's relatively rare, but it does happen. A lot of the time I've been working on something and I get pretty excited about it. So I really try to figure out the best way of getting it rolling. I usually start by asking a director, and in most cases they'll do a lot of the heavy lifting in terms of logistics, but I'll sort of tag along for the sake of conversation."

"Do you work with the same directors more than once?"

"Definitely. I know the handful who like my writing and the ones I know can work well with the type of thing I do. Sometimes I will sit and think about it and say 'hmm,' you know, 'who would be the right pick for this particular piece,' but most of the time I'm just at a party or something and I get talking to one of them and that's when a project begins."

"Is the director of this one here tonight?"

"Yeah," Dev waved over someone in the opposite corner. It took a few tries, but eventually he came over. "This is him, Toby. I'm sorry, remind me your name?"

"Wyatt," Wyatt said, not embarrassed at needing to remind him.

"Wyatt, right. He's a friend of Qat's."

"Cool, thanks for coming to the show." Toby was broad and taller than Wyatt. His skin was very dark and his hair was in neat, relaxed dreads.

"Yeah, definitely. I really enjoyed it. I've been sort of scooting around different theater scenes and a lot of times leave the auditorium feeling pretty lukewarm. This one really did it for me, a compelling piece of work."

"Well credit goes to Dev for the words."

"And obviously to you for everything else," Dev said back.

"I'm a writer and I've been interested in getting into theater."

"What do you usually write?" Dev asked.

"Prose, poetry. Just words on a page. I do some zines, had some short stories picked up here and there."

"Well, I don't know you and I don't know if you're any good," Toby said. "But I can tell you I don't necessarily have many projects lined up. I'd be willing to read something if you have it ready. Maybe we can talk about it."

"Really? That would...that's super cool. I can send you something right away. I have a piece I'm trying to get performed."

"What's the gist?" Dev asked.

"It's like a sort of post apocalyptic story with just a few people surviving in this wasteland, and one of the characters is a dog-person."

"Dog person?"

"Yeah, like an anthropomorphic dog."

Toby shrugged. "It's worth a look."

"I can email it over to you."

"I don't have email. I only read printed transcripts."

That would be annoying, but Wyatt begrudgingly respected the move. "Ok, no worries. I can get it printed. Where should I send it?"

"Send it to the Flying Buttress, c/o me. Tobias Bertrand."

"Well, neat," Dev said.

Wyatt, feeling the excitement of progress and the relief of having made more of a connection to a theater scene that he ever had before, was energized and his mind raced back to the evening's show. "So Dev," he said with glee, "did you have the renaissance setting in mind from the beginning of writing, or what was the conception of the idea?"

"It was a product of wanting to explore the idea of longing for death even if things are pretty good. So I wanted a very comfortable person trying to figure out how to die even though his life was really fine. It kind of went from there."

The discussion continued as did the drinks. People would morph in and out of their group, and by the end of the night Wyatt was talking to people he didn't recognize at all. The time came to go, and he made attempts to bid a farewell to anyone he'd engaged with for any length of time. He couldn't find Qat or Dev or Toby, but maybe he had already said goodbye to them when they left and had forgotten.

His instincts started kicking in to get him home. Whenever he was this far north, and especially this close to the water, he usually took a boat home. With so many bridges and trains unreliable and inaccessible to most people, there had developed in the last decades a robust sort of boat taxi service around the shores. It was not far to the docks, and when he got there, Wyatt found that the area was well lit, bustling, and noisy. There were drunk people everywhere and taxi captains yelling for their attention. Wyatt strolled confidently through the riff raff and walked to the boat that he thought looked the coolest.

"Sunset Morning?"

The captain whistled dramatically. "Pretty far!" he said. This was standard procedure.

"$20 and a cigarette."

The captain laughed, patting Wyatt on the shoulder. "You've got yourself a taxi, partner."

They boarded and Wyatt handed a cigarette to the captain, a sort of advanced payment. A friendly gesture. And the ship kicked out from the dock. It was a pretty small boat. Seats had been retrofitted everywhere there was space and often where there wasn't. It might've been a small yacht for some mid-level finance bro 60 or 70 years ago. It was clear this captain loved the craft and did whatever he could to keep the old thing floating. Its maximum capacity was probably only around 10 people. Most of the time they try to pack in multiple passengers, especially for long trips like this, to save money. Probably the captain didn't want to take just one person.

Wyatt moved up to find a seat near the bow. As he did he noticed there were actually a couple drunks already passed out and buckled in. Apparently the captain already had packed in multiple passengers, but with them asleep he didn't consider himself to be in a rush and waited for one more. Wyatt lucked out and got to be the one more.

The boat bounced and chopped through the water, huge lights illuminated the way in front of them. The captain skillfully weaved around the bigger chunks of garbage, but these were unforgiving waters and they were forced to plow through a lot of it. The air smelled bad, but the wind was cool and refreshing on Wyatt's face as they cruised southward.

The captain stood at the helm, elevated above the middle of the boat, just behind Wyatt.

"You ever see the demons out on the water?" Wyatt shouted up to him.

"Sure I've been seeing them more and more," he yelled back. "At first they definitely stayed down on the south shore around that portal. But they've been moving further and further out. Crazy thing is I think they're actually cleaning up the water."

"What?"

"Yeah, I've definitely seen them filtering junk out. Spitting clean water back in."

"That's interesting," Wyatt tried to sound pensive while still yelling loud enough to be heard over the waves and the engine.

"I hear they're starting to wander around the city proper, over to the other side of the river."

"Really? Are they doing anything there?"

"Same as here I guess. Little stuff, big stuff. Just their weird changes. Turning apartments upside down or whatever it is. Building new."

Wyatt hadn't heard about the demons constructing anything new, only altering what was there. He wondered if Lena had heard about this. "You know anybody who has an answer for what's going on with all this?"

"No, of course not. Nobody knows, there's no way. I've got my theory though."

"What's that?"

"I think they're setting up a vacation home. Like a tourist destination for other demons. They're just fixing it up the way they like it. We're just like the monkeys or whatever that you'd have to clear out of a jungle beach to build a fancy hotel."

After too many rounds at the Tap & Mallet, that was enough for Wyatt. He spent the rest of the boat ride trying to come to terms with being wildlife in a jungle, watching a luxury hotel be built where he slept.

CHAPTER 9

IT WAS RAINING AND NOISY and Wyatt was on his way to Lil Old Betsy's for an overnight shift. Summer was ending, days were getting cooler but it didn't really get cold in the winter time anymore. Occasionally the temperature would crash for a day or two, sometimes only for an afternoon. It would dip down around freezing and sometimes it would snow for a little bit, but it never lasted. Tepid air would claw the atmosphere back and the snow just left everything damper than usual. Fucked the lizards up when it got that cold. They'd just die in the street. Seasons were inconsistent, tough to predict. This was definitely a fall rain though, felt like that, so Wyatt had a sweatshirt on under a raincoat. His hood was up and his tote bag was tucked into the jacket for protection.

He was relieving Marina, finishing her evening shift. Opened the door to the back of the shop and could see that she had had a few drinks; a little row of empty cans lined up on the counter. A rainy day like this meant people weren't walking around. It was probably a slow night. He stepped in, so she started to get her jacket on.

"Marina, how are you?"

"Hey, Wyatt. I'm good. I'm alright."

"Did that guy from the gallery ever get back to you? I was there with Lena a while back and he said they'd sold some pieces. Had some money for you."

"Yeah, I got the money."

"Cool, good. I loved that exhibit. Lena did too."

"Thanks," she said out of obligation.

"Did you get everything from there?"

"I mean I took it, yeah. I didn't have anywhere to put it, and it didn't make any sense any more, so I just gave it to a second hand shop."

"What? You gave it all to a thrift store? I would've fucking taken some."

"I dunno. I didn't want it anymore. When I looked at it all, I thought it was dumb. It made no sense."

"Made no sense."

"Just... shit. You know?"

"Uhhh. I guess so. Yeah. Sometimes I finish something that I like but then when I look back at it I don't really like it anymore. I think everyone gets that."

"No, it's just more than that. Like it straight up makes no sense. What was going on with that collection?"

"I dunno. It was evocative."

"Fuck evocative. That's what people say when something means nothing. A fart is evocative of something that smells like the inside of an ass."

"No," Wyatt protested. He had liked the pieces in that collection and felt undermined in having found something of value now that Marina was challenging him on it. "Ok, I get what you're saying. I mean I like art that's evocative. I think there's value to being just that. But also that collection really had something going on. There was the contrast in terms of detail. You had intricately detailed crowds and landscapes and then sketchy, broadly rendered monster figures. Sort of abstracting something horrific and really trying to crystalize or humanize the mundane and the small. There's something there, man."

Marina paused. "You're sweet, Wyatt. I appreciate that. I'm glad you liked it. Sorry, I've just been in this phase looking at everything I was working on and it all felt so trite. Inconsequential."

"Have you been working on anything new?"

"I've been sketching the demons. It's the only thing I think about and the only things my hands will let me do."

"How has that been turning out?"

"Stupid as shit, honestly. I don't feel like I'm bringing any value to it. It's so obvious, such a boring thing to be doing."

"Mhmm," Wyatt reached into the jar with the joints and pulled one out, lit it and took a drag, handing it to Marina who took some and handed it back. The smoke hung in the air with the door and window both closed. "That's what I've figured with writing about it. I have no idea what the point of it would be. I guess."

Marina stayed far past her shift. The two sat in the tiny space and talked about their work and their lack of work. They talked about the demons and how they'd started to see them in different neighborhoods further and further from the beach. Marina had seen a neighborhood where entire buildings were turned into a pillowy blue moss. People still lived there, but now they had to get water from somewhere else because the pipes were all blocked.

There had been so many stories about changes the demons had made. It seemed like everyone was just watching, sort of holding their breath. Curious to see what would happen next. People took note of what they saw, everyone had heard from someone about a weird thing they'd done in another area they hadn't seen. Roads smearing. Structures turned into bizarre new shapes and colors. Piles of crates so black it felt like you could fall in if you walked too close. The true stories mixed with the invented. Businesses had started selling merch: little plushies approximating their weird shapes, t-shirts for fat dads visiting the city from other places, hats for ironic teens.

Starting to fidget, Marina announced she needed to get going and so she did, leaving Wyatt by himself with the smoke. It was a slow shift from there. Nobody stopped at the window, so he sat alone in the shop. Some time was spent reading, some time writing and more with a puzzle game on his phone. He drank some whisky from a bottle that they kept in the shop because sometimes people came by just for a cup of it. When he finished a few fingers' worth he scanned his phone for payment. Almost enough to cover the amount he'd taken.

Outside the window of the shop the lights were bright and hectic. Things still flew and drove by constantly. Maybe even more at night. He heard a police siren in the distance get louder as it approached and saw some cop cars race by at the end of the block.

And then it was quiet again. Wyatt looked around, taking inventory of the shop and looking to see if anything new was worth being aware of. In the corner, under the desk, conspicuously hidden, so obviously trying to be out of the way, was a box still shut. He slid it out and looked to see that it had Paulie's name on the top and nothing else. It must be the box the cops had mentioned way back whenever. Right at the beginning of the book. They said they'd had something for him. This must be it. What was it?

The rest of the shift was spent arguing between Wyatt and Wyatt about whether or not to open the thing. For some reason it felt like the trouble would be big if he got mixed up in it. But then what could that even mean? What could they do? Would someone kill him about it? Felt like being in a gangster movie or something. But then it also felt very petty. Maybe months ago, before the arrival event, this would have been a thrill. Now it almost felt tedious. A touch of resentment flashed through his brain. How dare they keep this secret, build up this package like some big old story in a world like this. Who the fuck did they think they were to pretend like they have some big important business they're involved with. How important could this dumb ass little box be? Fuck the whole thing.

For the rest of his shift he pushed it out of his mind. Or more accurately under a counter and into a corner of his mind. Like in the shop, it sat there — small and easy to ignore, but still definitely there.

Every couple days for weeks Brent from down the hall had reminded Wyatt about his gig, to the point that it would be rude to not show up or come up with an excuse. No excuse presented itself and later that week was the night, so he hitched Talbot along and they went down to check it out.

"I can't promise any level of quality for this show," Wyatt said on their way to the venue. "Brent's a nice guy, and he listens to some cool stuff, but I don't know that he's really any good."

The place was called The Shipyard, and other than a large taxidermied marlin mounted on the wall behind the bar there was no detectable nautical theme. It was a simple, open space: a bar in the front half and a stage in the back. No separation. There were some barflies hunched over, drinking, and a few people leaning on tables in the stage area. The opener had started, and they were bad. Wyatt didn't count, but if he had he would've seen eight people, other than the band, Talbot and himself. Talbot and himself hung out at the bar.

The opening band played loud and filled the empty space with their earnestness. A few people over by the stage were holding beers and standing around with their hands in their pockets, quietly watching and bobbing their heads. Everybody there was white except for Wyatt, Talbot and one other guy who looked south Asian. Sitting at the bar they yelled over the band to talk during the set.

"So, work's been good?" Talbot shouted.

"Yeah it's been alright. I started wrapping up sandwiches a little differently. It's a lot tighter, I think keeps everything all together better."

"Hell yeah, man," Talbot cheersed him, with less sarcasm than you're probably imagining. "You gonna get a raise for that?"

Wyatt's chuckle was swallowed by the cacophony. "How about you? Things good in the office?"

"They've been pretty good. Had a lot of turnover lately so I've needed to sort of pick up a lot of extra work until people get rolling on their own stuff. But it's been alright. I saw one of the newer people was listening to the Brigands at her desk when I was walking by. You remember those guys?"

"Yeah, we saw them in a basement like 15 years ago or something, didn't we?"

"That we did! But yeah, work is fine. I've hit a good stride at this place,

I think. I've been able to change a few of the ways we do things to sort streamline stuff and that feels pretty good. That first little while after the demons showed up nothing got done, and honestly it was beautiful. Enough people were just too busy wrapping their heads around that shit that nobody could focus and a lot of the time we'd just go drink. A few people never recovered, but they're mostly just gone now. Things now are pretty much the way it was all along."

"Anybody talk about it any more?"

"Yeah, like over by the coffee machine type stuff. Things people've heard about them doing or whatever. It's like it's sports."

A middle-aged drunk next to them decided that was an invitation and leaned over to them saying, "You know what this means, right?"

"What *what* means?" Wyatt said.

"The demons. It means we're in hell now."

The bartender, obviously having heard this a hundred times, said while wiping a glass, "Where were they before?"

"Hm?" grunted the drunk.

"Where were those things before they showed up here? Were they somewhere?"

"Well, must've been in hell I guess."

"And now they're here, and we can see them. But truly what's the difference of them being here? They must've been somewhere already. The universe had them in it, was already what it is, and now we've just got demons for neighbors."

This idea steeped in the barflies' brains like it was tea. Elsewhere throughout the bar everything was normal. Wyatt looked at the murky corners by the ceiling just to check. Normal dark bar corners.

The opener stopped, and it was quiet for a minute. Everybody froze. The bar back played some old outlaw country from a computer hooked up to the soundsystem, and it gave people permission to move and talk again. The crowd had not filled in much, but there were some more patrons at the bar. From behind the stage the guys in the first band showed up and transformed back into regular people— not a band anymore. The members of the audience greeting them with shoulder pats and things like that. Wyatt and Talbot had more drinks and smoked cigarettes with strangers.

Brent took the stage, just him and a drummer. "Hey I'm S. Brent, got some songs for you dorks," and he started to play. Some of the crowd moved over to the stage, most people in the bar didn't move. The drummer put down a vaguely groovy beat, and Brent joined with twitching enthusiasm, noodling out his song on guitar and jumping around. During the first song, Wyatt brought his beer closer to the stage and Talbot followed. They posted up by a table, looking nonchalant but trying not to look like they were trying. Brent was wearing cut off jeans and a sweaty looking white t-shirt, and his drummer was wearing a blue polo shirt and had short cropped hair in a side part. Wyatt thought he looked boring, but he felt bad about making that assumption. Probably he was really cool. Definitely an adequate drummer, at least.

They absolutely plowed through a set. Some banter between songs, but Brent seemed more into it than the drummer did so mostly he'd just jump into the next thing. One after the other the songs were shot out at the audience like mortar rounds. There was some craft to them, seemed like. They were well structured, a couple catchy melodies here and there. Brent was pretty good at guitar actually. But the songs sort of disappeared like a cheap beer you could guzzle and left very little impression. Wyatt did some shots and that sort of helped. Brent was charming, and he cared so hard about these dumb songs that it was infectious when Wyatt gave himself to it, but the spell would break and he'd lose interest again, retreating into his phone or staring at a few choice spots on the wall he'd grown fond of.

Seemed like Talbot mostly felt the same. They chatted between songs, and at the conclusion of the set both of them shrugged and got more beer. Looking around, Wyatt saw the majority of the crowd shrug and go back to the bartender for more beer. Brent emerged victorious from the back and eagerly patted a bunch of shoulders, including Wyatt's, and thanked people for coming out. He asked Wyatt about the songs, and Wyatt thought of some things to say. Picked out the parts he remembered. The riffs he liked best, things like that. Brent was satisfied and disappeared into the slowly growing crowd as the final act of the night's bill took to the stage. This last band seemed to be neighborhood favorites, but to Wyatt they just looked like some boys who were in a band. Their music sucked, but the bar had filled out and everyone was really loving it. Talbot invited Wyatt out front for a smoke, and they got really high until both wandered back to their apartments and fell asleep.

There was a little print and courier business Wyatt used for zines and projects like that. It was a small group of guys and they seem to have hit a stride doing a thing just well enough to keep a business running. The owner must really be passionate about printing onto things. He collected all of this equipment, and he knew where to get large amounts of paper of different sizes and thicknesses. The store was brightly lit and always pretty clean. It was in a warehouse next to a bunch of other businesses that had moved into warehouses. A bustling little corner of Sunset Morning, near the Old Belt overpass. The walls had huge and beautifully printed art. Some of it was apparently original work, probably by someone who worked there. Some classic famous works and others just of characters from a very popular and very animated comedy show 20-somethings loved. Everything on display was rendered with glossy, high-resolution respect. The shop was pretty reliable and the price was good, so that's where he intended to print a copy of his play to send Toby at the theater. This was the first play he'd ever written, and he was never taught any formalities. When formatting it he just kind of guessed based on what he'd seen in other scripts.

They always ask him if this is going to be the next bestseller, the big hit that makes him a fortune, the breakthrough success. He always joked back with them. It was fun to play with them like that and he got a kick out of it, but every single time it also made him wonder what success would mean or look like if it really happened. When he came to print the play, they asked what this project was and so he sort of explained it like the way he would to an aunt or someone at the grocery store. Just the simplest way that would invite the fewest questions but still represent something he was proud to have made. So he sent them the file from his phone and the shop guys got started. He drank some coffee with one of them while he waited and they put tequila in it. The coffee was burnt and the tequila was cheap, but it was one of those things that kind of worked. For a print shop it was a good cuppa. The print shop guy talked about sports. Wyatt liked sports but he rarely followed anything specifically. He kind of kept up enough to know a few names and personalities to throw out in conversation. This team was missing that, this player needed to start doing this. Stuff along those lines. The guy seemed satisfied, but as the conversation went on Wyatt was clearly running pretty close to the end of his knowledge and it was stressing him out.

It took about a half hour to print and bind the play into something half respectable looking. Really looked like something, he liked it. They brought it in from the back and handed it to him. He nodded approvingly and told them they'd done a good job. This was one of the first times he'd ever needed to use their delivery service as well.

Most deliveries, particularly small parcels like this, were handled by automated drones. There was no longer any form of regulatory system to tell drones where to fly, so it was risky, but in general the big droners sort of settled on specific altitudes and that's where their business was so they only had to worry about their own scheduling. Collisions did happen fairly often, but considering how many drones were in the air, city this size at any given time, it was still a pretty good way to go. It was miraculous how often packages did arrive safely, a real feat. You take a risk doing any single thing, so you gotta just go for it. Leave your apartment and you could get hit by a bus, stay in bed and your building could burn down. Send something in a drone, sure it could crash, spilling your tiles on the street so some nobody picks them up and leaves them at his friend's apartment for a few months. But if you send it with a driver? Well you've got about a 50/50 shot that driver steals some of the cargo, or they get jacked by some teens in a clever outfit. You just gotta kinda pick the easiest option and hope for the best.

As he had been instructed, he ordered to have the printed transcript delivered to the Flying Buttress Theater in the care of Tobias Bertrand. The print shop dudes tapped around on their computers to get everything organized for the short flight across to the Tip neighborhood. While they were figuring it out, the guy who had been drinking with Wyatt handed him a little flyer for a show.

"What's this?"

"I'm part of a display at the Lux Prima gallery over in Village Neo," the print shop guy said, kind of matter of fact.

"Woah, for real?" that was a real deal gallery, right in the heart of it all, over in the City. It was impressive.

"Yeah, I've worked with one of those owners before, he has a smaller venue over there. They liked my stuff so I slid in. Starts next week."

"Awesome, dude," Wyatt really meant it. "That's a big deal. You still gonna work here?"

The guy laughed and said "yeah sure. Pays rent, you know?"

One of the guys who had been plugging into the computer said suddenly "alright man, it's all set. Should be there in about an hour. Maybe less."

"Right on, thanks as always."

Wyatt paid with a card after checking in with the bank app on his phone. He had about enough for this print job and should be able to hold out the rest of the week.

On the way home from the print shop there was a horrific noise above his head, and he looked up to see a burst of metal and sparks as two drones collided. Debris showered across the windows and buildings all around him. Wyatt frantically ducked for cover, holding his arms over his head to protect himself as well as he could. An echo, and then again the din of city quiet.

"Uh," he said out loud to nobody. "I guess I hope neither of those were mine."

Chapter 10

A FEW DAYS LATER HE got a text from Lena. It had been a while since he'd heard from her.

Hey I need your help, you still know that cable guy? was the text.

He responded that he did, and they made plans to meet there the next day.

Lena and Wyatt met at the breakfast cart in his neighborhood and both got sandwiches to start the day. Wyatt also got a cup of coffee. He was feeling drowsy and couldn't match Lena's energy. She had maybe already a morning coffee, but more likely this was just her energy right now, and he needed a little help to keep up.

"I'm really excited about the imagery I've gathered. I want to start getting ready to share it."

"Wow, what's it been like?"

"These things are just really- I dunno, baffling. They're baffling."

They ate the sandwiches and walked, Wyatt with his sandwich in one hand and the coffee in the other, trying in vain to avoid spilling coffee down his knuckles as they went. Lena told what she'd been up to. Basically living and traveling with the demons, spending all her time among them for weeks at a time.

"After the second time I went down to the beach, I realized I was going to need to really spend a lot of time to get what I wanted. It was going to take a long time just to be around them enough to have any context for what types of images were worth capturing, what I could do with it. So I brought some camping gear and I started sleeping down there."

"That's interesting. Did you go in to work?"

"Sometimes. I took most of the time off, but I'd go in once a week or so. It'd give me a chance to clean up and stuff. I have a bunch of extra batteries to charge my phone, and so I'd go in and fill those back up. I have one of those solar chargers, but they don't really work. They might out in the mountains, but around here not enough sun gets through the shog to really do anything. Still, if I kept my phone turned off while I slept and most of the time I was working, I could get enough battery to get by."

"What about food?"

"I'd just stop here and there. Wherever, restaurants, some groceries. Anything that didn't take too long and wasn't too hard to carry around for long. A few weeks ago I saw them cross the water over to the main part of the city, so I followed them over there and watched what they've been doing there."

"I'd heard they were over there now, from a boat taxi captain. What's your context, what have you learned? I mean dog knows the rest of us are out here pretty much contextless about it all still."

"Here's the thing: they are changing the world in ways we cannot understand. Their changes are getting stranger, and deeper, and I think we need to try to come to terms with the idea that it's going to keep going. I've seen parts of this city destroyed by madness, starving hysterical naked."

Even though Wyatt was the one who knew where to go, Lena was walking so fast that she was basically leading the way. He'd turn when they needed to, and from a pace and a half ahead Lena would adjust to follow, catch up and then again take in front of him, needing sometimes to cantor for a few steps to keep pace without breaking into an awkward jog. They made it to the shop. It was an old garage that had been turned into a sort of an electronics shop. When they first got there everything was dark and closed, so they took up residence on the stoop across the street and waited.

"It hasn't seemed like they're dangerous. Do you think they are?"

"Well, it's not like they are here to do us harm. I think. It really feels like they just don't care one way or the other. And I think it just depends on what they're here to do."

"So you've still got no idea what they're working on either."

"I am convinced there's no way to know. That might be the only thing I'm confident about having learned during my time with them."

"Tell me what you've seen," Wyatt was nervous to ask.

"I can't tell you. I'll show you. I've got a lot of pictures. And video. People have been talking about it since they showed up, stories of what they've seen or heard or what they've heard someone heard someone else has seen. That's not getting anywhere, and I'm not going to do it. I've been thinking a lot about what to do with it. Whatever it is, I think all of this is something that needs to be recorded and presented as art. People need to see it to make sense of it or something. Really to come to terms with not making sense of it. Frame it so you can just look and think and feel it out a little. I think I have to show the progression over time. The way the changes have developed, their progress towards their unintelligible goal."

He opened his mouth to respond but at that moment saw the shop's proprietor strolling down the street carrying two large bags. "Oh, that's him, that's our guy," and called out to him, "Our man of the hour!"

"Hm?" the man grunted. There was a stern look on his face but a sparkle in his eyes shining out from under bushy, grey eyebrows. There was no look of recognition but still to Wyatt he said, "You sold me a box of cables a year or so back, wasn't it? A few lovely finds in there. It was a good old box. So now, empty handed, you need something?"

"We're looking for some hookups and thought you'd be a good place to start."

"I'm the ONLY place to start, and I betcha I'll be the last stop too," he boasted.

The man was old and craggy. Very thin, his clothes were baggy and threadbare, he had a large beard and long hair tied loosely in a bun to keep it out of the way. It had probably been years since he'd had a trim of any kind. Everything about him looked weathered. Salted. Like he had spent a lifetime on a fishing boat instead of in a garage hocking computer parts.

"I've got digital media that I need to display for an art installation."

"Ahhh digital art. That's not something you hear every day," the man chuckled like an old wizard. "Come on inside and we'll have ourselves a look, and I'm sure you'll leave with something figured out."

He hoisted the heavy looking bags to the ground in front of the door and entered the code to open the shop. There was a large garage door that seemed to be sealed shut. It had aged and grown over and seemed to have bonded irreversibly with the rest of the building. He entered the shop door and they followed, finding inside a space that was deceptively large. There were shelves full of crates stacked and slid everywhere all the way up to the ceiling. Along the back wall was a rotating apparatus so he could cram everything in there. There was hardly any space to move, but he had ropes and handholds deliberately placed to assist him in jumping and swinging around and above the piles.

"So tell me what type of media you've got," he said, putting little glasses at the end of his nose.

"I've been doing pictures and video."

"What're you shooting on?"

Lena pulled the camera out of her bag and handed it to the shopkeeper.

"Hmmm," he looked at it. "Doesn't look like much, I know. Looks are deceptive, and it isn't the tools that make the art, you'd say, right?" He flicked open a latch and pulled out a memory card, inspecting it before putting it back in and observing every port and plug on the device. "Tell me, how much have you got on this memory card?"

"I've gone through several cards. I had two at the start, and I bought a box when I got close to filling up the second one. I think I have six now. Everything I've done is on the cards, and I haven't had a way to view them anywhere other than on the preview screen of the camera."

"Yes, of course. They don't make this stuff anymore, and it would be hard to come by except nobody cares about it so if anyone gets it they usually just keep it. Let's start here," he grabbed a handle and kicked off, rolling along a track secured to the ceiling and out of sight. He rummaged in one box, scuttled back across and again out of their view before returning. "This is a card reader. If you have a normal laptop you should be able to use this to get the media off of your cards and onto a computer." He handed it to Lena. "This," he said holding it up, "is an RCA cable. With this you can attach your camera directly to anything with these inputs." He pointed at the red, yellow and white ends of the cord. "Works in many old televisions and screens like that. So the next question is what do you have in mind for display? Projection?"

"I was hoping to source a bunch of TVs and have different batches of images on each. Like an exhibit."

"Well, that is compelling. That makes things difficult, but nothing is impossible even today. Let me think. Do you have an idea of where you are getting your screens?"

"Depends on who's asking."

"Sure, say no more, I don't need the details on the process. Here's what you'll need to do: each television is going to need something else attached. I'd recommend phones. They're small and cheap and honestly you can sell them after you're done and probably break even. Load your media onto the phones and connect them to the televisions."

They kept talking, and occasionally the shopkeep would disappear again into the recesses of the shop to reappear with some new cable or converter or something. He'd explain it, they'd discuss more, and he'd disappear again— leaving Lena with a growing tangle of cords squirming in her arms. One of the times he vanished into the shop, a lemur returned in his place, looking at them with the intensity of a confident animal greeting visitors into its territory. It leapt around, back and forth across aisles on the top of the shelving, pacing on all fours until finally taking a perch like a gargoyle, watching them. When the guy came back this time, he greeted the lemur casually by name and with a head pat before continuing the task.

Lena and Wyatt were invited deeper into the shop, which surprisingly descended into a labyrinth below the street level that seemed to continue on without end. It was hard to imagine where all of this equipment had come from, how long it had taken to be gathered, how it was organized. The elfish shopkeeper knew always where to go and what to look for. His arcane knowledge seemed vast. As they journeyed into the bowels of the collection, the lemur followed along. For every question Lena had the man provided an answer, and for every answer she had there was a further question. This stuff was his art, and there was a unique science to it. A perfectionism in the chaos of this place.

He produced a box for them, and Lena filled it with what he had supplied her with. The group made the expedition back out of the depths and returned to the front of the store. Turning on a computer that looked as weathered as he did, the keeper inventoried each item and assigned it a price. The resulting total was more than Wyatt made in a month, but he had never seen Lena flinch, and this didn't do it either. She paid with a card, and they got ready to go.

"Thank you for coming by," the guy said. "This was a fun riddle to explore."

"I appreciate your help," Lena said.

"Good to see you again," Wyatt nodded. "I hope I'll have a reason to come back again another time."

"I'm sure you will, son."

And with a box of new resources and fresh motivation, they grabbed a bus and brought the day's bounty back to Lena's apartment. The trip back to her neighborhood was as herky as it was jerky. People got on and off at every stop, shuffling in and out of each other's lives briefly. The bus was almost completely full for their entire ride, as many people would get on at each stop as exited. At one stop someone boarded that looked familiar to Wyatt without knowing at first why. He wore a neat fitting denim jacket over an oxford shirt and slacks, his dark curly hair tucked mostly under a black knit cap. On his back was a full looking backpack. After about half a stop Wyatt realized it was Kalman and broke bus protocol by almost shouting to get his attention (buses were so loud you had to yell, and it was generally understood to be best just not talk on the bus at all). On Kalman's face ran the same calculation of recognizing someone but not knowing from where, but when he placed the person to the memory, he siddled over to them, bouncing back and forth and holding steadfast to the handholds overhead.

"I found I've got at least a few of your zines, *Talmudic*. I read vol. 13 after we hung out that time. I really really enjoyed it."

"Oh, thank you! That one was from a few years ago, but I have only done two since then. I can get you a hold of some others if you're interested." While he spoke, Kalman looked around and seemed a little self conscious about being too loud in a space he usually remained silent. Wyatt noticed and planned to keep the conversation short as a courtesy.

"Where are you heading to?"

"A bookstore up around Stone Slope."

"Oh right on, we're going to that neighborhood. Wanna grab a drink?" This was an excuse to end the bus conversation but to talk more later.

Kalman agreed to the terms and instead of shouting something back answered with a stern nod and gave a thumbs up.

The bus ride was another 15 minutes from there. The path from the electronics emporium to Lena's neighborhood would be shorter as a drone flies, but the bus needed to circumvent Green Wood Forest. Eventually they arrived and the three got off the bus. Kalman hadn't noticed that Lena was part of the group until they were off the bus, and she stood by them. He remembered talking to her about photography and saw the box of cables she carried, understanding it to be a part of the project. After a brief exchange of pleasantries, she left to drop off her box at the apartment. The boys walked together to the book shop.

"So what do you have going on here?" Wyatt asked.

"I'm dropping off a few copies of this book of short stories I had published. Do you want one?"

"Oh congrats!"

"Yeah, it's a project I've been working on the last few months. Before the arrival."

"Weren't you working on a novel?"

"I was. I am. This had sort of also been cooking on the side and it ended up being easier to finish up. The novel is still coming along, I think. I'll focus on it again now, probably."

"How'd you get this collection published?"

"A buddy of mine runs this indie publisher. She was looking for content for collections, and I had just been polishing these stories all sort of loosely themed around the idea of repair. Different types of repair, upkeep, construction. That idea."

"That's awesome, sounds cool."

"I am actually pretty excited. This is the third time I've had something published by like some kind of printer other than myself and a copy shop. It's my first with this press, and I'm pretty happy with the job they did." He slung the backpack off of one shoulder as they walked, and he unzipped it to pull out a cellophane wrapped book to hand to Wyatt. "I can't give you these ones. They're all for this bookstore. But I can get you a hold of one. They sent a handful over that I can sort of give out at my discretion."

Wyatt took it to look at. The printing looked very profi, and he was impressed by it. It had a clean design that would attract him if he had picked it up at random in a store. "This looks really awesome," he said. "Even if I didn't know you, I'd be interested just by looking at it."

"What about you since last time? Reading anything you enjoy?"

"I sort of sift through zines and things like that here and there, and going out to theater more. I have been reading *Old Rage*, the Edna LeBlanc book."

"Oh my god, it's amazing isn't it?" a new excitement entered his voice.

"Man, it really is. This is the first thing I've read of hers, but it's really captivating."

"She's incredible. One of my favorite writers. Her prose is so sharp but still playful. It's really remarkable. I love her work. You should also read

Road to the Barn. That might be my favorite of hers. But *Old Rage* is a great place to start. That was the first thing of hers that I read."

"I guess it's just really exciting to know stuff like this is still being written."

"I know exactly what you mean. You've always got that nagging voice in the back of your head that all great literature has passed. There's no more to be done, and we're all just spinning our tires, or digging at bedrock."

"Yeah. It's cool, if humanity holds on through this next couple chapters of our history, future dorks are gonna read this the same way we get excited about like Hemingway or whatever."

They reached the bookstore. It didn't look like much, but there was a warmth to the place. The windows had not been cleaned in probably years, and there was a layer of grime so thick you'd feel like you could scrape some off with a knife and spread it onto toast. From the outside the store looked closed. There was no visible signage. Everything had faded away and the store appeared like an extension of the trash from the street, sprouting up from the sidewalk and growing into a building with no demarcation where one ended and the other began. It was a place you just had to know was there. Wyatt had no idea how Kalman knew about it. Seemed like the information that must have been passed down generationally or else lost to the dust and churn of the unforgiving city.

Kalman pushed the door open, it scaped harshly across the smooth stone floor inside. Wyatt was shocked to see there were a number of people inside— browsing through the shelves, standing to leaf through a book of interest, or taking up residence in one of multiple soft and shopworn seats. They each looked to the new arrivals, briefly and in their own time, before returning to their tasks already at hand. It was dark, but there were lights everywhere. Lamps hung overhead, sat in corners or atop shelves, or nestled amongst books on wide tables. The store was laid out with a fairly open area at the front of the store, walls lined with shelves and three large tables taking up most of the floor space. The tables were covered in books, somewhat organized in a way to draw the eye, built into an architecture as if by an ancient civilization long extinct. Behind this area, deeper into the store, was a series of narrow rows with shelves extending up into darkness and fading from view. Placards noted what type of book would be found in each aisle. The shelves were imposing, and though the aisles looked claustrophobic and constricting, they were alluring, magnetic.

Towards the wall on one side was a large desk, and behind it was a small, old woman. Beside the desk was a sleeping, yellow dog. They went to the desk and Kalman removed his backpack to retrieve his books. The old woman looked up from something she was reading to greet them, at first with blankness and then a smile.

"Kalman, dear! Lovely to see you," she said.

"Hi Nina!" he responded with the same curt tone of voice he always spoke in, but there was a new friendliness running through it. This must be a friend of parents or something. He gently placed the pile of books on the shelf in front of her. "I brought some copies of my book. Sealed, never touched. Fresh as paper."

"Wonderful! Very proud of you for this," she took one of the books in her hands and looked it over. "They look very nice, your friend did a good job with these. I may need to get in touch with her about other things from her press. These look very nice."

"Thank you, yes, she really does good work. I've got some other things she's printed that I've picked up along the line. I can definitely get you in touch."

"Well, you've got your first sale, darling," Nina said. She started tapping things into a tablet that sat on the desk. She added the books to the inventory. Kalman would receive payment when each book was purchased and not all at once when delivering the batch. This usually meant the author would get paid more per book, but obviously carried the risk of each book sitting on the shelf ignored. It was most likely that this arrangement stemmed from the relationship between the two of them, which obviously had many years of history behind it. Wyatt had not published anything officially enough to really know how any of this worked or how the publisher would be involved transactionally. She ran her payment information to purchase one of the books for herself, which produced a dinging tone on Kalman's phone to announce receipt, and she started to unwrap one. She gave it one last look without the plastic wrap and then looked quickly back up at them. "Nuh, and who's this, Kalman?"

"Oh, this is Wyatt. I met him through some of my musician friends. He's also a writer."

"Ah the best of its kind!" she said. "Hello, Wyatt."

"Nice to meet you. Lovely little oasis you have here."

"I thank you! Next time you need something to read you should come in. Next time you have something for others to read for that matter, we can talk about it! Kalman, anywhere specific you want me to put this?"

"No, no. You're the expert on that. I put the words on the page. It's up to you to put them in the store."

"It's what, short story collection?" she asked.

"Yeah, that's right."

"Ok, well, let's put it on one of these front tables. I have collections there. It will take some rearranging, but we'll bring people to this book." With some effort she stood up and shuffled out from behind the desk, steadying herself with a hand as she did.

The door scraped open again, and Lena entered. Each of the other customers again looked up as they did before. She saw them and joined the group, thoroughly observing the interior of the shop as she did.

"Well, thank you. I'll leave you to your business Nina. You're the best table stacker in the game. Thank you for taking the books," said Kalman.

"A pleasure, very excited to read the damn thing," she said as she carried the books to one of the tables.

"If you ever need something schlepped, you call me or someone, right? We're here to help. Don't do what you don't have to." There was seriousness in his voice when he said this.

More polite farewells were bade, and they left the bookshop. After some discussion, they agreed to go to a cafe Kalman knew about down the street.

The place was called la Petite Tasse, and it was very small. There were a few tables outside under an awning, and that's where they sat. Lena said she had walked by the place a hundred times but hardly noticed it.

The whole cafe was essentially one narrow corridor, with a bar along one side and small tables along the other. The walls were smudged mirrors, and the floors were smudged tiles. Wyatt ordered a beer, Lena a whisky soda, and Kalman a glass of dark red wine. The drinks were brought to them at their table on the sidewalk. The conversation began with Kalman updating Lena about the books he had dropped off at the bookstore and Lena updating Kalman on the adventure they had just completed collecting cables for her project.

"You know ever since we met at the Lantern that time I've been sort of waiting with bated breath for this photo essay project of yours," Kalman said to Lena.

"That's flattering," she replied.

"I mean it really is just... I don't know. It's something, and I don't know what to do with it. I need help with it in my brain, right? I haven't been able to square with it yet."

"Have you written about it?" she asked him.

"A bit, yes. I've sort of meditated on it with some prose poetry and that. I don't know that I've had anything insightful enough to share, and it hasn't gotten me any closer to getting a grip on it. Wyatt, are you writing about it?"

"I'm not. But I can't stop thinking about it either. I'm still pushing this play, but in the back of my stupid head I just keep thinking like what the hell does a play matter? Could anybody write anything that would matter a tenth as much as a demon carrying a mystery box around the city and turning buildings inside out?"

"Here's the thing," Kalman took a sip of his wine and put the glass down, "if they just finish their thing, or if they decide 'ok, we're ready' and just fucking swallow the whole city or world or galaxy up, that's just the curtains for all of us probably. Who knows? You said it yourself when we were talking about LeBlanc: her work will be poured over and loved by future generations but only if there even are future generations. She has crafted something beautiful, monumental even, with nothing but words. But further down the timeline it will wash away without anyone to read it. A master like her."

"Not much room for hope there," Wyatt said.

"No, and I don't feel that way entirely. You know, I'm not consumed by the dread of it I guess. I'm not living each moment in fear of a Lovecraftian inevitable. But I am fixated on the damn things. At least a bit."

"Do you think I could read some of what you've written since they showed up?" Lena asked. "It could help me contextualize as I finish putting together an exhibit."

"Sure, I can share some of it. Like I said, I don't know that there's enough insight to make it any worthwhile writing truly. There's honesty in there, but I don't think that gives it value on its own. At least for anyone other than me. There's value in the process, I always believe. But sometimes the value is just in furthering my mind along towards something that is more worth sharing. Wyatt, what's been your approach?"

"To the demons? Like I said, I haven't had any idea either. I haven't found any way in. I'm at a loss. I haven't grappled with it in any creative works. There are times when it's the only thing I can think about, and it's all anybody is talking about. The only time I'm productive is when I'm not thinking about them. It's a part of the world now, and there's nothing we can do about it. I don't know what that means for my work though."

"You're right. It's just a part of the world now. And I guess like it or not that means it will filter into everything. Like a spill on a table cloth. If I was writing about the table cloth, all of the sudden it's wet, and a different color, even if that's not what I was writing about in the first place," Kalman said.

"That's interesting," Wyatt retrieved half a joint from his pocket and lit it. "We're writing about the environment we're in, even when we're not. And if the environment changes, so does the work." He passed the joint around for the other two to both take a drag.

"I think so. That's definitely how I feel. There's a vastness that we all feel on the backs of our necks, and writing is a conduit into the truth of it. Artists are finding the conduits. You know what I'm saying, right Lena?"

"Sure, yes. I think there's always an element of our environment in the work we do, even if we are actively trying to work in escapism or subversion. Maybe the surrealists avoid it? But probably not even. It's all in there somewhere. In the approach if anything, right?"

"Writing for me is meditation. It's just like a form of self-reflection, the world and my place in it. The way some people write in a journal. As long as it is seeking perspective. I think that sharing it for readers to pick up and look at it is part of the meditation. Like a yoga instructor almost. There's an arrogance to the idea that I have a little struggle with. I'm just trying to share whatever it is I've been thinking about, not say it's the only way to think," Kalman said.

"So how can you tell if something's been successful? Does it need to have had an audience to have been worth doing?" Wyatt asked.

"No, there can be a success in having worked through it on my own. I feel a value in that. But you're right. If part of the process is the sharing of it then it does need to be engaged with in order to be fulfilling that part. For me, if I've done the due diligence of making it, getting it to hopefully evoke what I'm intending, I just have to take it on faith once it's out in the world that readers hold up their end of the bargain. What's your intention with this media project?" Kalman asked Lena. "Have you thought about it explicitly?"

"Well, I don't know that I've had a thesis statement or anything like that. When the arrival happened it sparked and I was drawn to it, same as others I guess. It was instinct driven. Like a reflex. But I definitely am approaching it with the intention of contextualizing the event. Capturing it for study."

"Sounds more scientific than artistic," Wyatt commented.

"Something can be both," she said. "I think there is art in the capture and the curation. There's art in the way it's consumed. Science can be art, I guess. Somebody documenting this so that others can engage with it will be important. I think others will do it, but it will be important. It's some-thing the culture will need. It's almost a natural response to it. A necessity that will happen automatically."

As they continued to chat, one of the Great Demons came into view over the nearby buildings. They all stopped to watch it and Kalman said "speak of the devil." Lena finished her whisky in a big gulp and pulled her camera from its sheath. She went into the street to get some pictures, even as traffic continued. The entire staff of the cafe emerged to the sidewalk to watch as well. The huge thing lumbered across the neighborhood, strafing into the streets, up the buildings and around the blocks. At once it stood on two huge legs and held it's other three legs up into the air into a formation. Wyatt wondered if he'd ever noticed the Great Demons have five limbs. Do they all? He couldn't remember. The demon stood, taller than any build-ings in sight, reaching up into the troposphere. Its figure was a statue for several minutes until it released a blaring sound that washed over the area. A sound like an enormous bell of pure silver being rung by an exquisite hammer. Oscillating, enveloping them, crushingly loud but soothing the ears so after an initial flinch nobody's instinct was to cover their ears. Then the immense sound ceased, and the world again knew silence. From the crown of the beast emitted a huge pulse of light, purple or grey -- a color Wyatt had never seen — that flew up into the sky and into a gaping hole in the sky that sealed up as if it had never been there.

At that, the Great Demon returned all its limbs to the ground and shiv-ered a twitch across its massive body before continuing a lumbering jour-ney north. Before it was out of view, the staff of the cafe went back inside. Kalman drank deeply from his wine glass and said something that Wyatt didn't hear, but he nodded in agreement. Lena and her camera appeared again and sat down with them. Both had forgotten that she had left.

"Holy shit," she said, out of breath.

She was already looking through what she captured, her eyes and her smile wide. A waiter came to ask if they wanted more drinks, and they all indicated that they obviously did, so more drinks were brought. The sound of birds in the distance started to grow louder, and the sky thickened as hundreds or thousands of birds of all kinds and sizes flew frantically from the south, following vaguely in the direction that the Great Demon had gone. As their numbers grew they blocked out the entire sky, and they were so loud that nobody could speak or be heard. Wyatt covered the top of his beer glass with his hand to keep feathers or bird shit from falling into it.

The birds passed, and the sky was revealed again, the same sick orange it always was. Drones continued to fly overhead. Traffic had hardly stopped during any of it, though buses had slowed to avoid the path of the Demon when it was near the streets.

"Well," Kalman said, picking up his drink.

And then they said nothing for a while. None were sure if this changed anything. But they had seen and heard something new. The spill on the tablecloth Kalman was talking about had gotten bigger, soaked deeply into the fabric right in front of them as they looked.

CHAPTER 11

AFTER THEY FINISHED AT the cafe, after having seen the Great Demon put on its show, Wyatt, Lena, and Kalman went their separate ways. Returned home or otherwise moved on. Wyatt went home, anyway. He made it back to his apartment around sundown. Still a bit shaken up, adrenaline still high, but not troubled. Not scared. Just fixated. He watched out the window as the sky darkened and the streetlamps flickered to life in all their different shades of yellowy-blues and whatever.

He plugged his record player in. The apartment was too small to have a place where it stayed ready for use, so it lived on a shelf near the front door until it was needed. This was a night that would need it. A vain side of him liked the prestige of physical media, the size of the damn things, so impractical in this world and especially in this city. But what he truly loved most about vinyl was the ceremony. The participation. There were nights that called for it, and this was one. Beyond the act of collecting records, a ritual on its own, today he needed to plug in the machine, ready the speakers, let the tubes warm up and place the needle down himself. He took great care in the way he took records from their sleeves and delicately put them back. Leafing through his collection, he shied away from 7" and 10" records. He'd want to pick something he could leave on for a little while. So, thumbing across the shelf he picked out six albums and carried them over to the little desk where his laptop often sat, the laptop now relegated to the chair for the night. He picked a record, lowered it onto the tray, turned it on and gently dropped the needle onto the wax.

Then he went to the kitchen and opened a jar where he kept some pre-rolled blunts. The good stuff, not the skunky shit from Lil ol' Betsy's. Not for walking around, for really just sitting back and enjoying. He lit one, experienced it deep into his lungs and exhaled it out the open window. The window faced south, southwest. He couldn't see the water or the main part of the city over on the island. Just the rest of this borough. Some ways into the distance were two Great Demons milling around each other, trotting casually in a strange pattern. Wyatt slid a chair to the window to watch. Their movements were unearthly, enchanting, playful, deliberate.

For two hours Wyatt watched from his apartment window, getting high, only breaking away from the Demons' show when a record reached the end of a side. The night was as dark as it ever was in the city. The sky wasn't totally black, and millions of lights from windows, lamps, drones and everything else lit the streets and buildings. Buses were still running and did all night. Still, as the darkness closed in around them it revealed something between the two Demons not apparent during the day: a tether of light flowed between the two, back and forth. A shimmering beam, some ethereal rope, somehow there but also not fully. It connected them, jostling like water in a dish. Its movements did not seem to match the movements of the beasts themselves, but it remained firm to them as they went about their business.

The Great Demons eventually began to move further and further apart in their dance. One moved back in the direction of the beach, and the other seemed maybe to be heading to Greenwood Forest, coming closer to the Sunset Morning neighborhood. As they separated, the tether stretched and faded until it was eventually gone, at least to Wyatt's eye. Perhaps it was still there, but it was imperceptible to him now.

The remaining Demon lingered in his view for much longer, and he watched it long into the night. It lumbered heavily across the landscape. Even after these months since the arrival, their shape was so mystifying that everything about their existence stood in sharp contrast with the world around them. Wyatt looked and noticed that there were others in his building sticking their heads out the window and watching. Some were also smoking. Others partook of other things, probably. One person waved to Wyatt, and he waved back.

After much lumbering, the thing had gone further than he could see. The night air was warm and pleasant, so the window was left open. Very faintly from the distance the tuneless song was carried from the demons and into his apartment. He left the record player on the desk but retrieved a notebook and sat on the floor. Feeling very foggy, but also very filled with the experience of watching the demon, he wanted to put something on the page, so he picked up a pen and forced it to do the work.

He didn't write about what he had seen, not necessarily. Just tried to write about what was in his head and on the far periphery of his mind. It was just words, but it did start to form into something with some bones. A setting started to be drawn in it, and characters became rendered and began to walk around. Other than changing records he did nothing else, and eventually the music stopped and he left the needle there, in the middle, nestled against the label, and didn't replace it with new music. He just sat there on the ground, back leaning against the wall, knees arched, with the notebook resting against his lap.

The sun slowly rose, and the shog started to glow. It jarred Wyatt from his concentration, and without much thought he performed the ritual of getting ready for bed, closing the curtains as tightly as they did, brushing his teeth in cold water and lying down to rest. He didn't work until much later, so he would be able to sleep most of the day, hopefully.

Sometime that week he heard from Lena that she would be going out on Long Island to start sourcing televisions. She would be gone for a while. One day while he was at work he noticed that the small package in the corner was gone. Paulie must have come to pick it up. It had been there for some time. Maybe it was only there as a place to hide temporarily. The reason it was there was to stay there for a little while before moving on to wherever it was supposed to go next. Wyatt was a little disappointed at the idea of never finding out what was inside the thing, but he tried to find a romance in the mystery of it. Could be anything: a dumb, beautiful, little question for poetic dorks to have theories about.

Later in the shift, a single, thick-necked cop came to the window. Wyatt put down the copy of LeBlanc's *Old Rage* he had been reading to give his attention. The cop demanded attention not with words but with his brick-house torso and the tattoos on his neck. He looked like an ex-neo-nazi, but that was being generous about the ex- part of it.

"Good morning sir," he said.

The cop gruffly said "It's 2:30."

"Mhmm. Ok, can I help you? Candy bar or something? Lose your head-phones on the bus?"

"There was a package delivered here for your boss. Is it here? Should be under the counter. I'm sure a smart kid like you can find it, not too many places to look."

"Yeah, it isn't here. It's been down here under the counter for a while, but it's not there anymore."

"It's not there," the cop stated back.

"Nossir."

The cop squinted only and left but returned to take a candy bar without paying for it.

These days the Demons, which were growing in numbers all the time, were a common sight all around every area of the city. Rarely was there a day without seeing at least one. While he worked, he continued to read, occasionally glancing out the window to see a demon pass by or taking a break to help a customer or two.

He had plans that evening to meet up with Talbot at a record store in the neighborhood called King City. This neighborhood had once been the epicenter of hipster culture. It grew in popularity until it was completely over-run by luxury skyscrapers. When things started to crash and the municipal authority crumbled it was one of the hardest hit. There was no reason left to be there and almost all culture fled. No one was left to take care of it. Some of the bankers or whatever else stayed and kept living there, the Subway Company maintained a beautiful trainline into the city and there was a population who used it every day to commute in and out for work. Other-wise the area emptied. Every restaurant closed. Every bookstore. Of course the emptier it got the more places there were for squatters to hide, so a parallel universe developed. Those with money who kept working and the poor who fought to just survive lived side by side, sharing the same space but never interacting as if they couldn't see each other. Obviously along with the squatters eventually came artists who just needed cheap places to live and work on their whatever. More artists lead to an underground econ-omy. Empty buildings were converted to shops, communes and farmers markets. Even farms popped up inside old buildings, growing produce was with magenta lights and hydroponics. If Wyat ever had a few extra dollars in the account he loved getting fruit from those farms.

Talbot was a liminal kind of guy. He had been friends with Wyatt since childhood, and the two grew up in the punk underground. But at some point he learned an office skill and as an adult entered that world. He was the only person Wyatt knew who worked in an office like that. It definitely made Talbot's life a little easier: his apartment was a little nicer, he didn't have to worry about food or transport as much. But Talbot wasn't rich and neither was anybody he worked with. They had unreliable access to clean water just like Wyatt. On the other side, Talbot was one of the only peo-ple in the offices who ever acknowledged or participated in the scummy underground. He kept one foot in both spaces and would dip in and out sometimes. This record store was a discovery of his, they knew his name there, held onto things they figured he'd like, gave recommendations, asked what he was looking for.

Wyatt had to take three different buses to get to King City. He rarely went there on his own anymore, and he was confused why Talbot spent so much time there. The record store was in a building that had once only been apartments. Inside they had sledgehammered through the walls to create whatever shapes and spaces they wanted and there were all kinds of markets. The basement connected to an underground that stretched on further than Wyatt had ever had the guts to explore. There were people who lived their whole lives in this community, never interacting with anyone else. They met up outside, in a little overgrown park across the street. Talbot was feeding stray dogs when Wyatt got there.

"Ayy, how's it?" said Talbot when he saw Wyatt approach.

"Things've been good. How're you?"

"You know, as ever, I guess."

They continued to chat as they walked together into the building and climbed the stairs to the fourth floor, where the record store was. Wyatt was a music gormandizer; he kept as up to date as he could on as many genres as possible, always seeking out new underground and upcoming bands to support. He put in effort to be a part of the city's music scene even though he had no aspirations of performing in it himself. Talbot, too, was a connoisseur. But unlike Wyatt, he was also an audio fidelity fiend. Where Wyatt bought records to support the scene, and because it was fun, Talbot put tremendous effort into collecting the highest quality gear, chasing the cleanest sound and hunting down rare pressings. He lived alone in a two bedroom apartment. The second room was devoted to music.

The girl behind the counter smiled and greeted Talbot when she saw him. She looked like at least one of her parents was East Asian. Her head was shaved, emphasizing her high cheekbones. She asked if he was looking for anything specific today, and he said that he wasn't — just browsing.

"We just got in a few new comps from Kumpel Gruppe. Eurofunk, post-disco, dance punk. Some really interesting stuff," she said, knowing that was exactly the type of thing Talbot couldn't help but collect.

"Ooo, let me take a look at that," he responded.

She pointed them out on a shelf across from her on the opposite wall, and Talbot made his way over to study them. Wyatt always made his way through this store in the same way: starting by thumbing through the new arrivals, moving to the section labeled "punk/hardcore" and then looking through the the hip hop section. Sometimes he'd mosy randomly around the store or search for something specific in another area, but it almost always started with those two areas.

They were the only shoppers, and the two chatted while they browsed. Wyatt updated him about Lena's project and how she had left the city for a while to get screens. He talked about sending his script to the theater up in the tip, the experience in Stone Slope with Lena and Kalman, and watching the demons from his apartment window. Talbot liked to hear about all this, and he asked questions and engaged with each part of it. After that, Wyatt asked what had been new with Talbot. Things didn't change much in Talbot's life, outside the occasional update about his extended family who lived out in the country somewhere. Usually when it was Talbot's turn he just talked about music he'd been listening to and very occasionally a show he had gone to, though he didn't frequent live music. For the most part Talbot went to work, found new places to eat for lunch, then went home. He had friends from the office and they'd get drinks on weekends, but that wasn't much to talk about. This was just the way it was.

By the end of it Wyatt had a record under his arm, and Talbot carried a stack of four or five. They went to the register, and while Wyatt paid with the cashier, Talbot looked through the glass of the counter to look through various vacuum tubes they had. Talbot loved tubes, and this place apparently was one of the best at sourcing and fixing reclaimed tubes from who knows where. That was a world Wyatt felt lightyears away from. It was a foreign language to him. He admired it but couldn't imagine having the energy for it.

He finished his turn paying, and Talbot stepped up, asking for the girl working to retrieve one of the tubes. While they settled the transaction, Wyatt looked out the window and down at the street. There were no demons in view from here. Lots of dogs wandered around in and out of the park. People walked and drove around, here to there. There were a few cop cars parked down the street. Many of the tall buildings around them appeared completely empty as far as he could see.

"Do you have anything in mind to work on next, if the play gets picked up? Are you writing anything new?"

"I have been writing, been getting back at it lately. I'm not sure I've settled on a project, but I have been putting pen to paper. I don't think I want to write about the demons, but I do think I will try sort of writing around them."

He tried explaining the spilled tablecloth thing but was having trouble making it make sense. So they talked about the records they had picked up for a while. Talbot was fun to talk to. He could effortlessly conversate with just about anybody, always kept it moving. And Wyatt could tell how much Talbot liked talking to him. He seemed to get excited about it. It made Wyatt feel good.

It was unseasonably warm outside. When they exited the building it was very hot and bright. They blinked as their eyes adjusted to the blaring sun. It was while they were blinking that they saw dark, uniformed figures approach from both sides. Two blinks later, Wyatt recognized them, obviously, as police. Talbot did not get into trouble with police, but they still looked to make trouble with him from time to time. They both got nervous. This wasn't good.

"Wyatt," one cop said.

"Um," he gulped. "What?" trying to sound fine.

"Where the fuck is the package?"

"What?" was all he could think to say again.

A cop shoved him. "You dumb fuck."

"Paulie's package?" he was confused. "He picked it up, right? It wasn't there."

"We know it wasn't there."

"I didn't touch it."

"OK, well, that doesn't help us."

Talbot stepped in, "Listen, if you need any help, we can talk to Wyatt's coworkers and see what we can figure out."

"We got a fucking detective here?" The cop was such a meathead. Such a dumb ass. Wyatt wanted to mock the shit out of him, but was too terrified to think about it.

"No," Talbot said, "I just mean, like maybe it would be easier for us to talk to them. Like among colleagues or.."

From behind, a cop threw Talbot down to the ground.

"Hey!" Wyatt put his hands out, pleading for calm. "He doesn't even work there, he has nothing to do with this, he doesn't know Paulie, hasn't seen..."

Wyatt, now, was on the ground. Blinking, sore. Unsure how he had gotten there.

"Paulie had the package, and now it's gone," a cop said.

A fist rattled the side of Wyatt's skull.

"You're going to tell us what happened to it."

The yelling continued amidst a flurry of stomps and punches. Wyatt and Talbot both curled up to try and protect their faces and stomachs. Things started to fade in and out. He saw Talbot getting hit, and he tried to crawl over to stop them but got kicked and vomited on the boots around him. It didn't make any sense. Talbot was just some guy. He had nothing to do with this. Putting out a hand towards Talbot, a heavy boot came down on it, and one more kick in the head turned everything dark. It stayed dark.

Drifting back into consciousness, Wyatt watched police cars drive away. He couldn't think to move and faded back out. Later, he heard a siren and saw an ambulance come to pick up Talbot, who had insurance from work, on a stretcher. He saw them load him in; Talbot was completely unconscious, bleeding. Wyatt didn't have money for an ambulance or a hospital, so they left him there. The ambulance drove away.

Night had descended when a searing pain sprang from Wyatt's head and pulled him awake. His body was sore. Looking around he saw hardly any indication that the attack had even happened. It just looked like a trash-covered sidewalk like any other all over the world. He patted his pockets. His phone had fallen out. Looking around he saw it smashed on the ground. It was destroyed, but he still picked it up and tried to turn it on. Nothing, not even a shiver of life in the thing, so he left it on the ground. His bag was nearby. The record he'd bought was smashed, but his notebook, his copy of *Old Rage* and a few pens seemed to be mostly ok. His wallet was gone. Talbot was gone. He looked around and saw no friendly faces.

Wyatt started to head home, completely spent. The walk truly felt like an odyssey after the violence of the evening. It took forever. On the way he went into a drug store to wash the blood off his hands and face in the bathroom. He tried not to look at himself in the mirror. It was rough. With no phone or wallet to pay for the bus he had to go on foot. It was a long walk on a normal day, and he had to stop often to rest his battered body. He was walking for hours.

With his phone destroyed he felt alone, and it made the night feel darker than normal. Finally he neared his neighborhood. There was a peculiar smell. Not the normal smell for this area. After the interminable journey by foot he finally approached his block, he saw also a slight strangeness in the air. The sky was orange, but not the usual shog orange. It was too early for sun anyway. It was hard to have a sense for the time, but it must have been sometime between one and three in the morning. People were running past him and toward him, a panic in every direction. The shouting made no sense, and he was too tired to pay it any special attention.

As he turned the corner he looked down the block to where his building was… *was.* That was the moment he identified the smell in the air as smoke. He saw before him the tumbling frame that had once been the building where he lived. The fire had mostly burned out by now. There was just a peaceful glow of ember. Orange and yellow pulsing, danced across the buildings in the area.

His body tingled. It felt hollow. His face was cold and numb. If he hadn't already thrown up during the beating he would've again. His stomach really wanted to but was empty and couldn't. He didn't remember tripping and falling at that moment, only awkwardly picking himself back up.

There was a crowd of people standing on the street watching. Wyatt joined them. After a time looking at the wreck, he found somebody he recognized and asked what happened.

"Will lost his mind, lit the whole thing," said a neighbor from down the hall. Wyatt didn't know anybody named Will in the building.

"Burned it down," Wyatt said, confirming it to himself.

"Yeah, he couldn't square with it. The demons just made him crazy. Changed the world too much for him. I talked to him about it a few times, I could tell it was bugging him out. But I didn't know it was eating him up so bad. He stayed inside. Poor Will."

And that was that. Wyatt hung around for a little while longer, but the crowd started to dissipate, and so he walked away. Everything he had was gone. Was it worth scrounging through the rubble to see if anything had survived? No, he told himself. There was nothing of anybody's left in there. In a fucked up way he was lucky he hadn't been home. There were people who hadn't made it out at all. Who knows how many. People had probably been sleeping. Probably people he'd known. Definitely at least people he'd seen. What a shitty way to go. Here in this old square building. At least he was standing here, looking at the remains of his burned down building. That was something. Everything that had been inside was gone: his clothes, his shitty laptop, his refrigerator, all his records and books, his fucking writing. Every page in every notebook. The whole thing about him was those stupid fucking notebooks and they were gone now. The words he'd spent so long spewing into them. The ideas he'd dropped onto the pages and forgotten about. Ash on the sidewalk. All he had left was the mostly empty notebook in the bag he was carrying.

It was time to figure out where he was going to sleep. Talbot would be in the hospital for weeks, maybe longer, but he had some family nearby, so probably they'd come get him and take him out to stay in the corpse that remained of the suburbs. It had been so long since Wyatt heard from Lena. Didn't feel like he had anywhere to go. So he just started to walk away.

CHAPTER 12

WITHOUT REALLY THINKING ABOUT it, Wyatt wandered to the empty cafe where he sometimes went to write, the cafe where he had nearly been crushed by a plummeting drone, and laid down on the ground in the entryway, using his tote bag as a pillow -- though the books inside didn't provide much more comfort than the ground would've. Even tired as he was, it took some time to get to sleep, after lying uncomfortably for some miserable amount of time he drifted to sleep. He slept the entire next day, waking up just as the street lamps were coming back on. He was sore, battered, his hand bruised and probably broken from getting stomped by a boot, and he was realizing now he was hungry. There was no infrastructure for taking care of people who didn't have money. He'd have to figure it out on his own.

The first place he thought of was the diner he had gone to with Roland. Where was Roland? Would it be worth trying to see if he could get in touch with him to stay with? He was out on tour, as far as Wyatt could remember. Hard to get a hold of anyway, and only really a couch surfer himself. Wouldn't have much to offer. He walked to the diner to check the dumpster around back. It was pretty gross. A lot of spoiled food, the smell was powerful. But there were some vegetables that didn't look too bad, piles of stale bread and then, the jackpot: a bag of uneaten food from plates. There was a good chance the food was going bad, and the bag smelled a little bit like cleaning chemicals, but it would definitely do.

He hoisted the bag out of the dumpster and carried it away to get some distance from the smell. He felt a pressure from each person that walked by. It was a new feeling. He was more aware of every other individual than he had ever felt the need to be, as if they posed a threat to him. Nobody looked or noticed him, he wasn't being treated differently today as any other day, but it did feel different today. Not a threat, maybe, but a challenge. Like walking by someone was accepting a duel to uphold his honor. He would need to be away from all eyes before he felt comfortable eating. But he was so hungry. Eventually there was an adequate corner, down an alley in some abandoned industrial part of town.

Finally looking into the bag Wyatt saw that there were messy, coffee dampened scraps of the food you find in a diner. Mixed in with used napkins were the ends of sandwiches, uneaten french fries, uninteresting salad, chunks of meat and loose cheese. Eagerly his hands reached in, picking at the biggest, freshest looking chunks.

Wyatt tried to even remember what day it was. Without his phone, he felt unconfident about that. He was going to have a shift that week. How was he going to do that? It would be good to go to work. It might be a risk going if Paulie was there. Paulie must know about what happened or at least have had an idea that it could happen. Wyatt was going to need money, and working was still a good way to do it. But without a wallet or phone he didn't know how to access his money. Where was it? It was going somewhere. And he had no idea about cleaning himself up somehow between then and now. All his clothes were gone except for what he had on.

There wasn't any food left that he could bring himself to eat, so he let the bag drop to the ground where he stood. He started looking around, trying to get a better bearing for where he was. He hadn't walked too far from his neighborhood. If he headed a little closer to Lil ol' Betsy's there was a group of federated homeless somewhere in that area. He didn't know exactly where, but he knew he'd seen their comings and goings. Maybe it was the ones who had the flower patches on their clothes, or could be the ones with the green bandanas tied around their left arms. There had been another he'd seen recently. Somebody had come by the shop back before the arrival event. It was an octopus pin. Maybe that was a new one. Or it was just that guy.

Wyatt was going to need some kind of help. It seemed like checking in with the vagrant federations was his best choice. Not totally sure what he was looking for or where to find it, he set off in the direction that seemed like the best bet.

There was hardly any traffic here, no pedestrians, no cars. It was strange how empty it felt. Wyatt had hardly ever felt a sense of privacy anywhere in the city. An odd sensation: being on a street without anyone to share it with. It felt relaxing, especially given his situation. He didn't want to be seen by passersby. The day before he had just been another guy in an apartment, and now he was another person without one. But then a switch flipped in his mind, at once, it wasn't a comfort anymore. Being alone out here he was probably more vulnerable than he'd ever been.

The emptiness stretched out in front of him, exaggerated and imposing. It took great effort to force himself forward, but he exerted himself to move into the new blank space.

From around a corner came three of the smaller demons, still towering over a human's stature but not like the building-sized demons. It put him at ease, like a familiar face at a party. They scurried toward him without making a sound, moving faster than a car. As they zoomed by, the air rushed by with such force it knocked him over. Then they were gone, around another corner, out of view.

Clambering back to his feet, Wyatt pushed on down the street. It was a cool day, the air felt wet, and he was still hungry. He knew that somewhere in this area there ought to be a vagrant collective. It had to be. Trying to form a mental map as he walked he drew from memory to guess what types of places would make the most sense for them to congregate. Somewhere dry, if possible. There were empty buildings everywhere. Could just be any one of those. Squats had to be picked carefully; buildings that were still owned could have cleaning crews sweep in to vacate the space. Or they could just have old buildings demolished, it was not procedure to check if anyone was inside. So sometimes empty buildings were too risky.

Eventually he was in the neighborhood near Lil Ol Betsy's. Wandering down useless streets he had never explored, the area felt brand new to him. There was something new and unforgiving to the landscape now. A false step would have long-reaching consequences with no safety net to fall back on. He saw a green area on the other side of the neighborhood that he had never noticed, just past a subway stop. And there it was. That must be it: an old post office. When post offices all shut down, most of that real estate was gobbled up by other things. But some just sat there. This one still had the barely noticeable blue sign and eagle logo. Nearby were other government-looking buildings that had also gone empty, and would also be well suited for repurposing.

So his aching body shuffled over to peek in the windows. They were covered so there was no way to see inside. He knocked on a door. There was nothing, no response. From above, a voice called out, "What do you want?"

He looked up and saw two heads peering out an upstairs window down at him. "My building burned down. Over in Sunset Morning. I don't need a handout or anything. I was just looking for some support. Or... um, pointers?"

They disappeared into the building, and he was again by himself. Looking around, he saw that there were people all around, walking and driving. It was a busy neighborhood, lots of comings and goings, here to there. The bustle and speed bore down on him. He felt afraid. It was with relief that a head returned to the window and said, "Ok, hold on. Come around behind the building and someone will let you in."

He followed the instructions and found himself waiting several minutes before the door was unlocked and he was allowed to enter. It was a big building. There were spaces that had previously been used to collect, sort and distribute mail. It was now filled with people. With the windows mostly covered with blankets, the air was stale and thick. It was very dark, but they had figured out how to get electricity from somewhere and a few lamps were on. He was led through the first floor and up the stairs, presumably to the room where he had been addressed from on the street. There were a few people sitting in the room. Some were smoking or drinking, some slept.

"Hello," one of them said. Wyatt figured it must have been one of the people he'd just been talking to, but it was hard to tell.

"Thanks for letting me in," Wyatt answered.

"Sure, no worries. That was your building the other night? We saw the smoke."

"Yeah it was. So now I'm here. Like I said, I'm not asking for anything. I guess I just needed a safe place to be for a minute."

"Sure. You can stay here if you can find a spot to lay down. There are some extra blankets, but not much else."

"Yeah. That's good. Thank you."

"You look like shit. Did you jump out during the fire or something?"

"No, I had a run in with the police. Same day. Right before."

"Damn, that's a hell of a thing. When's the last time you ate?"

"I got some leftovers from behind a diner. Sorta did the trick. What day is it today?"

"Umm. I think it's Sunday. Hey Rick," he yelled to someone down the hall, "is it Sunday?"

"Sunday!" was the response.

"Yeah, Sunday," the first guy said.

He had a shift at Lil ol' Betsy's on Tuesday. He had to go, probably. But for now he had to rest. He nodded and thanked the guy he'd been talking to and the one who'd let him in. There were people everywhere inside, tucked into every corner. Many sleeping, but many doing little things, keeping busy. There were middle aged people, lots of teenagers, and some children both alone and with parents. All genders and races. As he walked through he could feel the last grasp of energy leave his body, and he finally found a corner out of the way that was just big enough for him to lay down on. Very quickly he was asleep.

HE WOKE back up, unaware of the time. It took a few blinks to remember where he was and why. As the smell of the stale air set in, so did his awareness of what was happening and why he was waking in the cramped corner of a federated vagrant hideout. It was difficult to navigate the cluttered space in the dark, but he looked around to see if he could find any of the people he had talked to when he first arrived but wasn't able to recognize anybody. He was hungry. And thirsty. He hoped he could get some help from those here, so he picked a person at random and approached a woman who looked about in her late thirties and like she might know something. She had a layer of dirtiness on her skin, her hair was matted, and her fingernails rough and brown. But she wasn't gaunt or wasting away. It seemed like she'd been here for a while, but she did well enough to stay somewhat fit.

"Hey, can I ask you something?"

"Sure," she replied, with little interest.

"What are some good ways of getting, like, water?"

"To drink or clean?"

"Drink."

"That can be tough," she said. He knew it would be. People didn't even have enough clean water in apartment buildings. "You can try and shoplift some — sometimes if you're hanging around behind a shop when they are doing delivery you can snag some bottles." She gave Wyatt a quick visual examination. "You just got here, right?"

He nodded.

"Most stores don't let people in if they figure you're homeless. But you could probably still do it. You should take advantage of that. Find a store with narrow aisles, avoid cameras, and see if you can just grab a bottle or two and leave like you didn't find what you wanted."

"Ok, yeah. That's just about it?"

"Mostly. Sometimes when someone from the group gets a hold of a lot they bring it back to share it. But I don't think there's any extra right now. Sometimes if you ask for something people will give it to you."

It might be a good idea to just check Lil ol' Betsy's. There'd probably be someone he knew working there. It was the best chance to get something. He looked to make sure he had everything he'd brought with him, patting his pockets instinctually for his belongings before remembering that they were gone and he didn't have anything to leave behind. Just the tote bag he'd been using as a pillow. So he navigated the dark and cluttered space back to the alley door he had been let in and asked to be let out.

"Here," a person at the door said, handing him a sort of stamped medallion. They had a box full, all different sizes and colors of scrap metal. The image stamped was crudely drawn tophat. "It'll get you back in here, help out in general."

It felt very nice to hold. There was a comfort to having the thing. It was something at least. For whatever it meant, he was sort of, partially, at least a little bit accepted as part of the group. "Thanks," he said, trying to put the right amount of gratitude into his response.

The door was pushed open, and he staggered out into the day. It was intensely bright after the shadowy interior of the safehouse. His head spun a bit as his eyes tried to adjust. It took much longer than usual. Walking out to the street in front of the building, he tried to get his bearings, but he never really knew this neighborhood. There was a menace in the city around him that he still wasn't used to. A new adversarial quality to everything. Like any other day, traffic murmured in all directions. People in cars and on foot went about their ways. Drones continued to buzz. But there was definitely something to it. It was like he'd always been on the same team as all that clanging and chatter. And now it was on another team, and without trying or caring it wanted to crush and forget him.

As he walked, Wyatt thought about the writing he'd lost. It made his stomach feel sick. Made his eyes hurt. It had been so long since he'd pub-

lished anything anywhere. He'd never really published anything somewhere he was proud of. He had put his zines around, and they'd always
disappeared, so he hoped that they ended up in collections of other people
like him — or better yet people more impressive than him — but he knew it
was just as likely the barista or bartender had just pushed it off the counter
and right into the trash the minute he left. And that was it. That was the
fruit of his labors. When he introduced himself at parties, he'd always said
he was like a writer or something. It felt like that gave him permission to
be in the spaces he enjoyed being in. But there was no evidence of that
anymore. It had completely blown away in the ash. What was he without
those first draft poems? Those short stories that needed to be proofread
and polished? The notebook in his bag was more empty pages than not.
And he didn't like most of what was on the pages he'd filled in. Every writer
hopes that by adding their words they are increasing the value of a page.
These pages were worth less now than they had been blank.

After walking north for about six blocks, he realized he started to recognize things. If he started veering west, he'd end up in Green Wood. That
meant Lil ol' Betsy's was just further and a block or two east. So he pushed
up, avoiding eye contact and watching carefully where he stepped. Finally
he got to the street and approached the store.

It was someone he didn't know working the shop this shift. Must really
be someone new. There weren't that many people who worked there, and
he thought he'd met everybody. This made things harder. When he got to
the window, the person was facing away, looking back into the alley. He
turned his head to look at Wyatt with a blank, distracted face.

"Hey, I'm Wyatt," he said. "I work here."

"Ok."

"I was hoping I could just get a bottle or two of water."

"Who are you?"

"Wyatt. I work here."

From behind there was another voice, "Who'd they say?"

Shit, Wyatt thought. It was Paulie.

"Um, well. It's Wyatt."

Paulie appeared, pushing the other worker aside. "Well look at that. You are a dumb piece of shit aren't you, showing up like this."

"I'm sorry, Paulie."

"I bet. I had a real mess to clean up because of you."

"I don't know what happened, but it seriously was not my fault. I don't know where the thing went."

"Shut the hell up, there's no thing. Don't talk about any of it. It's done. And you for sure are done."

"I just needed some water. I'll be here for my shift Tuesday."

"The hell you will. That shift has been filled, and so has every other shift in perpetuity."

"Paulie, what the fuck? You can't fucking do that."

"This shit is a big fucking deal. Honestly you're lucky I'm firing you. Stay the hell out of all this. That's the best thing you can do. I'm still smoothing it all out, but I can't be dealing with any other, I dunno, confusions."

Wyatt couldn't think of anything to say. His mind couldn't get past variations of *what the fuck, Paulie?* This development seemed to be the inevitable conclusion of the previous 24 hours. Just...of fucking course, *this* now. So eventually his shoulders just sort of drooped and he said "ok, sure," and that was it.

"What'd you say you wanted? Water?" Paulie said, with no shift in tone, as combative as anything else he's ever said.

"Sure."

Paulie grabbed a bottle of water from the cooler and handed it out the window. It was a bit of a break. "You'll get paid up through your last shift. Minus the cost of the water. Now stop scaring customers away. I got candy bars to sell."

There was a bank down the street a ways, closer to a corner where a few subway lines crossed, just at the edge of the next neighborhood. He had an account with a banking company called Pan City Bank. They could probably run a biometric scan on him to ID him, fingerprint or ocular scan.

The name Pan City was supposed to mean they were in all the big cities, but the logo was pan flute that had been graphic designed into corporate anonymity so it just looked like a few stripes. Wyatt walked that way. He was parched and drank the entire bottle of water before Lil ol' Betsys was even out of view behind him.

When he arrived where the bank should be, he found instead an empty building, the shadow of the old sign and the silhouette of the name still visible on the front. It was black inside, and the doors were chained shut. He didn't know where any other branches were. There was an ATM outside, but it's screen was also dark and dead.

Banks didn't have many branches in this part of the city. Lots of ATMs, but very few full locations with tellers and bankers and that whole bit. Without a card, an ATM would be useless. He didn't know about any other locations in this area at all. He knew there were a few on the island in the main part of the city, but he hadn't been to one in years. With nothing else to do, that had to be his goal. He'd better make his way into the main city and find a bank. There wasn't much money in his account, but enough to... well, something. Enough to get some food. Once or twice at least.

In the meantime he had to scrounge for what he could find. He found a small grocery store and found the dumpster behind it. It was mostly rotten produce. It was lousy with fruit flies and who knows what other crawling things. But with some creative digging he found enough to hold himself over. After eating, he hiked into the center of this burrough. He found a department store to sneak into to use a bathroom. Accidentally saw himself in the mirror. Looked like a worn out rag. His face bruised, and his whole body hurt. With hand soap he cleaned his hair, feet and armpits before sneaking back out.

Getting across the river to the main burrough was difficult for anyone. Required some amount of planning. But without money it was almost impossible. The Subway Company was too well regulated, dangerous. Bus was hard to sneak onto. Couldn't walk the bridge without getting a pipe to the brain from some tween gang or another. Boats cost money. They wouldn't even look at you if you couldn't pay.

Feeling as refreshed as possible, Wyatt journeyed to the Broken Bridge. There had been a number of bridges on and off the main island, each with their own name and character. People had favorite bridges. They'd talk about which bridges they liked as a form of small talk. One by one they fell into disrepair and eventually into the river below. Only one remained on the east river, two on the west side of the island and legends of a tunnel somewhere over there. But the ruined bridges served their own purposes still, and they held vibrant communities for people without homes. Someone there would know the safest way across to the island.

Wyatt had done this walk, or similar distances, many times before. He liked to walk, and just as much he liked to save money even during his old, normal circumstances. He walked and biked here and there just as often as he biked or bussed. This trip felt much longer than it was. Maybe having the option of calling a car or hopping on a bus at the next stop made a regular walk feel shorter or more tolerable. This simple walk felt like a straining and exhausting exhibition. Each block felt wider than the previous, the destination running out ahead of him and coming no closer. Step after step it finally came into view.

The Broken Bridge was large and still ornate, collapsed as it was. It had been an iconic part of the landscape in previous eras. Now its skeletal remains still towered, but in the middle there was only nothing. Just the series of pulleys and buckets used to shuttle things from one side to the other. Sometimes it was supplies, often it was a cheap courier service for those who didn't want to pay the prices drone delivery charged.

It was a hive of activity. A hub of commerce and survival. The bridge was crowded like a market, and Wyatt shouldered his way through, looking for someone he thought could help him. He made it to the gap where the bridge had fallen away and saw people feverishly operating the pulleys to shuttle bins back and forth across the river. Each person had a small pile of things they were to send to the other side, and waiting by each pulley operator was a second person whose job it was to retrieve deliveries to finish their journey. Wyatt saw a person who was not busy but still looked like someone who knew what was what and how to. It was a tall broad shouldered man. He was unshaven and had long hair clumped behind him. His clothes were faded and dirty, but patched in a way that indicated resourcefulness and also the will to keep going instead of defeated resignation.

"Hey, I need some help," Wyatt said.

"And?"

"Well I need to get to the other side myself. I don't figure these bins are made for people."

"No they are not. You have any money at all?"

"Nothing. I took a police induced nap on the sidewalk and lost everything when I woke up."

The man grunted an acknowledgment. "Ok, well. There are kayaks. You can rent a boat and take it to the other side. Talk to them and maybe you can figure something out. Barter." He pointed down at the shore far below them where they could see a few tiny figures managing the boats.

Wyatt made his way there, crawling down to the bank below the bridge. The kayaks were a variety of sizes and colors, scrounged from wherever they could be found and collected. Some seemed to have been modified to be more resilient to the corrosive water of the river. The boats were being managed by a man and a woman, maybe a romantic couple, who were both at least in their 50s. They were as weathered looking as the boats, looked like seafarers themselves.

"Hey young man!" the woman said as he approached. "Can we help you?" Her voice was inviting but firm. She was welcoming a potential customer and warning a potential threat at the same time.

"I need to get across. Was hoping to borrow a boat. But I have no money."

"No money!" the man said and let out a belly laugh. "Nobody has any money!"

"Is there anything I can do?"

"Well," the woman said. "What *do* you have?"

"Um. Nothing. I can do some work for you or something. I don't know. Maybe try to go get you something."

"Are you federated?" the man asked.

"Oh," Wyatt remembered his medallion he had been given. "I suppose I sort of am. I have this medallion." He produced it from his pocket and showed it to them.

"Ahh yes! I know this crew. Some value to this coin."

"I don't really want to give it up," Wyatt was nervous to be without the only thing he had.

"Of course you don't! But if that's all you have to offer and you need a boat, this seems like the only deal."

"Well," Wyatt thought, "I'm going over to find a bank. I'm hoping I still have some money in it. My wallet and my apartment are gone, but I may still have a little money. If I get to a bank I can bring you money and get the coin back? How much is a usual passage?"

"How about we have that conversation when you come back. For now let's just say I'll hold onto the token and we'll look forward to seeing you again to discuss it further."

It was arranged. They picked out a boat they deemed appropriate for Wyatt's size and for the conditions of the water that day. It was a yellow kayak, long and slender. He was handed a paddle and he sat down on the seat inside the boat. Carefully he cinched his tote bag into a plastic bag they provided him with, tying a firm knot to try to keep the only things he had left dry. The couple pointed out across the water to the other shore, indicating his destination would be directly under the bridge's opposite abutment. They gave him a shove off from the crusty shore, and they waved farewell as he went. He pushed his paddle into the water and started out across the river to the island on the other side.

CHAPTER 13

THE WATER WAS RELATIVELY calm but deceptively unpredictable. The river was a mile wide at this point in its course. It still flowed like a river but the current moved and swayed in a way that was hard to navigate, and its every little jostle was felt and amplified by the tiny boat Wyatt piloted. The direction of the current changed daily, even hourly. At the moment it was flowing from the north, out towards the bay to his south. He had never been in a kayak and there was some learning curve to making it move, keeping it going the right direction and maintaining balance so not to tip over. He did not get the hang of it.

There were huge, unidentifiable masses floating by in the water, like ice floes. The river was teeming with activity. Large and small birds were picking at whatever they could find on the surface, fighting with each other for the most valuable bits. Though aquatic and amphibious life had gone extinct from the high levels of every imaginable pollutant, as the climate had warmed the region had become home to new reptiles. They were most often seen scampering across the surface clumps. Sometimes they scavenged for food amongst the garbage, but primarily they hunted the birds, snatching them from midair in a scuffle of feathers.

It was like paddling through a war zone, though the sound of the city was distant and it was one of the quietest places Wyatt had ever been. The quiet was unsettling. The going was very slow, and often he'd feel like he'd made good progress and gotten into the swing of it when he'd realize he had veered off course or been carried too far downstream. He'd have to strain the boat back in the correct direction and paddle vigorously to make up for the lost distance. After some minutes of this his arms would be too tired and he'd have to rest, drifting again in the river's current.

He looked back to see how far he had come and was disappointed to be so near the shore despite so much effort. He still had at least three quarters of a mile to the other side. The boat was jostled and knocked around by debris that floated by. Whenever a larger piece collided with him, the birds would soon follow, swarming around him and sometimes collecting the bravery to swoop down and peck for something to eat. He'd have to swing the paddle in the air frantically to ward them off.

When he neared the middle of the river, there were suddenly no birds, no lizards and there was no debris moving near him. For the first time he started to feel some confidence in his ability to get to the other side. The boat glided across the water here like a scissor across wrapping paper. It was completely silent around him until, in an instant, the water erupted near him. The river pulsed and jerked violently. A dome rose from the surface, breaking into a massive wave. Wyatt made a desperate turn to face the wave as directly as he could to avoid being capsized or washed over by it. It was like a city bus barreling toward him. His arms felt like rubber, and his chest tightened with panic.

The wall of chaotic water loomed in front of him, blocking his entire vision, lurching toward him with a sound and a stench that was completely overwhelming to the senses. Some tiny part of his brain made the decision to keep his jaw locked and mouth shut. The wrong splash from this could literally prove fatal.

Paddling as fast as he could to maintain momentum, he charged head on into the watery beast until it reached him, completely engulfing him.

The water was thick, and while inside the wave it was totally silent. Instinctually his eyes clamped shut, but his arms kept moving— rotating the paddles in vain, pushing back and forth against the wave that had swallowed him. The blackness of this moment felt endless. He wasn't sure if he had remembered to take a deep breath before going in. He didn't have any idea what his oxygen inventory was as time under the murk dragged on. His head was swirling. It felt like he was melting into the toxic water and losing his body into it. Hopelessness was there in the silence, and he stopped paddling. Time was stubborn, refused to move.

Finally he heard something again as the surface raced back toward him. The wave spat him back out. His eyes stayed shut. The river's surface was still choppy and upset. The boat rocked and jostled with it and eventually it moved so viciously that his eyes were pulled open, and he had to get once again to the business of staying steady. Looking back, he saw the churn continuing down the river behind him.

As things settled, the birds floated back, and Wyatt was again surrounded by mounds of detritus to navigate. He had no idea what had caused the commotion to arise from nothing. Could have been a factory or something suddenly emitting waste somewhere into the river. An air pocket could've broken loose. Or just something on the bed of the river was breaking down and caused a shift that created some sort of seismic activity.

Settled again, he looked around to try and locate himself. He found that he had been pushed very far downstream. The Broken Bridge was now much further north and the imposingly large monument looked small now. It would take a long time to make up the lost progress. He rested the paddle on the boat above his lap, giving his arms a break. The boat bobbed calmly up and down. When he felt like he'd gotten it back in him to continue, he took the paddle in hand and pushed it back into the water.

His hands were getting sore and blistered from the paddle. His entire upper body cried out for rest. This was an exercise his body had never been tasked with, and it was resigning in protest. Still he nudged the little boat forward and forward and forward in spite of it. Eventually he reached what seemed to be a somewhat stable pile of rubbish peaking above the surface, and he wedged the boat next to it for a break. It was pieces of metal and plastic that tangled and melded together after months or years of being tossed around in the water. They had apparently built up enough to snag on the riverbed.

With this moment to breath, Wyatt looked around at the landscape. Buildings in the main part of the city were much taller and denser than on his side of the river. A little more than half still had people in them. There were millions of people going back and forth between apartments and offices. Old buildings, now almost ancient, stood alongside newer constructions. The buildings that lay empty were drifting into complete disrepair, like so much else in the world. Others were lucky enough to still have people paying for at least some level of maintenance. Every year there were more broken windows that would never be replaced. Still, these enormous giants reached up to the sky, often through and beyond the shog. He wondered what it looked like up there. Did any go above the shog into clear sky, or was there no more clear sky left?

It was with some reluctance that Wyatt allowed himself to notice that the sun was beginning to set. He was still wedged against the mound in the middle of the river, hoping the old couple he had rented the kayak from did not see his struggle. How embarrassing. Knowing it was now or never he told his arms this was the time, pushed the boat so that its nose pointed once again to the western abutment of the Broken Bridge, and with some renewed strength he started the sojourn again.

The wildlife changed somewhat as the sky darkened. The lizards remained, but birds were replaced by insects and bats. Insects had probably been there all along; there were tiny floating bugs everywhere. But at night the insects were bigger, flapping things. Bats swooped around erratically grabbing them from the air. The bats had no interest in Wyatt or the Kayak so he never needed to swipe them away as he had with the birds. As he went, he needed to steer around chunky floaters, but otherwise he was able to keep the little boat moving constantly and in the right direction. He still wasn't any good at it, but the boat was moving and that would get him there eventually.

Night set in fully, city lights flickered on, and many windows were still glowing, but their light did little for him. Fear of the darkness took root at the back of Wyatt's neck. It was so much darker down here on the water than it was almost anywhere else he had ever been. So dark and so quiet. It made it harder to see things coming toward him, but once his eyes adjusted, he learned how to watch the surface of the water. He got used to looking for the reflection and realized that where he couldn't see the undulating light on the surface of the river there must be something else there, and he managed his way around it.

Finally the Broken Bridge loomed large above him as he drew near his destination. He couldn't even see the eastern shore anymore. There was a light on at the makeshift boatyard under the bridge where he needed to go. His mind fixated on it and blocked out everything else: the fear of the dark and sick water, the fatigue in his limbs. The last hundred yards felt as long as any other part of the way. It felt like an hour, and the light drew no closer. Pushing, pushing, pushing, he saw it ahead until he was able to see the shadow of someone there waiting for him, waving.

He lurched the boat onto the shore, and it was pulled up and out of the water by the man waiting there. He gave the man the paddle and tried to stand, stumbling out of the boat and onto his hands and knees on the ground. He let himself fall, rolled onto his back on the dark murk next to the river.

"You made it," the guy congratulated him, probably having watched the journey.

Wyatt only nodded, even though nobody could see it in the dark.

"Well, thanks for your business. Have a good night, son."

He never saw the guy's face. The only moment that he even tried to look, a bright light was directly behind him so all he saw was a backlit, silhouetted shape. Shape of a guy. He gathered a little bit more strength, the fumes in the tank, just to get back up and scramble away from the river. Above him was a mess of highways. In front of him was the emptiness below those highways. It was mostly dark, except for a few street lights here and there and some cars running with headlights on. He dragged himself lethargically forward, found a space between two support beams, laid down and fell asleep.

It had already started raining when Wyatt woke up, and it was impossible to tell what time of day it was. He was still wet from the paddle over. After blinking awake and looking around, he saw that there were probably dozens of other people tucked into edges and corners all around him. Some were awake, others still sleeping, and for some he couldn't tell one or the other. Carefully he pulled at the knot of the plastic bag he had tucked his tote bag into and was pleased to find its contents only a little damp. His mostly empty notebook and his copy of *Old Fury* were still in decent shape, despite having been submerged in the unspeakable murk of the river the day before.

He stood up and started to make his way into the city proper. The edge of the overpass was a curtain from rain, and there were a number of people standing on the dry side of the line looking out beyond it. He approached them.

"How long do you think it'll rain for?" Wyatt asked. "Think it's worth waiting here?"

One of the people waiting there— a tall, pale woman— said, "Depends on how urgent it is you get anywhere."

"How long has it been raining?"

"Hours."

It could just keep raining. There was no point in waiting. He was already wet. "Any idea what time it is now?" was his last question.

Shrugs as a response.

So he took a deep breath, as if jumping into a pool, and ventured out into the rainy metropolis. It felt very different here than in his neighborhood. His old neighborhood. It had been developed for hundreds and hundreds of years. Growing taller and taller with each generation, the grid of impossibly high buildings was really a testament of...something. Wyatt didn't know what to take from it. A testament to how tall things could be? Yeah, something like that. This part of the city also had identifiable and distinct neighborhoods, with personalities and populations of their own.

The street level was completely dominated by shops, both active and dormant. There were restaurants and stores and little places that just sold every type of thing. Compared to the other parts of the city, across the rivers there were many more chains and conglomerates. Places that could afford the competitive real estate. Even with many places shuttered, it was often more valuable as an empty store front than to be owned by some riff raff. Above the first few floors there were offices and apartments. And empty floors intended for offices and apartments. Companies would rent out buildings by the floor and could share a building with all kinds of things: other offices, sometimes art studios, rich people who found the empty space of an office layout liberating, even teenage gangs if they could scratch together enough money or if they knew somebody who could hook them up with a space to use as a hideout or HQ. Wyatt had been to parties on some of these empty floors, some of which devolved into orgies and he'd pretty much flip a coin on the night to see if he was in the mood to stay or if he'd just sort of disappear into an elevator and go get a coffee or something. Anything you could ever think of was somewhere at any given moment, on one of these floors, if you just knew where to look.

He had not been over here for banking business in years. Without a phone for navigation he had no idea how to find his bank, and the people who were out in the rain were not interested in stopping to give directions. The roads were a little bit smoother here, plows would come through maybe once a week and push all the trash out of the way. Nobody knew where it went. Probably someone bought it to do something with it. Crush it down and sell it as jewelry or something. And then sometimes a steamroller would smoosh everything down as much as it could, and they roll out hot, new road right out on top of it all. They never did that on the other side of the river. Wyatt remembered having seen it once when he was eight or nine. He was excited to see a steamroller. You could see the way the road had risen up layer upon layer over the years. All this meant that there was much more motor traffic. More busses, more cars. The network of subways was much more robust here, and the tickets were more expensive. He'd only been in the subways in this part of the city a few times, usually accompanying someone else who could afford the passes. Everything was just more crowded.

Steady, he weaved through the city streets, zigging west and zagging north again. His head was on a swivel looking for the familiar logo of his bank. He found nothing. He saw other banks with different logos. Banks from other countries. Banks that had bought and merged with other banks. Banks with different color schemes and branding guidelines. Maybe a blue lobby would make people like this bank more than the one with the red lobby. Or a soft orange bank would be exciting, yet soothing.

Wyatt traversed many blocks and crossed from one neighborhood to another and into another, as the sky shifted to the deep, threatening grey-blue of a storm and the rain became heavier. The storm mingled with the shog, and electricity ran through the clouds. In the distance he heard the low rumble of thunder echo through the city corridors. He wondered if he should've stayed under the bridge.

Around him he noticed three different responses as the storm grew: there were the people that had somewhere to go who quickened their pace with purpose, those who didn't have anywhere to go but scrambled to find one, and those who had resigned to stay in the weather and did not change their pace. He had to make the decision at that moment to be one of the ones who didn't have anywhere to go, but who cared enough to try and find somewhere. So he quickened to a jog and tucked his bag under his arm like a football.

He noticed almost every space that could have someone hiding from the rain did have someone. Even two or three where space and occupants permitted. He didn't want to try and negotiate his way into a shared space, so he kept searching. After running several more blocks, he reached one of the main arterial streets and one of the dividing lines between neighborhoods. It was frantic with cars, but it seemed hopeful that somewhere on the other side there would be a place to take shelter and wait out the storm before it got any worse. The storm's first strike of lightning jumped out from the sky. The clap of thunder was the loudest Wyatt had ever heard. Shockingly loud, even in this noisy landscape.

Every door he tried was locked, even the empty buildings. The rain picked up into a torrent. He was again as wet as he had been in the kayak. Water seeped into his shoes. The sky was as dark as dusk, but this early in the day most street lamps were not on. As he scampered through the rain, he found a mildewy playground that had a sort of play tower. It would be good enough. He climbed the child-sized ladder to get inside, and he sat in the empty space under the plastic roof that had once been a bright yellow. Mostly he was protected from the rain. The playground was covered in a durable rubber meant to keep kids safe when they fell and smashed their little noses. It should do the trick to keep any errant lightning bolts away from him. He was dripping wet, droplets ran down from his hair and down his neck.

Wyatt sat on the floor of the playground platform, hugging his knees. Hours went by, the only change was that the street lights came on. People with umbrellas continued to walk by. A few times it looked like people checked to see if his space was available but turned when they saw him and kept looking for another shelter. Puddles formed, and cars drove through them. It started to get cold. As night settled in, the rain continued to pound, making a constant percussive rhythm on the arched, plastic roof above him.

He never made the decision to try and fall asleep, but at some point his body made the choice for him. He woke up some time later, leaning against a post. It was still raining, and still dark, but apparently now morning. Without a clue of where to go, he figured it would just be best to wait it out. And so he waited the entire day as the storm rolled on with no change.

The storm seemed caught by the city, like the buildings grabbed it on the way through and held on, not letting it pass.

In the height of the day, he carefully untied the bag and pulled out his book. He sat as close to the middle of the tower as he could to stay as far from any wetness as possible, and he read until it was too dark to see the words any more. Another night came. It was harder to fall asleep this time because he was so hungry. It got very dark but felt even noisier than usual. Every sound felt amplified. The whole world had the volume turned up in the dark.

The next day, demons showed up in the neighborhood. They were already trudging around when Wyatt woke up. One Great Demon was accompanied by three of the others. The three smaller demons were themselves more diverse than he'd noticed before, different sizes and shapes. One was much taller than the other two, still only a fraction the size of the great demon, with longer limbs that couldn't quite be described as tentacles but had way more joints than really made sense. It was hard to tell if they had already started working in the area. Wyatt didn't notice if anything was different at first. The rain was still coming, and the demons seemed nonplussed about it. His brain took a long time to wake up, and seeing the demons suddenly in a space where they hadn't been the day before was disorienting. Somewhere, a logical part of his brain knew that they just walked over during the night, simple as that, but their presence was jarring in a way that made him forget where he was and why.

With the rain unrelenting, he had nothing to do but watch the demons as they went about their indecipherable business. For several hours they were just all moving, going over every area of the block in great detail, up and down buildings, across rooftops. Stepping carefully and occasionally taking swift and unpredictable leaps. Then he noticed two of the smaller demons had stopped their patrol, and they were now working at something on the ground. They were swaying back and forth as if in a ritual dance. It looked like the mating habits of a rainforest bird or something. The demons were moving their hands along the ground, and as they did, they smoothed beneath whatever they touched. The trash, the street, the bits of shrubbery growing up from corners all become flat, smooth and smudged. Everywhere they worked was no longer wet. Rain would fall, hit the ground, and then seem to pass right through, leaving the strange new surface dry. They moved studiously around the area, smoothing everything as they went. Their pattern was deliberate and methodical.

The tallest of the three Minor Demons was not moving at all, and Wyatt forgot about it as he watched the two go about their process. When he looked at the tall demon again, he realized it had been standing still but in a bizarre sculpture-like pose. It reached its arms into the air forming an odd shape, its silhouette appearing like an arcane glyph. The rain continued to pour down on the beast. It was glistening and wet. The shape of it was so compelling to him. Wyatt fixated on it. There was something to the pose this demon had struck, something runic, something about it that he couldn't escape. He felt like if some linguist could understand this pose it would be the key to knowing where they came from, why they were here, and what they were doing.

Without warning, the tall demon called down lightning upon itself. A huge bolt shot down and into the Demon's waiting hands. It shook the windows, and Wyatt flinched back, violently. The flash was blinding and was immediately followed by a bellowing crash of enormous thunder. It called down a second strike, a third, and then a fourth and then a series of bolts too rapid to distinguish or count. Wyatt felt the breath get knocked out of him from the force of it all. His eyes were wide but could still only see light-induced globs in his eyes as they tried to adjust. When it had settled and he could see again, what he saw was the tall Demon, now squatting on all limbs, low and wide, ringed by a buzzing, electrical residue from the strikes.

Above him, now, the Great Demon started its work. The hundred foot tall thing moved its massive limbs and, with seemingly no effort, took hold of the top of one of the neighboring buildings and bent it over like clay. He stretched the shape of the building, pulling it until it was arched over where it hung in a way that it shouldn't have been able to. The windows did not break. It all simply bent to the demon's hands. The demon lumbered over to another building when it reached up, again, grabbing hold of the structure and molding it out towards the first. With flawless precision it brought the two ends together, gently pushing them against one another until they bonded into one. The two buildings that had this morning been standing straight up, just up and down like a regular ass building, were now twisted across the block forming a shimmering, smooth archway of glass.

When the Great Demon had finished re-constructing the buildings, it stepped back and stood still, apparently satisfied. The smaller demons all stopped as well, but Wyatt couldn't tell if they were looking at the new arch or what they were doing. There was no way to tell where they were directing their attention at any time. After a few minutes, they all began to gyrate, moving almost too fast to see, sort of just buzzing in place. This went on for what felt like a long time until they stopped and moved on to another area and out of his view.

Wyatt sat in the playground staring at the work the demons had left behind. He studied the ground that had been smoothed. He studied the modified structure far above him, the two buildings now joined. The rain was still drumming constantly on the vinyl, castle tower shaped roof above him, but in the stillness of the moment Wyatt trained his ears to listen past that. He heard, so faintly, the demons' humming musicality left behind in the air around him. As if they had pushed it into the flattened ground so that as a part of their grand project it now sang. His eyes followed one of the buildings from the ground floor and up through the stretched and molded arch. Had there been people in those buildings? He wanted to go see. He looked back and forth between the two to try and determine which was closer to his hideaway from the rain. Neither building was obviously vacant, but neither looked particularly well maintained. Both probably had electronic locking systems on the door, but it was impossible to tell from here if they were active. He noticed that one of the buildings' doors was not quite closed all the way, probably just some chunk of whatever had gotten stuck in on someone's way out and caught the door.

So, with his books back in his plastic bag, he tightly cinched the handles once again to prepare for a trip back out into the rain. He climbed down the yellow playground apparatus ladder and scuttled as quickly as he could to the door of the building that had once just been a building but stood now as a testament to the demons' influence. As he jogged, his path ran across the area that had been smoothed by the smaller demons' hands. He almost tripped over his first few steps on it. It was still flat, just a floor, but somehow very strange to walk on. It wasn't slippery, and it wasn't sticky. Just so incredibly flat it was like nothing he had ever stepped on. He had to catch himself and reorientate, holding both hands out for balance, and then when he stepped off the modified terrain and back onto normal ground he again had to readjust and remember how to walk.

He reached the building and pulled on the door to find that it was, indeed, unlocked. He dragged it across the cluttered sidewalk and stepped into the building. It was an office building with a front desk for a receptionist that was vacant. The ground floor appeared to be entirely empty. There was dust piled up so high in the corners you could bury a treasure in it. But the garbage cans were not overflowing, so apparently someone would empty them out occasionally. Deliveries were stacked up on the front desk and on the floor next to it. No way to know if that was just one day's worth of deliveries or if it had been a long time since they had been retrieved. He thought he'd seen people going in and out while he had been hiding in the park for the rain to stop. But he couldn't remember if he'd seen that many packages coming in or out. There were two elevators, but he had no idea if they would be working now or what would happen as it got closer to the top. Not worth the risk. So he headed for the stairs. The stairwell was narrow and dark.

After climbing three flights, he opened the door to see what was on the floor. It was an office, full and active. An open floor plan with a grid of desks with people on computers or on phones. Nothing seemed to be different. It hardly seemed like anyone was aware that anything had even happened. There were a couple people standing by the windows looking up at the building's new shape. But everyone else was back at their desks working, if they had gotten up at all. Some looked at him peeking from the doorway. They seemed more disturbed by his presence than anything else. So before causing any trouble, he gently closed the door and continued up the stairs. As he went higher, he noticed a subtle change in color to the walls — a slight purple seeped into the grey concrete. The higher he went, the stronger the purple, until eventually the entire stairwell was a wild, glowing violet. It felt like glass. Climbing became more difficult each floor he ascended. The stairs were uneven and so smooth his feet started to slide. There was a hum coming from the walls. Checking a door once again, he found that even though the walls were completely transformed into the glass-like crystal, the door knob and hinges still worked as usual if only with a harsher sound. Looking in, he found another office floor, similar to the first. This had more private offices with doors and windows looking out into the middle of the floor. The desk spaces were more varied and laid out with some level of creativity. He could see that the building was now much more affected by demons here. The walls were sloping and curved and everything was beginning to be pulled to the side. Everything was Demon crystal. Still, this office was also full of workers, and like those he had seen below, they were all still productively going about their business. Their phones, their computers, all still seemed to work. Their jobs kept them busy.

He could only climb up a few more flights until the stairs were so skewed and twisted that it was impossible to go any higher unless he had rock climbing gear or suction cups or something. Slowly he reached his hand for the door knob. Wyatt took a careful breath. He pushed the door open and saw that what must have been another normal office was now an unrecognizable labyrinth of glass. Everything was pulled and twisted and transformed. If there had been people, they had either left (taken the rest of the day off due to extenuating circumstances) or they had become part of the display. Eternally a part of the demons' design. Light reflected through every surface and off of every corner. The floor was now a steep angle. He crawled on his hands and knees, holding carefully to any surface that he could. What had been a gentle hum was now an intense, roaring sound. Gradually, he made his way toward a window, sliding along the smooth crystal surfaces as he did. He was completely surrounded by this surreal landscape. The twisted and warped edges formed into shapes that overwhelmed and confused every part of him. After a considerable effort he reached a window and found that he could not see out from it. He could not see the world below. He turned back and could not differentiate the door from anything else around it. The sound of this place, the new and nameless color that it brought into the world, he was surrounded by it.

CHAPTER 14

IT TOOK CONSIDERABLE EFFORT to navigate back to the door leading to the stairwell, but eventually Wyatt made it and climbed back down to the ground floor and exited the warped building. The rain was slowing, and the sky was growing light for the first time in days. He hadn't eaten since reaching the city. As the weather continued to clear, he restarted his search for a Pan City Bank location in hopes of restoring access to his money. There wouldn't be enough in there for a place to live, especially with no new money coming in any more. But at least he'd be able to get a meal and a new phone.

In his time in the city he'd never needed to learn his way around without his phone. Even when he knew where he was going, the weight of that battery-powered map in his pocket made every journey seem shorter, simpler. With no idea where to look, he just had to go about exploring. With no money for rides, he could only count on his own feet and legs. It made every decision physically taxing. He'd pick an area and zigzag back and forth across blocks, looking for that bank logo from his memory. Every corner felt like it could be the last corner he'd need to peer around, might be the street that revealed his goal. That feeling started to fade each time the corner did not turn out to be hiding his bank until eventually he had become so disconnected from the idea of finding it that he had to remind himself what he was doing at all.

The search continued for days. Each morning he'd wake up, look for some food and then go about searching block by block across the city. Dusk would come, and he'd find a place to sleep. Often if he was exploring the same neighborhood for multiple days he'd sleep in the same place and continue again when the sky became light again. His hair grew unkempt, his beard started to fill in. The injuries from the police had mostly faded into a constant dull ache. Some neighborhoods bore the influence of the demons. Modified in whatever way. He noticed road signs in the wrong place as streets had apparently been picked up and moved around. Many things just didn't match up. And then there were other blocks that were just the way they'd always been. No pattern he could see of why they had picked a certain area to work in or left another area alone.

Sometimes he'd find a spot to sit and rest for an afternoon. Usually he would just sit and that was all. Or he would sit and read *Old Fury*. It was a tremendous work of literature. He had already found it to be a great piece of writing. In this time, when it was the only thing he had, he gave himself fully to it. He wrapped his brain in the words. Dove right into the thing for hours at a time before coming up for air. Then he'd put the book back into his tote and continue on.

Wyatt felt incredibly alone, and he spent a lot of effort trying not to think about it. But there were times he wondered what Lena was doing and if she was back in town yet. He thought about Talbot and if he'd recovered yet and where he was. The world felt so hostile when he thought about the distance between himself and the people he knew. It was suffocating, the isolation.

Each day developed a deadening rhythm. Waking, searching for food and fruitless searches for a bank. Other people on the street would not look at him and wouldn't answer him if he asked them for direction. Eventually, he stopped talking to anyone.

One afternoon he was getting food behind a small cafe in a very bland looking area when a barista came out of a back door for a smoke break. His instinct was to panic at first. Startled, he let the lid of the dumpster fall shut with a harsh clatter and recoiled out of view for fear of some kind of punishment for taking from the place without paying, even when it was out of the trash. She was tall, looked cool. She was black and wore a loose buttoned shirt with a paisley pattern tucked into tight black jeans. Her hair was in braids and tied behind her head. Probably a year or two younger than he was.

When she heard the dumpster slam, it startled her, and the unlit cigarette dropped out of her mouth but she was able to catch it before it fell to the ground. She called out to him gently, putting the cigarette back in her mouth.

"Hey, no worries," she said. She casually lit the cigarette and said "You need some food?"

The words almost made no sense to him. It had been weeks since anyone was kind, and his brain had already forgotten what it sounded like. He peeked around the dumpster to see her. She had an intense look that wasn't immediately welcoming, but he could tell she was not trying to be hostile.

"Yeah, I was just looking at what was here." Wyatt hadn't thought about how he must look. He had not washed or slept indoors in a month or so by now. It wasn't long compared to some. But he definitely looked like he'd been out there. The city builds up on you fast when you don't have a chance to wash it off.

"I can get you a sandwich maybe. You want something to drink?"

"Oh my god. I mean just water would be great."

"Sure, you don't want coffee or anything?"

Coffee? "Thank you. Sure. Just black. Thank you so much."

She nodded and exhaled smoke.

"Could I...have a cigarette?" Was it too much? He regretted asking. But he wanted a cigarette so damn bad. The luxury of it. The idea of being able to ask for something that wasn't just barely surviving. She laughed out smoke and nodded, handing him one and her lighter. The smoke felt unbelievable. He almost felt like he wouldn't need the food.

"I'm Vanessa Kasongo. What's your name?" she asked.

"I'm Wyatt. Um, Harris."

"That sounds familiar."

"What does?"

"I don't know. I've heard that name. Are you a writer?"

That word knocked the wind out of him. He wasn't a writer. All he had was the notebook in his bag. Nothing he'd ever written could be read by anyone, so the answer to her question was no. "What?" was all he could say in response. Was there another writer named Wyatt Harris?

"Nevermind. I read something by someone named Wyatt. I thought the last name was Harris. It was a play."

"About, like… a dog guy?"

"Yeah!"

"How did you read that?"

"I used to be involved in the theater scene. My buddy Toby passed the script along to me. Told me it was the type of pretentious shit I get into."

His script. The printed copy he'd sent to Tobias at the Flying Buttress. The only piece of work that had escaped the fire. It had survived. "What did you do with theater?" he asked.

"I was a director. I used to work under the name Wolf Wolf."

"Holy shit!" Wyatt almost dropped the cigarette himself. "You're Wolf Wolf? Really?"

"Used to be, yeah. Did you see anything I did?"

"No. To be honest I was only barely getting into theater after I had written that thing. But my friends fucking worshipped you. I met a couple actors who were going to be in your next show, and I heard it was delayed after the arrival event."

"Delayed first, then canceled."

"Why?"

"Yeah, just the whole fucking thing," she shook her head, gesturing vaguely to the world at large.

"The demons?"

"It fucked things up, didn't it? But then, it was fucked up and I guess I never really fully thought about it. I haven't really talked to anyone about it much. I sort of just looked at the play we were working on, and I was like 'ok, what even is any of this?' and I walked away. Got this job. I haven't talked to any of those people since then."

"Do you want to talk about it? How much cigarette do you have left on your break?"

"Yeah you might understand. I'd always done my work, and I tried to make it interesting. I'd make work that was in conversation with what I was seeing and thinking about. We're all kind of commenting on the things around us, and art in context against other art. And that always felt vital, felt worth doing. People liked it, and I liked that they liked it. I was proud of it. But things just blew up when those Demons showed up and started their own little show. And they're just around now? Just doing whatever the fuck. Nobody has any idea. Nobody knows what or why. "

"Made the city feel small, right? Everything that used to feel big," he said.

"The whole world. The whole, I don't know, god damn universe. It became pointless. And after that I just couldn't focus on the play. The more the Demons did around the city the worse it was. Every time I'd see one of the blocks they changed, or I'd hear a story. You know? And then when you look around you're like 'damn it the whole thing has gone to shit.' Like you almost don't notice that things were already this dilapidating mess. Theater used to be the only thing, you know everything for me revolved around it. Then it just became an extra thing. Figured I'd just get a job and hang out."

"Mhmm. I get that."

"Have you still been writing?"

"No. I guess not. I mean definitely not since I've been out here."

"What happened to you?" she asked.

He explained everything. Everything that had brought him across two boroughs to eventually searching this area. It almost brought him to cry talking about it. He couldn't fully express that feeling of trying to understand that his writing was completely gone.

"Well it's not all gone," she said. "I think I've still got that play some-where. Do you want it?"

"Oh! Maybe. Yes!"

"Come back tomorrow. I'm working again. I can give you a little more food— not much because they count the slices of bread."

"Did you like it? What did you think?" he was nervous to ask.

"I remember liking it fine. It was interesting, I liked the ideas in it. When I read it I was already losing my grip on wanting to think about theater. It didn't feel like something that could work on stage. I've done a lot of avant garde things, but I couldn't imagine how someone would put that dog on stage in a way that was at all convincing for an audience, and everything hinged on that."

"I guess you're right. Hm," he slouched even more than he usually did.

"It's really close to being something decent though. Doesn't have to be a play that gets performed. I could see it as a closet drama. People would read it and feel smart to have an opinion."

That wasn't something he'd thought about. It was barely something he was aware of. The whole point had been to try and find a way to make peo-ple engage with his writing in real time, all at once, right in front of him so he could see what it felt like and hear their reactions in a shared space. This wouldn't do that. But maybe that was ok. He just wanted an audience for it. Maybe this was the way to do it. "That's an interesting idea."

She tossed her cigarette butt out into the alley and said, "Well let me go get you something to eat. You still want that coffee, too?"

"If the boss doesn't count coffee cups."

"No, it's fine. And a water. I'll be right back."

He sat alone in the alley smoking the rest of his cigarette, feeling more things than he had felt in a long time. He felt a feeling he could only de-scribe as "good" as well as a motivation that had been missing. He hadn't thought about writing or any of that in weeks. There was also a new anxiety that he couldn't pin down. He had never figured out how to publish any-thing before. How was he going to do it now without a phone or computer? Being handed a manuscript meant some piece of him as a writer existed.

But it was a new burden. She came back with a sandwich wrapped in plastic, a to-go cup of coffee and a plastic water bottle. He took them graciously, tucking the water bottle under his arm and taking a sip of the very hot coffee. It tasted glorious.

"You don't happen to know where there's a Pan City Bank, do you? I have an account there, and I'm hoping I can get access to it. Maybe get a phone back."

"None in this area, I think. I've seen a lot of empty ones. It's Sunday anyway, they'd be closed today."

Sunday.

He sipped more of the coffee, mostly just feeling and smelling it.

"Let me look it up," she pulled out her phone and tapped on it for a few minutes, sort of nodding impatiently as it loaded results. "Ok yeah, looks like there's one near Port Authority. On 10th and 42nd."

Wyatt looked for street signs to try and get his bearing of where he was and how long that would take. If he had a place he knew to go, it shouldn't take more than an afternoon to get there. "10th and 42nd. I can do that. Listen, thank you so much Vanessa." He said her name but in his head he still thought *Wolf Wolf.*

"If you want your script back, come back tomorrow though. It'll be Monday and then the bank'll be open."

And she disappeared into the cafe, leaving Wyatt in the alley with the warmth of coffee in his hand. He found a tree to sit under and nestled in among the feral roots that were clawing through the sidewalks. A few times he needed to shoo street dogs and lizards away, but mostly he was able to eat in peace. He hadn't had water in, well he'd lost track, but it had been a little while. His body exploded with gratitude as he drank it. He ate half the sandwich and felt full, so he wrapped it back up as well as he could and tucked it into his bag for later. It was a hazy, almost green day. The air was cool, and Wyatt's clothes were still wet so he felt cold.

There wasn't anything else for him to do. No goals he could really accomplish. He'd been fed, and he had an idea of where to go for the bank. So he sat the rest of the day and read, standing up and walking around a block when his legs got too stiff. These walks gave an opportunity to find some place to sleep, since he'd need to have somewhere to go when it got dark. He found a stairwell that led down to a cellar of some long-defunct bar. It smelled like shit down there, but it seemed like it would be a safe spot to stay for the night.

When he read, he devoured the text. His mind was ready to take it all in so fully, and so it eagerly did, page after page. As it went, he felt the book grow thicker in his left hand and thinner in his right, subconsciously counting down to the end from the sensation of this transfer. Close to the end, he paused. This was, in a way, the only book in the world right now. When he was done with it, he'd never be able to be reading it for the first time again. The question of where any new possession would come from had no answer, and so there was no guarantee of another book to swap in as soon as he was done the way there always had been. Losing track of time, he just stared at the book for a while, turning it over in his hands. Looking again at the cover, reading the back summary, flipping through those first few liminal pages at the beginning before the book really starts, looking at the dedication and wondering who those people were.

It was starting to get dark anyway. So he put the book away and hoofed back over to the basement entryway he'd picked out for the night. In the dim, popping light of the street, he rummaged around in the trash a bit and found some sources of the smell he had detected. A few dead animals, some rotting food and some actual, literal shit. Doing his best not to touch any of it, he wrapped the things up in other garbage and hoisted it out onto the street level at the top of the stairs. It took several trips to do safely and a bit of something did get on his hands. He just had to wipe it off and hope for the best. The smell lingered, but he felt better knowing he'd done something about it.

For the first few hours of darkness he just sat and looked up at the sidewalk, watching people and cars pass. He'd been so disconnected these last weeks that these things had become part of the wallpaper. Tonight he was seeing them all again as he hadn't in some time. It was so busy. The lights of cars hurrying frantic back and forth. The shadows of people on their way. He'd forgotten how crowded these streets were. Night deepened and he began to settle into sleep. It didn't come right away but when he did fall asleep it was a more restful sleep than he had remembered recently.

He was a little worried he didn't remember where the cafe from yesterday was. After checking a few alleys that did not look familiar he found one that he felt confident was the right place. Having never seen the front of the place, he didn't know the name of it. Hadn't even thought to check that before leaving the previous day. He sat far enough away to be invisible but close enough that he could see the door. He was pretty sure it was the same door that Venessa fka Wolf Wolf had emerged from and returned to.

Hours went by, and he opened his writing notebook for the first time since the fire. He looked at a blank page and wondered if there was anything in his head worth putting there on it. He clicked the pen, and pushed it across the whiteness, only to find the pen didn't work anymore. He shook it, touched it to his tongue, you know; all the things people try to do to get a pen to work again. But there was nothing to it, so he just tossed the pen back into his bag and went back to not writing.

The door squealed open and Venessa appeared for a smoke break, so he stood up to greet her. She was startled at first, not immediately recognizing him. "Shit, hey. How was your night?" she asked.

He shrugged. "You know. Just gotta figure it out as I go and it just is what it is I guess. It's whatever."

"I have your thing. I put it in a little binder, it had just been in that manilla envelope. Here," she handed him the cigarette she had just lit. "You can have this one. I'll be right back."

She went back into the cafe and Wyatt took the cigarette. The intimacy of the shared smoke was almost overwhelming to him. It felt like love and maybe in some kind of way it was, a little bit. When she came back she had a new cigarette in her mouth and the black binder tucked under her arm.

"It was cool bumping into you," he said as he took the copy of his play from her. "You really have no idea how much help you've been."

"Glad I could. Good luck with the bank and with the play if you end up being able to try and do something with it."

"Do you think the door is totally closed for you having any part of the scene again?"

"Hmmm. I dunno," she was wistful. "Maybe not. Sometimes I hope so, just settle in to not feeling the pressure. But I definitely miss something about it on occasion."

"I'm sure you'll find something to engage with, if you look for it. The art mattered before there must be a way it still does now."

"The question is if it did matter in any real way before."

"Might be worth just checking in on it. Even as Vanessa."

She smiled. "The door is open. Who knows," she said as she went back inside.

And that was that. With the only known surviving piece of his writing now in his tote bag, he started the hike across town to where his bank should supposedly be. The binder made the tote too big to fit into the plastic bag. The walk was to a known destination, but was still a back and forth up streets and across avenues. Wyatt stopped for traffic as he got into the throbbing chaos at the city's center.

This was no longer a place people wrote songs about. It was just busy and that was it. The buildings were tall, the lights were oppressive and pedestrians as well as cars seemed to be an unceasing, singular unit. Shoulder to shoulder for miles. It moved with ruthless efficiency. Entire crowds could cross through each other with no one bumping into anyone else. Adjustments would be made effortlessly and usually nobody even needed to slow down. There were more cops here too. He felt a terror in his throat whenever he saw one. It was his hope that even though he looked like he'd been sleeping on the streets, as he had, if he moved with purpose he could blend into the crowd in a way that would not draw their attention or their anger. It seemed to work.

Each block he'd double check the road signs as often as they were there and he calculated what felt like the most direct route to 10th and 42nd. He looked for clocks to measure his time and could only hope that the bank would even be open still when he arrived. The shog grew dark, and there was a light rain. He stopped to tuck the plastic bag over the top of his tote's contents: the notebook, *Old Fury*, and the binder. He desperately hoped to keep them as dry as he could. The rain continued the rest of the walk there, and everything smelled bad. His hair and scruffy beard soaked up and dripped from it. Then came that last corner. He turned and he saw that logo. It was the same. That lame and unrecognizable pan flute. Without realizing it, he broke into a jog, weaving and dodging through the crowd and not waiting for crossing lights.

As soon as Wyatt entered the door, a tall bank employee wearing a fine suit confidently and gently pushed him back out onto the street. Before he knew what was happening, Wyatt was simply back on the sidewalk surrounded again by the city's chaos, and it had happened so convincingly that he almost thought he had done what he came there to do and was finished. He shook his head to jog his memory and headed back in to see the same man with arms folded.

"I have an account here."

"Do you now?"

"I do. I think so. A little while back my building burned down, and I don't have a phone or cards or anything. I was hoping there was something you could do here to help me get access to my account again."

The man stood there like a statue, eyes fixed on Wyatt, apparently running calculations on how credible the story seemed. Clearly the bank guy didn't want someone who liked the way he looked coming into the bank. Annoying for customers and probably bad for business. It was with obvious reluctance that he was invited in.

"Don't sit on any of the furniture, and don't stand by the windows. We'll have someone here for you soon."

Obediently, Wyatt stood in a corner looking as invisible as he could, uncomfortable to be in such a clean indoor space. Another tall, bland looking banker walked over with the soft-boiled politeness of obligation.

"So you've got an account with us, but you've lost access to your card, is that correct?"

"Yessir," Wyatt felt like an asshole for saying sir but it slipped out.

"Do you have any form of identification at all?"

"No, I lost my wallet and my apartment."

"Ok. Well, we can do biometric confirmation. Ocular and finger prints. You'll need to wash your hands and face for them to work. There's a bathroom over here. I'll be waiting outside."

Wyatt could tell they didn't really want him to use the bathroom, but the opportunity truly felt like a gift. The bathroom itself was lit with a toxic-feeling incandescence and was aggressively unstylish, but the privacy was a luxury that weakened his knees when he locked the door behind himself. He took off his shirt and hung it on that little hook in there. He washed his hands first, letting the water get as warm as it could and lathering his hands with so much soap that bubbles lingered in the bottom of the sink when he was done. Then he rinsed and washed his face in slow motion, like he was in a commercial. When he had finished, he did it again, scrubbing behind his ears and rubbing the soap into his beard and hair. It felt wonderful. He dried off with paper towels, careful to dry as best he could for fear of being a wet mess when he left. Before putting his shirt back on he stared at himself in the mirror and saw a body that did not look familiar. He looked thin, hungry, tired, stretched, broken. His face looked rough, even after the wash. The toll of these weeks was immediately and visibly apparent on him. With a shiver he turned away and put his shirt back on, picked up his tote and headed back out to find the bank employee there waiting for him and the first man still watching him from the front door.

Together they walked to a desk that was partially obscured by some temporary looking office walls. There were two comfortable looking chairs that had been pushed aside and a plastic folding chair that he was indicated to sit in. The banker sat down behind a table with a computer on it and started typing.

"Ok, what's your name?"

"Wyatt Harris."

Typing.

"Mhmm. We do have a couple people with that name with accounts associated with them. First let's do the finger prints." The man retrieved a tablet from a drawer and held it out in Wyatt's direction. "Put your hand on this when the screen turns blue."

The screen was red, then blue, so Wyatt placed his hand on it as instructed. There was a gentle electronic tone and a pulse of light to announce that it was finished. The banker put the thing back and produced another contraption: a tripod with a sort of face mask attached. The banker put a disposable plastic cover over the side that faced Wyatt.

"Ok, keep your eyes open and slowly approach the device. Get as close as you can without touching it."

He followed the instruction and looked into the device as it shone a jittering and blinking red light across both of his eyes. Startled at first, he blinked and heard the banker exhale in frustration.

"Don't move please," and he touched some buttons to restart the process.

It scanned his eyes, and the red beams disappeared.

"Ok. We'll submit this for decoding. It will take two weeks for confirmation. You can come back to this or any other Pan City Bank locations in two weeks, and we will be able to restore access to your account and issue you new cards."

"Great, thank you," Wyatt said without really realizing what had been said. "Wait, two weeks?"

"Yes, it takes two weeks for the data to be confirmed. It's for your own security."

"My own security? I don't have anywhere to live between now and then."

"I understand that, sir." He didn't understand that. "And we're sorry." They weren't sorry. The banker stood up, indicating Wyatt should also, and so he did. Defiantly, he took one of the mints from the bowl on the desk.

In a slow blur Wyatt was ushered back out onto the sidewalk outside the bank, but he did not remember it happening. This was supposed to be it.

This was supposed to be the way out of this whole thing. End of the journey. At least the end of this chapter of it. But now he was told at least two more weeks. Still no means of contacting anybody he knew, still unsure where any of his close friends even were. And stuck over here on the island, he didn't even know anybody who lived in this part of the city. With shoes that hadn't fully dried in over a month, his feet suddenly felt very sore. They were announcing in advance that they weren't going to be getting him out of this situation without putting up a protest.

This was a very dense and busy part of the city. Almost all traffic in and out of the city came through this bus station or the nearby bridges. It would be hard to find a place that he could borrow for the night that wasn't already occupied. He tried to develop a strategy before embarking. He didn't really know this area well, especially without navigation. It was a much closer walk to the west shore of the island from where he stood. It was possible there would be something over there. There were a ton of piers and many were in disuse. It was the only thing he could think of, the only destination he was sure he could find without too much wandering.

His feet certainly did not want to do it, but he knew he had to make them walk. Every block or so he ran out of steam and had to lean on a wall or sit on a stoop to build up the motivation to continue. It was hard. He had lost all concept of time of day. Like a slug he dragged himself west until he found a bench beside an old running trail. There was no one around and he collapsed onto it. It wasn't sleep, but it was close. With eyes open and mind empty, his body began a slow and total shut down. The day became dark.

With no announcement, morning returned. Wyatt woke up hungry, but he ignored it. Instead he just sat there on the bench looking around. He couldn't quite see the river, but he could just barely hear the waves. Like many other parks, the trees had grown tall and thick. As it grew brighter he pulled the binder containing his script from the tote bag. He flipped through it. Parts of it seemed good; lots of it he didn't like. But as he read it he got ideas of how things could work. Changing it to something intended to be printed and read opened it up for him. It seemed like it could really be an interesting work if he fixed it up a little. Then he took out *Old Fury*. There was not much left. He decided to finish it and he did. It was one of the most tremendously impactful pieces of fiction he'd ever engaged with. Something verging on a masterpiece.

After the last word it felt hard to close the book, so he kept leafing around in it again. He read the "About the Author," and it said Edna LeBlanc lived in a place called Beacon, New York. That was up in the valley from here. A little far, but there were trains that went there. Maybe he should go, he thought. There must be a way to catch a train. He'd never been to Beacon. It was a proper town in its own right, but it wasn't a big place. Not a city. Maybe somehow he could find Edna and talk to her. He had no reason why, certainly no reason why she'd want to talk to him, but in that moment his mind fixated completely on the idea of going to that place and seeking out this writer who was to him a master of her craft. He had to do it. Without a plan, his mind was made up. He would take a train and go there.

CHAPTER 15

WYATT HAD NEVER HOPPED a train, but he knew some buddies who had so he basically knew how to start. It had been a common source of transportation for crust punks for close to a century. Once he decided to head upstate he needed to find out which train to hop and how. So he hiked across the city to Onion Square, a busy hub for much of the city's traffic, a crossroad of many of the active train lines and most importantly a long-standing headquarters for the transient oogle population. He was able to find out which train yard to go to, how to avoid the railyard bulls and which train to get on. There happened to be a couple other punks on their way up into the valley, or who just didn't have anything else going on and figure they'd go up for the hell of it, that agreed to accompany him on the trip. The train they took was a series of standard freight cars, bringing cargo in and out of the city. They sneaked on at dusk, before the lights came up but as the sun was setting. While they were in the city, they needed to stay hidden and completely out of sight. Quiet and invisible.

The crust punk community had not necessarily thrived in the last few decades. Many were still around, but crust as an aesthetic and lifestyle dwindled as more and more families fell out of the upper and middle classes and social safety net programs withered away. Without the security of a suburban home to fall back on, fewer people took the leap into full gutter punk. So, for the most part when you found a crust punk they were the real deal. Lifers.

Once they had gotten out of the city and onto the rails proper they emerged from their hiding places and convened in a freight car for the duration of the trip. They passed around a flask of indeterminate liquor and a seemingly endless supply of cigarettes. It felt like the lap of luxury, getting drunk with those crusties. They just wiled away the time, shouting about shows they'd been to. The punks talked about places they'd been. They had no interest in the impact of the Demons on their city or any other. It truly just did not matter to them.

The train reached his destination, and Wyatt carefully dropped from the train as it slowed to enter the freight yard in Beacon. He was instructed to get off the train before it stopped because it would be less likely he'd be seen and run into trouble. Jump when the ground is flat, tuck and roll. The landing was rough and left him in a daze but he was not hurt. Knowing it was not smart to stay there on the ground for long, he hurried to his feet and made off in the direction of buildings in the distance. The rest of the punks continued on to their destination, wherever it ended up being.

Beacon was a small city, barely a city at all to his eyes. It was one of several towns like it along the river. There wasn't much of a skyline but there was a cluster of buildings at the city's center. They were short, only a few any taller than four or five stories. The town was surrounded by wilderness and coffee farms. As the climate had rapidly changed, the types of things that grew changed also. The forest of this region had undergone a slapdash and incomplete transition that left things looking strange and messy. There were still old trees hanging on and irregular new growth filling in around it all.

No public roads in the wilderness had been maintained. The only roads that existed between cities were toll roads that belonged to a company. Wyatt didn't know the specifics of it all, but he had heard about the competition between these road companies, fighting to have the most valuable routes. If a town wasn't worth having a road go to it, there was no road. From the train yard to the city proper there was only a wide dirt path for trucks. Wyatt followed along the edge of the dusty road. He could see far enough in both directions to know if anyone was coming and figured he could hide in the brush if he had to, but nobody came and he didn't have to. It was a windy day and it made for a difficult walk. The place seemed so small that it continued to feel very far away even as he hiked toward it in the morning sun.

There was no sign that said "Welcome to Beacon" or anything like that. He just had to know that he was there by realizing it himself. The town was spread out, houses and yards, varying degrees of neglect or care. No stop signs, no traffic lights. Cars were around but very infrequent. Nobody was walking on the streets at first. There was the feeling of people around though, even if he couldn't see many. These houses had people in them. People who paid mortgages or rented. The streets and sidewalks did have less garbage, but only because there were fewer people. It was the same garbage per capita as it was back in the city.

Walking through, looking for a main street or town square, he thought just now for the first time that he had no idea how he was going to find Edna LeBlanc. Every building around him was just a building, and any one of them could have her in it, smoking a cigarette and typing away on a vintage typewriter spilling out her next illuminative piece of grand literature. On an unassuming corner he found a gas station with a convenience store and decided to go in to ask. The man at the counter shooed him away before he even got to the door.

"Wait, wait!" Wyatt shouted. "I was just looking for directions! I don't even need to come in. I'm not here for anything."

The man met Wyatt at the door with his hands held out to keep him away.

"Not here for anything, of course! Get the hell out of my store!" Honestly he did seem like a nice guy, despite it all.

"I'm just looking for somebody. She's supposed to live in this town."

"I don't know, I don't know who," the shop guy said.

"I'm just trying to find the writer," Wyatt pulled out his copy of *Old Fury*, "I'm trying to find Edna LeBlanc. Do you happen to have any idea how I can get in touch with her?"

He did pause, but still kept his hands up, barring Wyatt from approaching. "I don't know any writers. There's a little shop, kind of a general store, old fashioned, off main street. It is called LeBlanc's. I've never been in. They're sort of competition except they don't sell gas. Maybe they know her. Now go!"

"Thank you!" Wyatt said, turning and looking around with no idea what to do with this new intel. He looked back over his shoulder.

"That way!" the man yelled.

Wyatt pointed himself that way and went. The shog here was less dense and patches of sky were sometimes visible, but it didn't quite look blue. Maybe it just wasn't anymore. We'd sold out the atmosphere, and the sky moved to another neighborhood. As he neared the busier center of Beacon, there were more and more cars and people. Many corners had panhandlers with signs, and benches had people sleeping on them. There were a few office buildings, but it was hard to tell how full of offices they were. More common were business parks, like office buildings sort of spread out around a parking lot. They were full of doctors and lawyers, or manufacturing firms and things like that. Honestly it looked similar to the town Wyatt had grown up in.

Main street seemed to be about half empty shops, though the variation in store fronts was subtle and some of the shops that looked closed might not have been. Each window was coated with a film of grime. The gutters were overflowing with kipple, windblown rubbish was piled up in every corner. The trash was old. Some of it dating back to that first week garbage trucks didn't come. Faded from the years of sun and wind. The central street was wide, with narrow side streets cutting out from it irregularly. Every major intersection was marked by tall, old churches, most of them empty. Some had been turned into other things. One looked like a weird house probably for some rich eccentric who had fled the city. What had once been a church parking lot was now a driveway for two expensive sports cars; one classic and one new. Even with the shog above, the sky felt vast and wide. Much wider than he was used to. Nestled in a valley along the river, Wyatt could feel the intense and vibrant forest bearing down on them from all sides. He'd heard stories about how the immense and ancient forests of the world had all been hewn and driven to dust. The world needed its lungs though, and earth was growing new jungle wherever it could. Pedestrians were seldom, but each one eyed him with suspicion. Finally he saw some punks and felt comfortable for the first time since rolling off the train. They were sitting on the stoop of a closed shop, drinking beer, three boys and a girl all probably in their mid-30s. They had two dogs with them, and the dogs were laying on their sides, fully asleep and snoring.

"Hey, can you help me?" he said to them.

"Who knows?" one of them said, another kind of giggling.

"I'm just looking for Edna LeBlanc."

"Who?" said another.

"Edna LeBlanc, the writer. She's supposed to live around here."

"Man I hate to say it again, but honestly who knows?" the first said again.

"Oh. She's like, a really great writer," he again produced his tattered copy of *Old Fury* to show it. "In her bio it says she lives here. I was hoping she still did. Maybe she doesn't."

"I've never heard of her. There is a shop called LeBlanc's around the corner, over there, two blocks. You can check that out."

"What's that book?" the girl punk chimed in.

"Oh, I don't really know how to explain it. It's just really good, she's an incredible writer. I just finished it a couple days ago and I came up from the city."

"I'll see if I can track down a copy," she said.

"I recommend it."

"You wanna beer?" the second punk said.

"Yeah, actually I really do."

He was handed a can of beer with a label so generic it might as well be completely blank. Many regions had a beer that was standard issue for the punk community, and this must be the valley's.

"Good luck, man," the first punk said.

Cracking into the beer and moseying in the direction he'd been guided, Wyatt turned the corner to see a dingy storefront with an unlit neon sign that said "LeBlanc's," and obviously it was the place. Standing there in front of it, he didn't know what he hoped he'd find inside. With a deep breath he pushed the door and siddled inside.

It was dim, and cramped. Looked about like halfway between a bodega and a very small grocery store. There were some refrigerators along two walls, rows of racks and shelves stacked with boxes and cans of food, crates of mostly fresh produce and a counter with a convenience store coffee pot. There was nobody around. Somewhere unseen, a speaker was playing some kind of contemporary post bop jazz, just melodic enough to hold onto but all over the place rhythmically. Out of instinct and anxiety, he started browsing the store as if he was there for something. Most of the stock wasn't dusty or old looking. Looked like people shopped in this place, stuff seemed to be moving in and out. As he wandered through the aisles nobody appeared, and so he went to the counter to pour himself some coffee, an old habit, before remembering he still had no money and left coffee unpoured. In the back he heard what he imagined must have been the sound of a delivery being dropped off, and then a very loud truck drove by the front of the store. Someone appeared from behind a beaded doorframe. It was an older white woman, must have been in her 60s. She looked strong, and her back was straight. Her shoulders were broad and her posture was so much better than Wyatt's that he suddenly noticed his slouch and pulled his shoulders up to correct it. Her grey hair was tied in a ponytail that went just past the collar of her bomber jacket.

"Hello," she said, assessing Wyatt. "Can I help you?"

"Um," he faltered. "I'm.. I was looking for Edna LeBlanc. Do you know if there's a way I could talk to her?"

"Sure, go ahead. Can I help you?"

"Are you Edna LeBlanc?"

"Yes."

"Hi. I just finished reading *Old Fury*. I thought it was incredible, I'm sort of a writer, well I mean I'm working on writing, and I guess I just thought I should come try to talk to you."

"Where did you come from?"

"Up from the city. I took a train."

"Just like that, huh? I've never had anybody familiar with my books stop in here. You dropped everything and caught a train upstate."

"Well, I didn't have anything to drop. Everything I have is here. My building burned down a month or so ago. I've sort of lost track of the time to be honest. I haven't had a phone or any money. I just had my notebook and a copy of this and when I finished it I saw it said you lived in Beacon so I wanted to come."

"What do you want me to do, sign it?"

"No…"

The door opened, and a woman came in with a child, maybe … 8? Wyatt had no idea the ages of children.

"Hi Edna!" she said.

"Hey Darcy, what's for dinner tonight?" Edna said.

"Figured we take a look and see what you had. What's fresh this time of day?"

"Just got in some boxes of greens from Gold Stone Farm. You want first picks at that?"

"Sure!"

"I'll go get 'em."

Edna disappeared into the back and the woman started to put groceries into a bag she carried. When Edna was gone, the customer saw Wyatt with some noticeable apprehension. She made an effort to keep herself between Wyatt and the kid. Wyatt tried to disappear into the corner so as to not appear threatening. He didn't feel threatening.

Edna came back with one of the new boxes and opened it up. The customer pulled out two bundles of greenery and put them down on the counter, along with everything else she'd picked up. The two made small talk as Edna rang up a total and the woman paid. She and the child left, leaving Wyatt again alone with Edna.

"Do people around here think it's cool that you're, like, a prominent author?"

"I'm not a prominent author. People around here think I have reliable groceries, and I like running a good shop so they think that's cool."

"Are you still writing? Or do you just do the grocery thing now?"

"Yeah I'm working on a few projects. The store makes enough money to fill in the gaps. I couldn't really do either on their own and get by."

"Oh so the store isn't just something you do because you dig it? You don't make enough from your books?"

"Man, it's expensive as hell to exist. I don't know many writers who don't have to do something else. Even since before, most people I knew were professors or some other sturdy day job like that. There's definitely a few around, but I don't know them personally. You know as long as there's airports there'll be airport books, and they seem to still sell well enough to give those people big old houses somewhere."

"Hm."

"Where are you staying while you're up in the valley?"

"I hadn't figured that out yet."

Another customer came in, around 20 years old or so. He picked up a few items, knew exactly what he was looking for and where it was, did no browsing. Some snacks and a drink. With them in his arms he addressed the counter and the two politely carried out the transaction of payment. Edna said, "Have a good one," and he said, "Thanks, you too," and left.

"You don't know where you're going to sleep?"

Wyatt shook his head.

"No leads?"

"Usually I just look for a park or an empty shop with an awning or something. Someplace dry and out of the way."

"Shit, no don't do that. Look, there's a cheap hotel over near the train station, one of those really bland ones with the same name in every city. I'll put you up for a few days. I'll call down and take care of it. You can hang out, wash up, get some breakfasts maybe. I can't help much but maybe we can get you on your feet a tiny bit."

"I can't…" It was overwhelming. "That is so kind."

"I know."

Edna pulled out her phone and tapped around on it for a second to call up the hotel. She told them she needed a room for a few days and pulled the phone away from her mouth.

"What's your name?"

"Wyatt Harris."

She swiveled the phone back to her mouth. "Wyatt Harris. Ok good, thank you." She hung up and put the phone back in her pocket. "Ok they'll get a room ready for you. It'll be about an hour. You said you came in from the train station?"

"No, I took a freight train. I hopped off before the train yard and walked up a dirt road from there."

"Haha. Ok, sure. You're young, why not? Ok, well to get to the hotel you'd need to go back to where the train station is. You take Main Street toward the river, all the way to the end. Go past the court house, the road kind of loops around, but then you'll end up at West Main Street. Follow that and you'll see the hotel. Got it?"

"I think so, yeah."

"Good."

"Mrs. LeBlanc…"

"Shit, just call me Edna," she muttered as she put a cigarette in her mouth. "Mrs. Shit."

"Edna. I was wondering if you'd be willing to read this thing I have. It's the only piece of my writing I've got. It's a play I'd sent to a theater not long before my apartment burned down. Somebody gave it back to me. I felt pretty good about it when I finished it, but I don't really know if it's any good."

She exhaled smoke. "You have it with you?"

"It's right here," Wyatt pulled it out of his bag. "I wrote it to be a play, but I think it might work best just printed and read."

"Uhh, sure I can take a look at it," she reluctantly took the binder and put it down on the counter next to her.

"It was an honor meeting you. If I can ever get in touch with my friends in the city again, they'll think it's really wild."

"Honestly, don't go telling everyone they can just come to Beacon and find a store with my name on it. I sell cans of food, I don't need this place being some hipster pilgrimage or something."

Another customer came in. It was an East Asian woman, probably about the same age as Edna. "Hi Edna, how's it going today?"

"Good, Kelly, yourself?"

"I'm good. Getting some coffee, taking a quick break." She looked at Wyatt. "Who's the tourist?"

"Actually, I guess this kid's a fan of my books."

"Ohh, yeah that makes sense," Kelly laughed.

"Kelly is one of the only people around here who knows I'm an author," Edna told him.

"Are you a writer, too?" he asked.

"No, I'm a gardener."

"She used to be a painter."

"30 years ago.

"Why'd you stop?" Wyatt said.

"Didn't have to do it anymore. I had a few galleries, and then one of my collections just took off with the right critics and the right collectors. I had a few pieces sell for, well, a lot of money. And that did the trick. I've basically been in the greenhouse ever since."

"And you've never wanted to paint again?"

"No, do you want to know the secret?"

"If you know it," he said.

"The trick is, I buy my coffee here instead of the trendy coffee place.

It's much cheaper. That way, the money I made lasts longer. I get to keep growing things, planting flowers." She swiped her card to pay for the coffee she had put into her travel mug. "Good seeing you Edna. Nice to meet your admirer." She left, sipping the coffee on her way out the door.

"Well I've got inventory to take care of," Edna said. "You'll find your way?"

"Down Main Street and toward the train station? I can find it I think."

"Ok. They'll have it under your name. Tell them who you are. I assume you don't have ID?"

"No."

"Should be okay. Have them call me if it isn't."

"Thanks again. Honestly, I'm sure you know, but you really have no idea how much it means to me."

"I do know."

"I'm excited to hear what you think of my piece."

"Right, that too. Yeah, well. I guess we'll see. I'm interested to take a look."

Edna's stern eyes watched for him to go, and so he turned and left. It had turned out to be a somewhat gloomy day, just sort of a vague, drab sky. Very humid. Reaching Main Street, he tried to orient himself and started off down the opposite direction he had come from, hopefully heading toward the river as he'd been instructed. It must have been the middle of the office work day. Cars were parked everywhere, and windows were all lit, but there weren't many cars on the street and pedestrians were scarce. Sometimes a big truck or a bus would go by, rumbling and rattling over the crumbling street.

He walked by a white middle-aged punk, head shaved, dressed in all black, tattoos peeking out his sleeves and spilling onto his hands. The old punk carried a bucket of hot asphalt and a few tools. He located a pot hole and started filling it in, flattening it out with care and pounding the asphalt into place. It took about 20 minutes, and then he moved on to another. Infrastructure was even worse here than it was in the city. The bus companies probably had less money to devote to keeping the roads up. The anarchist road crew was all they had. Maybe there were others like him, but it was a tall order for somebody doing it just because he had the time and the will for it.

The buildings got fancier as he got closer to the river. There were a few taller commercial buildings. They were still only five or six floors high, but they towered over everything else around them. Many apartments looked expensive. The cars got nicer, too. The roads were no better.

At the end of Main Street was a wide and busy intersection that seemed to be the artery leading from the heart of Beacon to the nearby highway. Looking south, he could see a standard issue suburban plaza full of large chain stores and local iterations of things you found in every plaza like it everywhere in the world. There was no traffic light as there had once been. Cars just had to have the confidence to believe it was their turn. Wyatt waited for a long time before he felt he could safely make it across. Rising above him on the other side of the street was the old Court House— a big, ugly brick building. It looked old but it had no style or character to it. It was plain and square like an old school. Behind it, as he had been told, was West Main Street, and by now he could smell the river.

When he reached the hotel, he was surprised to see that it seemed to have many people coming in and out of it. Some might've lived there, at least temporarily. Some probably worked there. But there were other hotel patrons, just staying for a visit. There were broad, sliding glass doors at the entrance that he saw open to receive visitors before him as he approached. The doors remained stubborn and shut for Wyatt. He was confused and looked around to see what was wrong, waving his hands and stepping back and forth to try and trigger the sensor. Next to the door was an intercom, so he pushed the button and heard a ring.

"Welcome to the Inn, can we help you?" said a distant voice.

"I wanted to check in. Someone made a reservation for me."

"Name please?"

"Wyatt Harris. Edna LeBlanc made a reservation."

"Come inside, please!"

The doors opened with reluctance, and Wyatt hurried in as they shut again behind him before ever fully opening. With a bare minimum of courtesy and little to no eye contact, he was issued a card and a room number. It was at the furthest end of the second floor. Entering the room, Wyatt fell asleep immediately on the couch.

CHAPTER 16

WHEN WYATT WOKE UP he saw the crisp red glow of a digital clock and knew definitively what time it was for the first time in weeks. 9:41. The hotel room was exceedingly bland. There was no art on the walls, no extra pillows. There was a bed, a couch, a small desk with a stool, a dresser with a television and a rack to hang clothes.

The bathroom was small and dark but looked clean and smelled like nothing. Turning on the shower, Wyatt was delighted to find hot, relatively clear water. He took off his clothes and got in, washing himself over and over for as long as the warmth lasted, felt like an eternity. Even longer than it used to in his bathroom in the old apartment. He'd wash, rinse, stand in the water, and then wash again. After getting out of the shower he used bottles of hotel shampoo to wash his clothes which he then hung on the shower curtain rod to drip. Standing naked in front of the sink, he brushed his teeth using the little disposable toothbrush wrapped in plastic.

Tucking a towel around his waist and leaving the bathroom, he turned on the TV only to find that every single channel needed to be purchased with the use of a card. He only had access to a running loop of some local commercials that the hotel had accumulated and been paid to run. He left it on, hung the towel up on the bathroom door and laid down on the bed on top of the sheets, naked. The garbled sound of the TV washed over him with attorney's slogans, promotions for dry cleaners, bus companies, on-line clothing stores and before long it was just like the sound of waves on a beach. The electricity blinked occasionally. He laid on his back for an hour, falling completely into the ambient sound of the television.

When he climbed out of the bed he opened the square-patterned curtains to reveal a chilly, forgettable day. From this window he didn't really have a view from the river or the town of Beacon. If he leaned to the glass one way he could see the river as it disappeared around a bend in the distance, and the other way he could just barely see the busy intersection he had crossed to get here the day before. Stretching in front of him was a low grid of grey and brown buildings, the highway, and beyond that the aggressive green of the chaotic new jungle growth. From here he could see a dozen or so drones of different sizes criss-crossing across the valley, some venturing out toward another town, others coming in from elsewhere. As he surveyed the landscape, he noticed a building with that familiar striped logo of the Pan City Bank. It was a small local branch. There were probably people who lived here and commuted by train into the city, and it made sense to have city banks out here. It hadn't crossed his mind to look for one here.

Wyatt checked his clothes to find they were still basically soaking, and the fan in the bathroom just wasn't going to do the trick. Looking to the window, he found that it didn't even have a latch. It was just a window cemented into a wall. Further exploration of the room uncovered a hairdryer, tucked under the bathroom counter, so he started using that to dry his clothes. It took what felt like a long time. He put on the warm, stiff clothes hoping they seemed as clean as they felt to him. It was 12:16.

It was with some hesitation that he gathered the motivation to venture out of the safety and privacy of the hotel room and back out into the world. First he looked in the lobby to see if there was some kind of complimentary breakfast, but there wasn't. He asked about it and found out that it was put away hours earlier. When asked if there was anything from it left, he was given a single-serve box of colorful cereal. Wyatt carefully lifted the tab on the top of the box and peeled open the bag inside and started crunching on it as he left the hotel. The sweetness was overwhelming, but it felt good to have something resembling food in his very empty stomach. It was much colder outside than it had been the day before.

Trying to navigate the strange, old streets, he attempted to find the bank he had seen from his window. Unlike the grid he was used to in the city, these old towns on the river were just sort built as they went along, curving around the landscape to produce baffling twists and turns of a roadmap. He couldn't tell what the buildings around him were. They seemed clean and maintained, but most looked completely empty. There were no cars on the road, but there was trash.

After bending and curving along the roads, he came upon the bank. There was no sign of anybody inside or out, but it was lit and apparently open. He pulled the door open and entered the grey and green bank lobby. It was carpeted, and there was a waiting area with green chairs and a few toys in a box in the corner. There was nobody inside, it seemed.

"Can I help you?" called a woman's voice.

"Um, yes," he answered, not sure who he was talking to.

Stepping further into the bank, he saw that there was a teller sitting at the counter along the side, out of view of the front door. He approached the counter.

"What can we do for you this morning?" she said, and then checking a clock behind her, corrected herself, "Oh, this afternoon!"

"Well, I have an account here, but I recently lost all of my cards and every form of ID. I went to the branch on 10th Avenue in the city a couple days ago. They took these scans but said it would take two weeks, and I guess I was just looking for a second opinion. It'd be a hard couple weeks."

"Sure! Well, technically they are right. Security checks, especially at city branches, take two to three weeks to confirm. But If they've gotten started, I might be able to double check those things from here. Let's go give it a try."

She was an older woman, older than most people Wyatt had ever seen. Most people didn't live much past 50 on average, and she looked well beyond that. She slid down from the stool and led Wyatt to a partially enclosed cubicle, not dissimilar to that he'd sat in earlier that week in the other branch. She walked with delicacy, keeping a hand on walls or ledges whenever possible, but she moved with confidence and purpose. She gestured for him to take a seat, and he did while she dug around in the drawers behind the desk. The device she produced was clearly much older than the other he had used, but the idea seemed the same. It was basically a tablet that she held out for him and indicated that he was to put his hand on it. After it was done, the banker returned the device to its place and sat down at the desk's computer. She typed some things for a few minutes, and other than the click of the keyboard, it was quiet.

"What's your name, son?"

"Wyatt Harris."

"Yes, that's correct. Good job! Ok, well I've got your identity confirmed here. It looks like you did ocular and finger print scans at the city branch. I should be able to use those two checks to finalize everything here and see what happens next."

Wyatt felt hungry.

She clicked more for another several minutes.

While she worked Wyatt stared out the tinted window behind her. The already gloomy day looked almost like night through the dim glass.

"Ok!" she said.

"Ok?"

"It's all set, let's print you a new card."

More typing, then she disappeared into the back. Wyatt sat alone there for a long moment that he spent continuing to stare at the window, his eyes focused on the reflection rather than the outside. When she returned she had an envelope and before handing it to Wyatt she said "don't lose this one!" It felt heavy in his hand, and he flinched taking it.

"Shit," he was overwhelmed by the plastic thing he'd been given. "Thank you. You really… thank you very much. You have been such a big help, you don't know."

"Just doing my job. Anything else while you're here?"

He didn't hear what she said, but on autopilot his brain went ahead and made his mouth say "no, thank you, that'll be it for today I think," and he left.

With a new card in his tote bag, he was suddenly famished, hungrier than he'd been in weeks now that food had for the first time become a possibility. Across the street was a pink and orange coffee chain, so without even making the decision he found himself inside ordering a bacon, egg and cheese sandwich on a bagel, a big black coffee and some of the weird little hashbrown nuggets the place served. He sat at a table in the furthest corner and attempted to fully disappear to the world while he quickly ate the cheap, greasy food he'd been given. Feeling more satisfied than he had since his building burned down, he knew the next thing he'd need to do was get another phone. And then probably need to stop spending money altogether. There wasn't much left.

He headed back to the plaza he had seen the day before, knowing there would be a place to buy a phone. The intersection and intercity highway was as busy as it had been the first time he crossed. He walked alongside the road on the other side of a bent and bruised guardrail heading south toward the plaza, waiting for the long enough pause in traffic to cross. It wasn't until reaching the plaza and waiting on the opposite side of the street for another five or ten minutes before there was any opportunity to dash across, a car in the final lane needing to make a frantic swerve around him before he reached the other side, the air rushing by as it zipped by behind him.

The plaza was white and clean. Each store's brand shone like lighthouses, the color bright and the typography clear and evocative. There were huge stores — multiple department stores, a grocery store with locations in almost every city of this size, a hardware store, huge empty storefronts — and then a number of smaller shops. Tucked in among a row of these small stores was a storefront Wyatt spotted with a logo of an old phone (with a number pad? Wyatt had never even seen a phone like that) and the word "mobile" in the name. He went in and worked with the lone shop employee to track down his account and attach a new — well, a cheap refurbished — phone and activate it. After getting the new phone, he had to stand in the store awkwardly and let it charge the battery. When it was finally charged enough to turn on, he finished the process of activating his existing phone plan on the device.

The old phone was sleepy and not eager to get back to work. Once it was turned on, it stuttered to get to a home screen and then sat there for a little while. Finally the thing got up and running, and Wyatt left the store. Standing on the sidewalk, he stared at the blank screen, waiting for some activity until the phone buzzed to receive the texts that had been waiting up in space or wherever they wait until they can be delivered. It buzzed over and over, five times in a row, and then it stopped. He had four messages from Talbot, one from Lena, one from Roland and one from a spam number telling him about a new credit card offer. Then the phone sat still again, and that was it.

Talbot texted him once from the hospital and twice a few weeks later when he was discharged. He was checking to make sure Wyatt was ok. His final text was very concerned, and there was nothing from him after that. Lena had texted to check in after returning to the city from her trip sourcing screened devices for her exhibition. She was wondering if he had any suggestions of venues to check out. He thought of a couple but probably she had already sorted it out by now. Roland politely saying they were heading out and to see you around next time. The final text claimed to be from a person named "Rebeccah" who said they had heard about a great deal on a low interest credit card, and they thought Wyatt needed to know about it. He marked it as spam and blocked the number.

There wasn't enough fuel in his tank emotionally to deal with the idea of responding to any of the messages. He spent an hour or so wandering around Beacon, trying to learn the layout of the strange little city until his feet started to hurt so he just went back to the hotel and fell back asleep. The next morning he looked at his phone again and gathered up the motivation to message back. He wrote multiple drafts, deleting them and starting over each time before he replied. Talbot he messaged first, letting him know that he was alive, and he told him about his building burning down and that he was currently upstate in a hotel and that he'd probably be back in the city in a few days or something. With Lena he just checked in, asking if she'd gotten a venue and apologizing for the delayed response. He'd tell her the rest later.

For the next two days, he woke up early enough to catch the free breakfast in the lobby. He'd make himself coffee in his room and sit watching the commercials loop on the television while he drank it. In the afternoons, he'd walk around and get to know the town. He found a few book stores, a decent record shop, a dingy looking internet cafe, another big grocery store on the edge of things. There was even an art gallery on the second story above an empty storefront on Main Street. The artist currently on display wasn't very interesting to him, but he still spent two hours in the gallery looking at every piece. They were peddling traditional Americana, and he didn't find any of it particularly inspiring. Probably there was a market for that type of thing. The pieces had prices listed next to them.

On his fourth day in Beacon he decided to go back to see Edna LeBlanc at her shop. He woke up, ate breakfast and drank coffee in his room again before taking a shower and putting his clothes back on. The clothes had become so worn out they weren't going to last much longer. Pants and shirt he could pick up for pretty cheap, probably, but shoes were more difficult, and he'd either end up buying a pair that would just break after a few weeks of constant use and need to be replaced again, or he'd have to buy something better that would wipe out a good chunk of what was left in his account.

This town had started to feel comfortable to him as he'd continued to get to know it during his time walking the streets. It felt smaller and smaller the more he explored it, unlike the city he had come from. That place was built on itself. It had layers going up and down and extending out in all directions. It felt as though it grew bigger the more you got to know it, the more you realized how far the city's ecosystems continued. It was infinite. But here there was an edge. A border you could see from almost anywhere you stood. The valley rising around you was a wall the town couldn't grow any bigger than. And there had been no touch of the demonic invaders here. In a way that, too, seemed to shrink things down a bit.

The little bell on the door tinkled as Wyatt entered LeBlanc's. Edna was there, and she didn't recognize Wyatt at first when he came in. He must've looked completely different before he'd had the chance to clean up a bit. She'd only seen him the once.

"Thank you so much for the room," he said.

"Glad I could be helpful," she said in her stern voice.

"It really, I mean you really can't know how much it meant to have a bed and a shower. And breakfast. Thank you."

She nodded.

"I got my bank account back up, I'll probably catch a train back for the city when the reservation runs up."

"I read your piece," she said, pulling the binder out from beneath the counter and sliding it to him. "I put some notes in there. I hope you don't mind I wrote right on it. I did the old red pen business inside."

"Of course I don't mind! Thank you for looking at it. What did you think?"

"I think it's alright. Feels unpolished. But I get it. I see what you're going for."

"What do you think I should do with it?"

"I don't know. I think it's pretty good, but it's not good enough to be finished. I don't have anything for you other than that. Look, I've been working with the same publisher and had the same agent, the same editor, for 25 years, and they don't have it in them to look at anybody new. I've only ever published novels. I'm not really a part of this world that way. I just don't have anything else for you other than I read it, and I think it's alright. My notes are in there if you want to take a look."

"Yeah, yeah. Of course I'll look at the notes. I really appreciate it!"

"It was fun reading it. Thanks for dropping it off with me," she said. "Honestly it's been a while since I've read anyone's drafts but my own. Like I said the other day when you were here, most people don't know I'm a writer. I try and keep up with what's going on in the lit world, but even though I get printed and sold I'm not really part of it."

"I mean, you're like a modern legend though! It's strange to think of you as being on the outside looking in."

"Probably there's no '*in*' like that. Just rings of windows, everyone's on the outside all looking another level deeper in from where they are. At the center there's just, I dunno, Gertrude Stein's bones or something."

Wyatt nodded. He had spent his entire adult life trying to be better at taking feedback on his work. He'd never had a piece reviewed by a writer that he considered the caliber of Edna LeBlanc, and her opinion felt like gospel to him. This play was something he'd finished and read and revised and polished for months, and he felt like it was really ready, like it was really the thing. But now he knew it wasn't, and thinking back on it as far as he could remember, he hated what was there. He thought of possible structural issues. Pacing problems. Unclear character motivations. Without even looking at a single letter of her red pen, he started thinking about everything that he guessed must be wrong with it. It was daunting at first. He felt a little knot developing at the base of his stomach, but it gave way to some kind of excitement. A new energy. Then he asked "how can you tell if something you wrote is successful?"

"That's the question sometimes isn't it? I try not to let myself wonder about it too much at this point in my life. Basically with each book I've got an idea, or a theme or question I really want to explore. Make the reader think about a certain thing or feel a certain way. I do my best to get the piece to a point where it does that effectively and it's still interesting to read hopefully. And then if the people who read it honestly find something of value in it, that's it. We all want to find a definition for artistic success that doesn't include the artists who we personally think are shit. The disappointing thing is I don't know if there's an answer like that. Hacks sell more books, make TV deals, make more money. I'm sure they have found themselves to be successful. And even shallow, edgy goons have fans who really connect with their work. So who's to say? You do your best, listen to the critics and see if you agree— if there's anything you should do better— and just start working on the next thing as long as you have another in you that's worth working on. Anyway, now that you've got money attached to you again, can I get you anything from the shop?"

Thinking about it all, he looked around. The store had most things. In the back there was a small shelf that had just a few bottles of wine, and his body demanded it. He grabbed one that had a screw off lid instead of a cork. "I'll take this. More to celebrate than I've had in a while."

"Nice outlook," she said as she rang him up.

"Thank you for everything, Edna LeBlanc. I know it's corny as shit, but it's been an honor."

"You're welcome, Wyatt. I'll keep my eyes open for your work. And don't wait 'till your building burns down again to come back for a visit upstate. Interesting stuff going on up here from time to time."

And he left LeBlanc's, tucking the binder into his tote and carefully sliding the bottle in next to it. Eager to take a look at the notes, he settled onto the steps of an abandoned government building and retrieved the binder back into the daylight. She had written quite a bit inside, the margins were filled with red ink, sometimes even scrawled directly on top of his writing. The insights were clear, efficient. He agreed with most of it. Not all of it. Page after page he flipped across the manuscript, reading her notes first and then referring back to his original text. The floor was open for debate, the printed words on the page, her notes and his thoughts. They conversed, battled, compromised. There was in his brain a churning like water being chopped by massive propellers of a cargo ship.

The deeper into the play he got, her notes became more specific and longer. She had figured out what he was trying to do with the piece and had learned his habits. Could really point out what he was doing wrong, what opportunities he was missing, what was a waste of space. At the end were a few sentences, addressed to him. She summed up her thoughts, told him what was missing to really make it work, at least in her mind. And that was it.

There was so much here to do. He had a good idea how to really get the thing where it needed to be. Hopefully. It would probably take another couple passes, but his fingers were itching for it, and he had the energy. There was that internet cafe somewhere. He'd seen it. Just had to remember where it was. One of these streets. Some zigzagging and wrong turns did bring him there, and he went into the place. It was dark and stale inside. Ceiling fans were running, but they were just moving around the same dusty air that had been swirling in and out of computers and customers for years. Wyatt went to the front desk and asked for a day rate. They didn't really do that, the guy said, but if he bought five hours he'd give him the sixth free. They'd be closing around then anyway. That was good enough. He ordered a coffee, mostly for the mug. A computer was assigned, and Wyatt took his seat.

Wyatt pushed the monitor as far back as he could to make room for his binder on the desk in front of him and still have room to type. After logging into the borrowed computer, he opened up the generic word processing program that was installed on the machine. Taking a breath, he started. The notes helped him filter his thoughts. Having had another reader experience it really did show him how it felt to read the thing, what he'd need to do to have it do what he wanted it to do. He knew what he wanted from it, and he thought he'd already been there. But without a reader it would just be a journal. A meditation. He needed to talk to the audience, he wanted someone to listen. It was important that he was saying what he wanted to be saying. It didn't take long to finish his coffee, so he opened up the bottle of wine and poured it into the mug.

From the first page he'd start by transcribing what he'd already had, but as he went he'd change phrasing, eliminate words that he used too much, try to make the different characters sound different when they talked. He lingered on each of the red pen's notes. Grappled with its suggestion. Worked with it, discarded it, returned to it. Every page was a struggle, but the process was exciting and he was focused. The thing was growing before his eyes like a timelapse of a houseplant. It was the same story as the previous draft had been. A story about a small group of weirdos, acquaintances in a desolate wasteland who after being thrust into each other's company are forced to learn to survive. A story about meaninglessness. Trying to find humanity in a hostile world. A story about what if there was a dog-person, like it was a dog but it just acted like a person and it wasn't weird to the other characters.

Half the bottle in, he checked the time and saw he only had about forty minutes left, so he tried to wrap up the sequence he was writing. Just as the place was closing he had the time to save the file, email it to himself and then delete it from the computer he'd been working on. He checked the email from his phone to make sure the file was there. There wasn't anyone else left when Wyatt was signing out. All the other computers had gone dark. Walking by the front desk, Wyatt held up the half-empty bottle by the neck, sloshed the wine around and said, "See you tomorrow," before leaving. It was dark outside.

On the way back to his hotel he passed the punks he had met on his first day in Beacon. They were in a similar position circled around a street lamp with their dogs, drinking and smoking. They called out to him as he passed by.

"Hey you're that book guy, right?"

"Hell yeah," he said.

"Did you find that person you were looking for?"

"I did, she runs that place."

"Nice, good. You hanging out somewhere tonight?"

"Nah, probably not. I'm working on something I have to finish up tomorrow."

"Oh, what is it?"

"It's this play I wrote, but I'm rewriting it now."

"Woah, the *theatre*," one said with an affected English accent, miming a cup of tea.

"So you're a writer, too?" another said.

"Yeah, sort of. I'm writing now. We'll see where it goes."

"Hang out for a minute!"

He relented. "I sort of owe you a drink already, but all I have is this half bottle of wine. I was really planning on finishing it while I worked."

"They got cheap beer over there," a punk pointed at a vending machine across the street. "You get three for the price of two if you elbow the thing just right. I'll show you."

They crossed the street together, and Wyatt scanned his new card. The punk pushed some buttons and as the transaction was processed bumped the machine so three tall cans of beer dropped out. They were the same very generic looking brand as he'd seen them drinking the other day.

"Thanks, brother," the punk said. "You wanna smoke?" holding out a cigarette.

"Yes, please."

They joined the circle across the street. Even though they were in the middle of town, it was completely still and almost overwhelmingly quiet. There were a few people out and about, a bar was open several blocks away, but the streets were empty and the air was still. It was a beautiful night to be outside with a little group of punks.

"Y'all live nearby?" Wyatt asked.

"Right here," one of them gestured to the next building. The street lamp in front of their building was burned out, so they were sitting next door.

"You're up from the city or something?"

"Yeah, that's right."

He told the story. Even though he'd already had to explain it a few times he still sort of got a minor thrill out of it. It was a crazy thing, and there was some pleasure in relaying the tragedy of it. Especially now that he knew Talbot was still alive.

"What's the scene like around here?" he asked.

One of them gestured around at the group. "You're pretty much looking at it, man! Some people come through, but they don't stay too long. A lot of old timers in the houses. Tons of old hippies who got fancy when they retired."

"You dig it here?" Wyatt asked.

"It's alright. Not too expensive. The hiking whips."

"I saw a record shop while I was walking around the last couple days. Is it pretty good?"

Another punk chimed in, "I work down there! Randy is the guy who runs it. He's a good dude. He was my babysitter before he transitioned, got me into punk by accident back when I was a little kid. It's a cool spot. Randy does his best to keep good things in there and a bunch of like dad records for the tourists or bankers who come up for vacation and shit like that."

"Any of you play in bands or anything?"

"Not right now. There was only one drummer in town, and he hitched a ride out west last year and stayed out there."

"I get that. I've got buddies out in those mountains, there's something to them," Wyatt nodded.

"This is pretty much it most of the time. Gwyn and I work at one of the coffee co-ops in the valley. It's just sort of hang out, work, get shows together when it's possible. We try to activate some mutual aid if we can and it's needed, but otherwise I guess we're just watching the water circle the drain. Same as everyone else."

"Pete used to do video stuff," one of the punks pointed at whoever was apparently Pete.

"Oh, really?"

Pete seemed reluctant to talk about it, "Yeah, I used to be into film. I wanted to make movies and stuff."

"Woah, that rules. Why not anymore?"

"I was working on a project, and the camera broke. That was pretty much it. There's just not enough cameras anymore, I don't think they've made new ones in like seven years at least."

"Nah, I know!" Wyatt said. "One of my buddies back in the city found like a little point and shoot photo camera. Must be ancient. She's working on a display with pictures of the demons."

The punks responded with a chorus of "holy shit!" and "that fucking rules!" and things like that.

"You should come check it out. I think she's just about ready with a venue. Should be any day now or something. Pete, you can talk to her about camera gear. She's gotten sorta into that world."

"So the demons are real?"

"Yeah, yes they are."

"Did you see any down there?"

"I did. Lena and I went to the beach and saw them the first day they showed up. It was fucking wild. You really haven't seen anything of them at all up here?"

"No sign of them around here. Not yet."

"What did you see?" Pete asked.

Wyatt tried to summarize what he'd experienced, but it must have made no sense even as he said it. He couldn't figure out a way to explain it with any clarity. In the middle of describing one thing about them, or some thing he'd seen or heard about, he'd remember some other thing about the demons and the riddle of their activity. Each tangent spiraled into another. They stared at him as they listened, each with differing mixtures of fascination and fear.

"I do kind of want to see your friend's exhibit," Pete said after. "When are you going back down?"

"I have one more night in the hotel after tonight. So tomorrow will be my last day in Beacon, and then the next morning I'll figure out how to get down there. I don't know if I can navigate hopping a train without guides like I did on the way up, but I wasn't looking forward to buying a train ticket. Must be expensive as hell from here."

"Yeah, the train is pricey if you just buy a single ticket. Cheapest way is to hitchhike," said one of the still nameless punks.

"Look, if you can split gas I'll borrow my brother's car and take you down," Pete offered. "Anyone else wanna do a trip into the city?"

Plans were made, and beers were finished. Wyatt had a ride back home. Or back to the city as it were, home or otherwise, he'd just have to go from there. The night was crisp and clear, and he walked back to the hotel.

The next morning, Wyatt barely woke up in time for the free breakfast and he skipped the morning coffee in his room knowing he'd need to order coffee again in the internet cafe. With half a bottle of wine waiting in his tote, Wyatt got his coffee and a computer for the day and sat down to continue his work.

After first opening the document, Wyatt stared at it for some time before he put his hands near the keyboard. It took several attempts before the approach stuck, retreating from the keys multiple times until being able to type. He'd type out a few words or spend some time reformatting something or reviewing yesterday's work before again taking a break to sip some coffee and stare at the screen or look around the cafe.

He was only a page and half further along when he was already out of coffee, but at that point the gears had warmed up and things were progressing smoothly. People around him came and went, quickly taking care of their business or printing or whatever they needed to do and didn't have access to elsewhere. It started to loudly rain outside. Water accumulated in the streets and loosened the trash so that it floated around in the current. The rain blocked out the rest of the world; it gave him something to retreat into when he was losing momentum but helped him return to writing refocused.

Line upon line and page upon page, the work took shape in his hands. Some sections were carried over from the old page with minor tweaks, but huge swaths of text were completely retooled and rewritten. The wine bottle emptied as the document grew. Wyatt had been in the internet cafe for five hours when he typed the final stage direction and hit the period key on the keyboard to finish it. He'd need to proofread it at least one more time, and wanted to have it reviewed again. But the draft was done. It was close. Close to final.

There was a little bit of wine still when he had finished writing, so he drank it straight from the bottle. He again saved the document and emailed it to himself, cleared everything off of the computer and signed out. The guy at the front desk processed his payment, and with a deep breath Wyatt clutched his tote tightly to his chest and ran out into the rain, trying his best to keep it dry. He ducked strategically under every awning or roof he could find along the way to the hotel but was still mostly drenched by the time he got there.

The rain continued, and the temperature dropped dramatically that night. Ice formed around the edges of things. He was glad to have a room with a ceiling and bed to sleep in. It had not been this cold in his time sleeping outside in the city. In that way he'd been very lucky. This was his last night in the hotel. The next morning he texted Talbot and Lena to let them know he was going to be back in the city. To Lena, he asked where her show was going to be and when it started. He also told her he'd need a place to stay that night, if possible.

He met up with Pete and the two others who'd planned to make the trip down. They got into a Toyota Camry that was probably a little over 10 years old and in the type of shape as you'd expect from a car that had been driven for 10 years on roads that were only maintained by hobbyists. It was a two or three hour drive and more or less a straight shot once they got on the highway. Pete drove. Wyatt wondered what it would be like to have access to a car and the knowledge of how to drive it. A foreign idea to him.

Like the subway, the highways in this part of the world were run by a ruthless private business. The company was called "The Highway Company." They charged admission for access and in return provided the bare minimum in terms of comfort and charm but a maximum emphasis on security. There were police every few miles, cement walls along the sides that were often topped with barbed wire to prevent intruders like freeloaders or thieves. Literal highwaymen. The average patron of these highways tended not to be particularly wealthy, so it wasn't usually worth the risk of stealing from them. The actually wealthy flew everywhere. Every once in a while some lunatic gang who had gotten a hold of old military gear from somewhere would make a go of it, but that was rare since the police would respond brutally.

They listened to a Waylon Jennings cassette as they drove. Along the way, they stopped twice for gas at the Highway Company's rest stops. Wyatt paid once. He'd never paid for gas before. He didn't know that it was much more expensive on the highway than it was at other gas stations. Splitting the gas for the trip was still much cheaper than a train ticket would have been. The punks were pleasant company, but keeping up conversation with strangers was tiring as was the activity of just sitting in a car cruising on a highway. Often, Wyatt would need to zone out and recharge.

After an hour and half the city started to come into view in the distance, and the shog started getting thicker in the air. The traffic got thicker, too. As they got closer it was bumper to bumper, stop and go, the rest of the way to the bridge. Through the boredom of the traffic there was a palpable excitement in the car. Moving against the foggy skyline was the lumbering shadow of a Great Demon, walking across the East River. Wyatt had made it back.

CHAPTER 17

IT HAD ONLY BEEN about a week since Wyatt had left the city but things felt very different upon his return. Perhaps it was the time spent in a land yet untouched, but the Demons' changes seemed stark to his refreshed eyes. The punks dropped him off, and he sent a text to Lena to let her know he was back in town. They disappeared to link up with whomever it was they knew. He told them the name of Lena's venue, and he never saw or heard from them again. Alone again, he had nothing to do but wait for Lena to respond and hopefully meet up with him. He wandered to a neighborhood where he thought she might be and started to cycle through some of her regular spots. He spent the afternoon peeking in the cloudy windows of cafes, hungry but still with no money for food and with no promise of income.

When Lena's response arrived to his phone, he had sat down on a bench in what had once been a park but was now a rusted pile of shopping carts just surrounded by benches. He'd been sitting there and lost track of time. Lena said she was with Qat and suggested they all meet for a coffee or something, and Wyatt agreed. He had guessed the wrong neighborhood in his wandering. They were up in the Tip. He checked on his phone to see it would be about an hour walk. Usually he'd take the bus—there was a pretty direct route—but this time a walk would do. It was manageable.

The shoes on his feet were now so worn after relentless walking that there was almost nothing between his feet and the ground. They wouldn't last much longer like this. What did people do? He thought about the Triangle Silhouette, the bookstore. He couldn't even think of the last time he'd been in there, but he remembered suggesting to a homeless person at the window of Lil ol' Betsy's that he could look there for help with shoes. Now he was that guy. Had they helped that other person those months ago? Hopefully they had. Hopefully they could help him now.

They met at a coffee shop called The Acorn. It was a trendy looking place, exquisitely cozy inside, leaning heavily into the forest motif implied by the name— complete with fake trees built into the walls and around the support posts throughout the space. Lena and Qat were already inside when he got there, and seeing them flooded his chest with an unimaginable warmth and comfort. He hadn't seen anybody he knew since the night of the fire, other than Paulie firing him. He had been so lonely that his soul had hardened to it. It was so pleasant to see them, and his knees almost gave out from the surprise of something pleasant as he pulled the door open to enter the shop. Qat saw him first but didn't seem to know him as he approached. Seeing the confused look on their face, Lena turned to see what they were looking at.

"Wyatt, looking shaggy, my man," Lena said.

His hair, usually tightly cropped and edged, had grown unkempt and frizzy in the period since the assault. His curly beard had grown wide and wild looking. "Yeah, I am. It's been a shaggy time." He knew he was going to have to again explain what happened, and he had grown exhausted of the conversation now.

"You look so different," Qat said. "I didn't mean to be rude. I just really didn't even recognize you."

"It's ok, I haven't seen anyone in a while, so I honestly sort of forgot that I would look different."

"What have you been up to? What's going on?" Lena asked.

"Well," here goes. "A little while ago. I don't remember. Since I saw you last, I guess. I was hanging out with Talbot. We were at the record store he likes in King City in that big old building. And on the way out we got jumped by some cops. Something with a package for Paulie at Lil ol' Betsy's. They kicked the shit out of both of us. I got knocked unconscious, and they left me on the sidewalk. Talbot's been in the hospital. I haven't seen him again yet."

"Holy shit! Are you fucking ok?" Qat was furious.

"I dunno, it's hard to tell. I mean, I am. I'm alive. Still moving and all that."

"Fuck."

"Yeah. Then that night, after I came back to, my phone and wallet were gone. I went back home, and, well, someone had burned down my building. Someone who lived there. Went nuts and set it on fire."

"Wait, are you kidding?" Lena knew he wasn't but it still didn't make sense to her.

"Mm mm," Wyatt shook his head.

"Where've you been staying?" she asked.

He shrugged and sort of gestured to the air around him. "Just, around. Wherever I can find. Spent a night with a vagrant federation, then I went over to the main part of the city to try and find a bank. That took like a few weeks and I spent a while just in a playground to stay out of the rain. Then I caught a train up to the Valley. I met Edna LeBlanc."

This was all a lot. "Edna LeBlanc? You met her? How? Wait, hold on. Why didn't you come find me or something?" Lena was working hard to process this.

"You were out of town, and I didn't have a phone. I didn't have access to my bank. I didn't have anything I could do."

They sat there for a little while.

"Do you want a coffee?" Qat asked. "Let me get you something. Or like a bite?"

"I mean, yeah all of that would be great. Just a coffee and anything to eat."

Qat went to the counter to order.

"Ok, so," Lena was gesturing wildly with her hands, "tell me about Edna LeBlanc. How did that happen?"

"The only stuff I had was just what I had with me and what didn't get stolen while I was knocked out. So I had my tote bag with a notebook and my copy of *Old Fury*. When I finished reading it, I saw that she lived in Beacon and I was like 'hey the train goes right up there,' so I found some gutter punks who could help me hop a train, and we went up. She runs a general store. I just went in and talked to her."

Qat came back with coffee in a mug and a dry scone on a plate. He took a bite of the very stale baked good, and it was delicious. He thanked Qat profusely.

"She read my play. Oh shit, I forgot! I met Wolf Wolf, too!"

"What?" Qat was shocked. "Nobody has seen her for months."

"I got that impression, yeah. She works at a cafe over in the city. She had the copy of my play that I sent up for Toby to read. She gave it back to me, and I gave it to Edna LeBlanc to read."

He pulled the binder out and put it on the table. Lena picked it up and looked at the notes inside. "Edna LeBlanc reviewed your piece? This is her feedback?"

"Yeah. She put me up in a hotel for a few days while I was in the valley."

"Makes me want to burn my house down almost," Lena joked.

"Vanessa read it too. She suggested it as a closet drama instead of trying to actually get it performed."

"Who?"

"Wolf Wolf. She doesn't go by that anymore. She's just Vanessa."

"Interesting," Qat said. They seemed disappointed.

"That's funny, the whole point of this project was so you could see your words in a live space for an audience. And now it's back to being trapped on a page."

"I know, I've been coming to terms with that. But I think I agree that it's what the thing needs. Maybe I can write something else to perform after I'm done with this. How about you both, what's been going on here?"

Qat answered first. "I've just been up to more of the same as last time I saw you. Back and forth to work and then as much as possible out to shows and stuff. There's been a few fun things."

"How did your screen gathering safari go, Lena?"

"It was good. Took a long time. I was out of the city for three weeks. Getting them together was one thing, and then figuring out how to bring them all back safely was another. That was hard. But it's done! I've got a venue lined up. The TVs are in the basement over there and we'll start setting up in a few days. Opening is November 21."

"Yo, congrats! That rules, Lena. I'll be there, obviously!"

They sat and talked for a little while. It was refreshing and tiring at the same time. It required social muscles for Wyatt that had atrophied.

"So that's why you were looking for a space to stay tonight," Lena realized.

"Yeah that's the story."

"Yeah, come to me. The apartment is crowded right now. We've actually already got a few extra bodies at the moment, but we'll figure something out! I'll set up something on the floor of my bedroom. It'll be like a slumber party."

Lena called for a car to keep things simple. She lived in a three bedroom apartment with eight other people already there. It was a bit of a rotating door. Wyatt only ever knew one or two of her roommates at a time. There was only one who'd been there the whole time Lena had lived there. A guy named Rich who worked as an administrative assistant and seemed to have no further aspirations. He was a nice guy. Big comic book reader. Sometimes Wyatt would talk to him about that.

In her bedroom while Lena was fashioning a bed from blankets and pillows, Wyatt saw the ceramic tiles he'd left there the day the Demons arrived. He'd completely forgotten about them. They had become part of the general population of the room.

"Those dumb tiles!" he said. "I'm so sorry I left them here. What a pain."

She turned to look. "Oh, right! Don't worry about it. I actually used them to test some stuff with the camera a few times. Did a little home studio photoshoot. If you don't mind I can just hold on to them until you're back on your feet. Unless you want to hock them or something."

"Hold onto them for now. We'll see. I'd be interested in seeing those pictures sometime."

They hung out and drank, listening to music and talking about their projects. He talked about the work he'd been doing on the play since getting Edna LeBlanc's notes. He wanted to do one more round of revisions himself and then have it reviewed by some other people, and he offered to let Lena read it at that point. She was interested. Without realizing it he fell asleep. Lena would probably let him stay here as long as he wanted, but he knew it would be difficult for her and he was too paranoid to impose on her in that way. He'd need to find something else.

The next morning he texted Talbot and found out he was at work, but they made plans to meet after. He left Lena's apartment and started to walk to the bookstore, the Triangle Silhouette. He would need to look for a job, also. It had been a long time that he'd just been working at Lil ol' Betsy's, and he found that job because he knew a musician who worked there. Griffin. A squirrelly little guy, but a dynamite hardcore drummer. He had gotten hit by a bus and killed three or four years ago. So, all that's to say Wyatt didn't really know where to start when looking for a job.

Wyatt didn't recognize anybody in the bookshop when he got there. He asked if Marcy was there. They said she was in the back, and someone went and got her. Marcy also didn't remember him when she appeared. She had long red hair, was tall and heavy set, her pale skin covered in freckles.

"Can I help you?"

"Hey, Marcy, I'm Wyatt. Sorry, we met at a few Lenin and Engels readings here a while back."

"Oh, Wyatt, sure! I think I remember that. Were you a writer or something?"

"Sure. I mean, yes, but I guess who isn't, you know?"

"Well, the people who aren't writing aren't writers. Is there anything I can help you with?"

"Ok, so. My building burned down a while ago. I was just looking for a favor, I was wondering if you had any shoes. I have a little money. Not much, but I've been wearing these shoes for a month straight and they weren't new then. It's been a lot of walking."

"Haha, are you the one who sent that other guy? Li?"

"I am. I used to work over at a bodega around the neighborhood."

"I was wondering about it when he came in. Let me go take a look. We've got the mutual aid Free Store stuff. There might be something in there."

She asked for his size and retreated again to the back of the store. Wyatt started browsing the shelves. There was a section for local and independent press. Some things looked interesting, a lot of it looked bad.

She came back with some dusty looking sneakers. They were used, but in much better shape than his current shoes. She offered them to him to try on, and they fit pretty well. They felt unbelievable. His feet sighed with relief.

"So, what else? Other than wearing out your old shoes, what have you been up to?" she asked. "Are you still a writer, i.e. have you been writing?"

"Actually I have. I'm pretty close to having a draft of something I'm looking to publish."

He explained it to her, and she seemed into it. She told him to bring it around, and if he ever had the thing printed and in hand, they'd stock it. With his new shoes Wyatt set back out into the world to find a place to sit in the neighborhood where Talbot worked now until they were able to meet up.

Talbot worked in an area called the Bridge District. It was connected to the last functioning bridge across to the city as well as the Broken Bridge. Towering skyscrapers clustered around the busy streets, the tallest buildings on this side of the river. There was a huge train station, a big sports arena, clusters of offices and luxury apartments only for the last remaining wealthy. Most of the apartments were empty, simply value held as real estate. Wyatt never came here. He did not know his way around. During the day it was bustling and chaotic. Every day around 7 p.m. when the office workers had left for the day the neighborhood emptied out almost completely. Streets became barren, aside from street dogs and vagrants who'd shuffle through and pick up the scraps left behind during the day. There were no commercial businesses. Restaurants closed after lunch. No bars. Wyatt never understood the point of the place. Even now, arriving in the peak of the afternoon as it was alive with activity, it felt so useless. There were deliveries being picked up and dropped off, power lunches and business meetings over coffee, deals being made. It felt like everyone was intent on being busy just for its own sake. Everything around him was moving like it was in fast forward. There were a number of corporate, manicured areas resembling parks. They had seating areas, running water, maintained greenery and boasted a brutalist aesthetic that shouted, "We're serious here, and we demand you behave seriously as well." Wyatt found one that was just populated enough that he could slip in unnoticed, and he sat down at a table with his notebook and started to jot down things for a new project. He sat there long enough to become completely invisible.

Things in the neighborhood became particularly chaotic on the hour each hour throughout the afternoon as different shifts ended and people frantically escaped to home. Around six during one such swarming exodus, Talbot showed up, limping and smiling.

"Wow," Talbot said, "look who's back from the dead."

"Same for you, huh?"

"I was worried when I didn't hear back from you. Last I saw you were basically just a smear on the pavement, and I was getting carted into an ambulance."

"How long were you in the hospital?"

"A few weeks. I was in pretty rough shape. Busted ankle and shoulder, broken ribs."

"This isn't where you worked before, is it?"

"No. I lost the old job while I was in the hospital. Out of the office for too long. It didn't take too long to find this one, it is less money though. Been here a couple weeks."

"That's a drag, damn."

Talbot shrugged.

"Lost my job, too."

"Really? Same kinda thing?"

"No. It was just because of whatever happened with that package. Paulie wanted me out of there. He was acting like he was doing me a favor by firing me."

"Shit."

They kept chatting, and Wyatt talked about what had been going on and how he ended up in Beacon. Talbot had been in the hospital most of that time. He had been much more seriously injured. It started to rain, so Talbot brought Wyatt back to his apartment in a neighborhood called the Bush. He offered him a place there until Wyatt figured something else out. Luckily, Talbot hadn't been down and out long enough to lose his apartment. Everything was just the way it had been the day they met up at the record shop.

The next day, Talbot went back to work, and Wyatt stayed in his apartment. He used Talbot's computer to review, proof and edit his manuscript again. It took most of the day with lots of time spent scrolling his phone or pacing the small landscape of the apartment or leafing through Talbot's records or looking out the window. He finished and read it to himself one more time before emailing it to Lena, Qat and Kalman for review. Not long after, a response came in from Kalman commenting that it had been a while, and he was excited to read the thing.

Talbot gave him a spare key, and for the next few days he slept on the couch in Talbot's apartment. When Talbot would go to work, Wyatt would sometimes stay in and read, and when he could gather the will for it he'd venture out into hostile feeling streets. There wasn't much to do out there, so inevitably he'd just head back to the apartment after a few hours. He was looking for "Now Hiring" signs in windows, but he didn't find any. This is how things went for a few weeks. At some point an email came back from Kalman that said he'd passed the play along to someone he knew at an indie publisher. They'd looked at it and had some notes, but they were interested in it. Initial excitement faded to skepticism when he didn't ever hear from them.

On one of these wandering days, out of nowhere, Marina texted him and said she had borrowed a copy of the Coen brothers' *A Serious Man*, and she wanted to return it. He didn't remember lending that to her, but he did remember that he had owned it. Must have been years ago that he gave it to her. They made plans to meet up, she told him to meet her down at Corn Beach, the beach where the demons had first arrived. It was very far away from Talbot's neighborhood, and it was going to be a pain to get there. He found an abandoned bike and rode down, as he had that first day. It took about an hour and a half. When he arrived he found that she was already there waiting for him, sitting on a bench on the boardwalk.

The music of the demons had grown loud in the months since they'd arrived. They were still here, coming in and out of the gate. The beach felt completely different. The air felt different. Since that day Wyatt had first been here, the demons had removed most of the garbage. The sand was now totally flat and smooth. It was a greyish-purple now. What was that color? Mauve? Along the shore were huge towers of the demons' construction, stretching up into the sky higher than any human structures. The towers' shapes were irregular, in a way similar to the demons' antlers. Still, it was the same place. Changed as it was, it felt the same as it ever had. Just a mostly empty beach, framed by the looming carcass of the abandoned amusement park. He waved to Marina as he approached. She acknowledged him only by returning his gaze.

"Hey, how've you been?" he asked.

"I've been alright. Just tired I guess."

"Have you done any more painting since I talked to you?"

"Nothing new. You don't work at the shop anymore?" she said, a statement more than a question.

"No, Paulie fired me because of the thing with that package."

"He did? I think they found it."

"Are the cops still mad about it?"

"I can't tell. It seems weird still. Paulie has been on edge since that thing."

"Do you know what it was?"

She shrugged.

She handed him the movie. He took it and put it in his bag—another possession to add to his short list.

They sat there for a little while.

"I'm not gonna work there anymore either."

"Did you get a new gig?" he asked, excited.

"No, I'm just gonna leave."

"Oh. Alright, cool. I get that. Get out for a recharge. I was just upstate for a little while. It seemed nice up there."

"Mhmm."

She seemed distant. Fixated somewhere else.

"I just wanted to make sure you had the thing back. I've been trying to make sure there wasn't anything left in my apartment that wasn't mine. This was the last thing I think."

"Yeah, ok. Cool. Did you ever watch it?"

"I did. It's good."

"It is."

Again, the two sat. Then Marina stood up and said, "Ok, well. I'm gonna go."

"Alright!" Wyatt was trying hard to be cool and friendly. To lighten the mood. "It was good to see you. Lemme know if you're ever back in the city."

"Sure," she said, knowing she would not be.

She reached down and took hold of what had appeared to Wyatt as a part of the anonymous population of garbage but turned out to be a kayak. It seemed like she had brought it here with her. Marina labored to drag the kayak across the unnaturally smooth beach and climbed in when she reached the water. Wyatt watched in confusion. As she started to paddle, he got up from the bench and hurried to the shore. He called out to her but she did not respond or change course. She continued to paddle out into the water, south, away from the city.

The line she followed was straight and decisive. His brain knew where the line pointed, but it refused to understand. It took a long time, maybe an hour, but he stood watching while her figure got smaller and smaller. Out of helplessness he would sometimes shout to her again, even after she was much too far to hear him and even as he knew she was not listening. There were no demons around, but the gate remained an alluring, swirling maw. As Marina drew nearer she was tiny in contrast to the immense shape of the thing. Still, Wyatt stared, squinting to watch, holding his breath until his chest burned. The little boat pushed further out into the water and did not slow down as it reached the demons' portal. She steered the kayak directly towards it, and he watched as Marina disappeared into the gate and was gone from sight.

There was no visible indication that she had entered it. Its color or shape did not change in any way. She was just gone. As his body demanded he breath again, his heart started to race and he stumbled, feeling light headed, gasping for air. He would look out across the water at the gate and then, too overwhelmed to see it, look back at the sand between his feet again. He crouched, staring at the ground for some time, trying to catch his breath. It was a drawn, heavy moment until he was able to move again to find the bike and find his way back to Talbot's apartment. He fell immediately asleep on the couch and didn't wake up until Talbot had already left for work again the next morning.

With the bike waiting outside where he had left it, Wyatt decided that he wanted to visit his old neighborhood for the first time since the night of the fire. In no hurry he weaved across neighborhoods to get there, passing through Stone Slope, Sludgetown and past Greenwood Forest. Sunset Morning was largely unchanged. Things had more or less continued on without him as they had been. On a utility pole he saw his old neighbor Brent's name on a poster. Wyatt checked the date on it: he had a show coming up. Turned out he had survived the fire, and he was back out there and still on that grind. "Son of a bitch, good for him," Wyatt said to himself. He hadn't heard of the venue or any of the other bands on the bill.

The block where his building had been was already cleaned and fenced off, and new construction was getting ready to begin. There was no one around and Wyatt saw no value in standing around looking at the empty space where his home used to be. He biked around a bit more, doing a tour of his old places. Passing The Diner he saw that elusive sign he'd already given up hope finding in the wild: the help wanted sign. The stark red and white. Runic in its simplicity.

He went in to inquire and learned that one of their line cooks was leaving to join a collective somewhere outside Albuquerque in a week. A manager sat down with him at a booth and poured him a coffee. She was a broad, gruff white woman. Probably had worked in kitchens for decades. She had an old-fashioned quality to the way she ran the restaurant that hinted to the fact that she'd probably started in this business before the collapse of the old rules and regulations. They drank coffee, and she asked him questions. He talked about what he had done for work at Lil ol' Betsy's and did his best to explain why he had been fired. She seemed satisfied. There was apparently one other person she'd talked to, so she was going to discuss things with the other owner and then let him know what decision was to be made. He left his number and rode back to Talbot's neighborhood. The next day they said "welcome aboard" and told him when his first day would be. Talbot was excited to hear the news. They sort of celebrated that evening by turning up the volume on some records and drinking the fancier beer Talbot sometimes got.

When Lena's exhibit opened he met up with Qat to go. Qat was eager to talk about his play when they met up. They had read it quickly. Mostly they thought it worked but wanted to talk about Wyatt's intentions with the piece to make sure it was doing what he wanted. It seemed like Qat had picked up on most of what he was trying to bake into the text. They could tell what it was thinking about. They had some feedback that made sense to help him really get it there.

"So what's your goal for it now?" they asked.

"I'm still figuring that out. I definitely think I want it published. I want people to be able to hold it and know that it exists. I think that's really the goal."

"What if people don't like it? Or don't get it or whatever."

"Yeah. I mean, I've been thinking about that. I want people to think it's good. I want the people who *I want* to like it to read it and to like it, you know? But ultimately if I feel like I've got it where I want it that's all I can do I think. If it's out there, people can read it, they can engage with it, it's theirs now."

"Until the demons kill us all."

"Until then at least, yeah."

The venue was in a recently revitalized industrial area on the east side of King City. Another neighborhood that had once been warehouses and factories, which closed and gave way to artists' lofts, which gave way to corporate salad chains and apartments, which withered up and left the buildings empty again. Before long they had started to become industry once more. Shipping holdovers, urban farms, offices. Nestled onto a blank street in this area was the venue. It wasn't an art gallery or a music venue. It was just some place that hosted events. Wedding receptions, office parties. It was big and blank. Perfect for Lena to work with.

Lena had transformed the space to exactly create the experience she desired. There were no overhead lights, only light filling in the floor so that people could absent-mindedly wander without needing to worry about where to step. All distractions were expertly removed. Most of the light in the space came from the screens themselves. Screens of different sizes placed throughout the venue in a way that naturally drew a viewer through. There were galleries of small laptop screens with photos, large television screens, and in the back a projector's images illuminated the darkest corner of the room.

Upon first stepping into the gallery Wyatt was completely captivated just by the entirety of it. The light, the color, the movement and the darkness were from any perspective a work of art just as Wyatt stood looking into the gallery. There was a crowd but it wasn't crowded. He looked to Qat who was already starting to move to the closest screen. He followed loosely in their wake but the two drifted apart and back together over and over as they experienced the gallery. The first display was an imposing television— a narrow pool of light on the ground indicated a spot for viewers to gravitate towards, and when Wyatt stood in it the screen took up almost his entire view. The screen showed large, vibrant photos of the beach, the demons and the gate that Marina had disappeared into.

Laid out before Wyatt was a record of the chaos that followed the arrival of the Demons into the world. Early in the exhibit, the majority of the media depicted focused on the Demons themselves. The different kinds. Their sizes and shapes. The peculiar way they moved. He looked at the lumbering figure of the Great Demons that towered over the landscape. Lena had gotten evocative footage from the ground that showed the scope of their figures and had found vantage points level with and from above the beasts to force the viewer to truly study them. A station contained headphones with her makeshift field recordings of the music that emitted from their bodies. The demons were maddening, and these images, in their attempt to capture them, made them even more baffling.

Further into the exhibit Lena focused on the changes the demons had been making to the city. She had video footage of the various tasks they'd been working on: the strange objects they carried, the holes they'd dug, the buildings they'd changed or removed, the wildlife they'd altered. Somehow, miraculously, she had captured an image of a skyline before it had been changed and gotten a picture after two large buildings had been completely removed and another turned into some kind of immense, crystalline spiral. The before and after from the same angle, the same time of day, the only difference in the photo being that which the demons had produced. There were things he'd heard rumors about but not seen, and many were here on display.

The next screens Wyatt moved to showed the demons framed within the landscape of the city itself. Photos of Minor Demons climbing up buildings, sitting atop them, or lurking in alleys in who knows what neighborhood. One small screen showed the picture Lena had taken of Wyatt with demons behind him at the beach that first day. He was proud to have made a little cameo. In the photos, one saw the demons as less unfathomable but mundane new residents of the city. A new community of immigrants as so many before them. What new world they were looking for was a mystery, but here they were. They were shaping the city to their designs. These images placed the demons and city in the same space, joining them together as parts of the same thing.

In these pictures were pedestrians, cars and buses simply continuing their ways. One screen showed a video of a Great Demon walking through dense traffic on a busy street in the main city and walking through a stream of cars simply parting around the beast's feet as it moved. The video repeated on a hypnotic loop. There was a video of a demon doing carving a hole in a building and the crowded sidewalk ignoring it on their way.

Then there was a screen that depicted people not ignoring the demons, not going on about their day. Lena had edited together a series of videos of people reacting to the demons' business. Normal looking people losing their minds, screaming, weeping. The clips became short, more manic, as the montage progressed until finally a long, steady wide shot of a person, their figure tiny in the frame, jumping from an eighth story window and plummeting to the street. Lena mercifully kept the camera lingering on the open window instead of leering at the splattered body. How she managed to get the footage was a mystery.

On the furthest wall was the projector making Lena's final statement. She had deliberately kept herself anonymous in the gallery itself, never appearing in any way in the displays. But her vision and voice was inextricable from the curation. And so this final display stood as her conclusion on the subject. Her thesis. Wyatt stepped into the light and faced the illuminated screen, the projector above his head with its fan whirring. It showed simply a view of the demon's gate from the beach. This was where it all started but probably not where most people saw them first. Most people in this city probably just saw them in their neighborhood, or from a window at work, as the demons started to move further out into the world. The video was a very long loop. Wyatt stood watching it, unable to tell when it ended, and it looped back to the beginning. The composition of the frame was painstaking and deliberate. On the screen he watched the portal swirling for several minutes, nothing else in view but some litter tossed by the wind. Then a few demons came into view. One walked by, another out onto the water and into the portal. Again, there was nothing. From above came the legs of a great demon, crossing from behind and then disappearing from view. As the camera lingered he watched the gate. Then he began to watch the waves, regular and irregular as they had ever been. The comforting sound of the waves, crashing at random intervals. A beach, an ocean, the demons and their gate. He closed his eyes and listened. He could still see the light from the projector through his eyelids.

When Wyatt turned around to migrate back to the front door, he saw that the gallery was quite full. He didn't see Qat around right away, but they must be around. He also couldn't find Lena. Probably she was hiding in the back somewhere or in the front smoking a cigarette and trying not to be too noticed. She didn't like to interact with people in these settings. He wanted a cigarette but didn't have any. Heading back to the outside door, he saw faces he recognized but did not know and many he didn't recognize at all. Outside were small groups smoking, drinking and talking. Lena and Qat were in one of them, and he joined the circle. They weren't talking about the gallery, and he joined in the conversation when he had something to say. Somebody offered him a cigarette, and he gratefully took it. After talking for a while he went back to Talbot's apartment to sleep.

In order to be ready for work, Wyatt decided he needed at least one new pair of pants and a couple new shirts. Talbot had let him borrow some clothes, but he needed something else. One day he went to a second hand shop to pick up some things. The clothes were sorted by color, rather than by size, so the store looked kind of nice when you viewed it from a distance but finding something that fit was unnecessarily difficult. With a pair of black jeans and a couple shirts slung over his arm, he browsed through the rest of the store. In the housewares section he found a painting that looked like one of Marina's. Looking closer, he did indeed find her sloppy initials at the bottom. It was from the gallery that had been in Sludgetown. A little orange sticker applied directly to the canvas said $6. He bought it, too.

A few days later Wyatt had his first day at the Diner. There were a lot of new recipes to learn, and it was overwhelming. The kitchen was way bigger than anything he'd ever worked in, and he'd only ever worked alone in a shop. But the staff seemed like good people. There was another writer, a couple anarchists who ran an info shop in the back of a bodega somewhere, a comedian, and then some folks who just worked there. At the end of his first shift he was completely exhausted, but after a few more he got into the rhythm of the place and started to find the pleasure in being back at it. He started to figure out ways to do the thing well, to find the best ways to be a line cook, and it was rewarding to feel like he was getting better at a new thing.

Riding in to work one day, a message came in from the indie publisher that Kalman had sent the manuscript to. They thought it seemed worth their time but felt it needed work. They'd sent some notes back to look at. The document was big and marked up, and it was overwhelming to look at on his phone so he had to put it down for now and just get through work for the day. After thanking them for looking at it, working through the notes took the better part of a week. He didn't hear back from them again for a while.

Living with Talbot was good. Wyatt was constantly paranoid that he was a burden, but it seemed like it was good for Talbot to have him around too. In the quiet moments Wyatt could tell that he hadn't recovered from the trauma of that night in King City. He needed someone around. Talbot didn't like his new job. It seemed like a shitty and stressful office. Now that Wyatt was working too, he contributed to rent a bit and bought food sometimes. If Wyatt wasn't working a dinner shift they'd listen to records and get drunk.

After going back and forth with several new versions and changes, they arrived at a manuscript the publisher and Wyatt were both satisfied with. Months later he had a box of printed copies arrive at Talbot's apartment. The cover was a photo Lena had taken of the tiles that had nearly fallen on him. He leafed through it. It looked good. It felt good in his hand. Talbot was excited and said congratulations and poured some whiskey.

He dropped off a paper bag with six copies of the book at the Triangle Silhouette, telling them Marcy had indicated to bring it in. She wasn't there, so he left his name and number on a slip of paper in the bag and they took it to the back. With Kalman's help he brought some into the bookstore in Stone Slope they had gone to together. She paid him for the books up front. The publisher sent it around for reviews, but nobody printed reviews. He mailed a copy to Edna LeBlanc at her store. A few weeks later he got a note back from her that just said "much better."

The Diner scheduled him three or four days each week, usually much longer shifts than he'd been used to at Lil ol' Betsy's. He'd take a bus from Talbot's over to Sunset Morning, and it took about an hour and one transfer. On the way home he'd fall asleep on the bus. A couple times he missed the stop for the transfer and had to walk the second half of the trip. He'd started thinking about a new writing project and was starting to outline it. It was always his goal to use the time on the bus to work on this, but most of the time he was too tired or the ideas just weren't there, and instead he'd just sit. He never heard if any copies of the book had sold.

He saved as much money as he could and looked for apartments he could afford but couldn't find one. Occasionally it would snow. On a chilly night he and Lena met at a bar, and he gave her a copy of the book. She was excited to see how it turned out. Her gallery had since finished its run, and she was in the process of selling off a lot of the equipment. They talked a little about how it had gone. There were some art magazines that wrote favorably about it. Lena said it drew a decent crowd each night, and some people returned multiple times. Then it was over and all of the media just lived on a couple harddrives in her apartment.

"What're you going to work on next?"

"I'm not sure. More photography, probably, something with the camera. I don't have a subject in mind. So I'll just go back to work until I find a new idea."

He nodded. They chatted and drank, and then Wyatt went back to the apartment.

One day while Talbot was at work and Wyatt was not, he sat in the apartment and read through his play for the first time since it was printed. He found a few typos and couldn't tell if they were his fault or the publisher's. Some of the changes that had been agreed upon during editing took it a little further from his original idea, but reading it now he felt most of it worked. He thought it was pretty good, and he hoped if anyone else read it they would think so, too. He figured that just had to be enough. There was no real routine, but Wyatt settled into his current normal: going to and from Talbot's place, out to the Diner and very occasionally out for something else. On a few shelves around the city were copies of his dumb little play.

A few weeks later, just on some weekday, during an early morning bus run going from the Sunset Morning neighborhood up to the Bush, there was a Demon working in the street on the bus's path. The bus was forced to slow to a stop and wait for the Demon to finish or move along, but it did not. Wanting to get a move on, the driver carefully began to steer the bus around where the demon stood, inching the machine with all the delicacy she could muster. Without warning the Thing flailed one way, and then the other, and on its second thrash it smashed into the side of the bus which lifted briefly into the air before it fell hard onto its side on the street. Glass shattered and sprayed the entire block, the frame of the bus buckling under the new pressure. From the engine spewed thick, black smoke that billowed and joined the shog. People around reacted, startled or scared. Some ran away while others ran toward the wreck.

Bodies inside had been flung to one side. Passengers who were able to scrambled from out of the bus, frantic. Some inside were dead and others unconscious or injured, screaming, and some people tried to help them. The demon paid no attention to any of this, seemingly unaware that it had struck the bus at all. It lifted what appeared to be its hind legs into the air and stood still for a moment before carrying on with its task. The injured passengers who had been dragged from the bus laid on the sidewalk while people called for hospitals. Those who could walk and had somewhere to go walked away from the scene of the collision and headed wherever they were going.

Special thanks

I want to thank my wife Chelsea for the support while writing and working to publish this. I also would like to thank Lucas Gardner for the incredibly helpful feedback throughout the process, Madelyn Pawlowski for helping proof and edit, as well as Alana Dyson, Ross Johnson, Abdul Hadi and Benjamin Wayne Torrey for reading and helping me get the book to be as good as I could get it.

Charlie DeMott Wildey is a writer from upstate New York. He lives in the Rochester area with his wife, their daughter and their cat Pashmina. *Lightning Bolt* is his first novel.

Twitter: @charliewildey

Instagram: charliedw.poems